Sherman wasn't his usual self.

Sitting in that conference room with Talia Malone, he couldn't find the composure that saw him through every aspect of life.

"First," he began, relying on his notes, "what you said about Kent giving us messages... It fits with what his psychologist says. He thinks Kent's anger and acting out is his attempt to express some emotion he can't get across in a healthy way."

Her accuracy about his son excited him. Or something about her did. Maybe just the idea that at the end of this exercise in art therapy they might find a solution. A way to help Kent.

"I'd suggest that you take whatever you get from our meeting to Kent's counselor," she said. "Except for the collage he made. I promised to give it back to him by the end of the week. But you can ask Kent for it. Or take a picture of it here to email to his counselor."

He nodded.

"The real question is whether Kent should know that you've shown it to his psychologist," she said, frowning. "But keeping secrets, even when you think you're doing it for someone's good, can be far more harmful than telling him would've been."

She sounded as if she knew what she was talking about...

Dear Reader,

Once, many years ago, I wrote a story with a heroine who'd been a prostitute—*Her Secret, His Child*. Back then, I got handwritten fan letters in the mail and I answered every one of them. (I kept them, too, in notebooks that are now filed on a shelf.) After *Her Secret, His Child* was released, I was astonished to get letters asking me if I'd ever been a prostitute. A resounding *no*! But parts of me are in all my books. And I look back at that book now and realize some of the feelings—of not being good enough, of being used rather than cared about—resonated with me.

Child by Chance is the story of an ex-stripper. I'm just going to say it right out—*No*, I have never been a stripper. The closest I got to dancing was ballet class, for five years, three times a week. And I never once, ever, danced onstage.

But I learned to respect the physicality of dance. The athleticism of dancers. I learned about dedication. And I learned about finding my center and "pulling up." Talia, the heroine in *Child by Chance*, knows all these things. But this isn't a story about dance. It's a story about life's tough choices. About making mistakes. And making amends. About accepting the lemons life hands you and making lemonade. It's a story of heart, redemption and the true meaning of love. All kinds of love.

I'd really like to hear what you think about the Lemonade Stand and this series, Where Secrets Are Safe. You can reach me at staff@tarataylorquinn.com. And if you like friendship stories, take a look at *The Friendship Pact*. I tried something different, and the verdicts are in! I'd be thrilled to hear yours, too.

Tara Taylor Quinn

USA TODAY Bestselling Author

TARA TAYLOR QUINN

Child by Chance

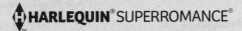
HARLEQUIN® SUPERROMANCE®

Recycling programs
for this product may
not exist in your area.

ISBN-13: 978-0-373-60890-4

Child by Chance

Copyright © 2014 by Tara Taylor Quinn

Printed in U.S.A.

With sixty-eight original novels published in more than twenty languages, **Tara Taylor Quinn** is a *USA TODAY* bestselling author. She is a winner of the 2008 National Reader's Choice Award, four-time finalist for a Romance Writers of America RITA® Award, a finalist for the Reviewer's Choice Award, the Bookseller's Best Award and the Holt Medallion, and appears regularly on Amazon bestseller lists. Tara is a supporter of the National Domestic Violence Hotline, and she and her husband, Tim, sponsor an annual in-line skating race in Phoenix to benefit the fight against domestic violence. When she's not at home in Arizona with Tim and their canine owners, Jerry Lee and Taylor Marie, or fulfilling speaking engagements, Tara spends her time traveling and in-line skating. For more information about Tara, visit her website, TaraTaylorQuinn.com.

Books by Tara Taylor Quinn
HARLEQUIN SUPERROMANCE
Where Secrets Are Safe

Wife by Design
Once a Family
Husband by Choice

Shelter Valley Stories

Sophie's Secret
Full Contact
It's Never Too Late
Second Time's the Charm
The Moment of Truth

It Happened in Comfort Cove

A Son's Tale
A Daughter's Story
The Truth About Comfort Cove

MIRA

Where the Road Ends
Street Smart
Hidden
In Plain Sight
Behind Closed Doors
At Close Range
The Second Lie
The Third Secret
The Fourth Victim
The Friendship Pact

Other titles by this author available in ebook format.

For Christina.

All children should be so lucky to have someone as devoted to them as you are to Emma, Claire and William. We are blessed to have you in our family and I hope you know how much you're loved.

CHAPTER ONE

SHE'D MOVED WITH confidence on some pretty exclusive Vegas stages. Had entertained moneyed and powerful men. With and without her clothes.

But as she walked down the hushed elementary-school hallway lined with short lockers that Friday afternoon, twenty-seven-year-old Talia Malone had never felt more uncomfortable in her life.

No one at that school was going to know that the ten-year-old boy in the classroom midway down that hall was her son.

She'd given birth once, ten years before, but she'd never been a mother.

Had no idea how to be one.

You were a mother when you were his age. Tanner's words from earlier that morning played over and over again in her head, much like his words had always done when she'd been growing up and her big brother had been a demigod in her life.

Before she'd grown deaf and dumb to his wisdom, slept with one of her high-school teachers and ended up pregnant.

She slowed her step, eyeing a deserted alcove

hosting a water fountain that was so low to the ground she'd have to bend in half to take a sip.

She hadn't technically been a mother at ten. Tanner, of all people, knew that. But she'd been ten when their baby sister, Tatum, had been born. Between her and Tanner and their brother Thomas they'd managed to make sure that baby girl was protected and loved.

But then Talia had run off. Abandoned the family. Abandoned Tatum. And her sweet baby sister had ended up a victim of domestic violence—drugged and pretty much raped, too—all because she'd been so desperate for love and acceptance that she'd believed the young rich creep who'd told her he loved her more than anyone else ever would.

She'd believed his hitting her had been her own fault…

Deep breath.

Talia didn't want the water she sipped. And didn't leave the alcove immediately, either.

Used to waiting in the wings for "showtime," Talia stood between the fountain and the wall, watching the quiet hallway for signs of life. A janitor crossed the hallway several yards down from her, on his way to a different part of the Santa Raquel, California, elementary school.

She was there to facilitate a class. Not teach.

Her class didn't start for another half hour. She'd arrived early. On purpose. Kent Paulson, adopted son of widower Sherman Paulson and his late wife, Brooke—who was killed in a car accident, her obituary had said—wasn't in the sixth-grade art class she'd be visiting. He was only in fourth grade. Two doors down from where she was standing.

All she wanted was a glimpse of him. She wasn't there to claim him.

She just needed to know that he was okay. Happy. Better off than he would have been growing up the bastard child of a teenage mother, and a drug-addicted, sometimes homeless prostitute grandmother. Or knowing that his biological father, who'd served time in prison for a host of crimes including statutory rape and child endangerment, was a registered sex offender and unable to work any job that would put him in the vicinity of minors.

"I don't care!" There was no mistaking the very adult anger in the childish voice as a door opened and a small arm pulled away from the larger hand that was holding it.

"Keep your voice down." A woman reached for the boy's hand.

"Ouch!" he cried, snatching his hand back before she'd even touched him. "You're hurting me and that's against the law. You aren't allowed to hurt me."

"Shhh."

"Why? So that all the other kids don't figure out that life sucks?"

The words struck a chord. One that hadn't played inside her in a long time, but was still achingly familiar. Growing up as the mostly destitute offspring of a prostitute, she'd learned quickly that she wasn't like the other kids. Wasn't naive. Or innocent.

Retreating farther into the alcove, Talia watched as the middle-aged, short-haired brunette escorted the small-boned, dark-haired boy past her—not even seeming to notice that she was there.

"This makes it four school days in a row that you've disrupted class. You're going to get yourself into some serious trouble here. I'm doing my best to help, but you're going to tie my hands if you aren't careful." The woman's words were hushed, but brimming with intensity. And, Talia kind of suspected, sincerity, too.

"I don't care," the boy said.

"You do, too, care, Kent."

Kent!

Surely there weren't two of them in the group of fourth-grade classrooms lining that hallway.

The couple had passed out of hearing range, and Talia stepped out from her alcove far enough to watch them until they turned a corner out of sight.

Had that little, short-haired preppy-looking boy in need of anger management been her kid?

Her *son*?

Biologically only, of course. She had no parental rights to him.

If he was even Kent Paulson. *The* Kent Paulson. She had to find out.

And if he was? If that troubled young man was the one she'd put here on earth? Had she just witnessed that scene for a reason? Her being there, hoping to catch a glimpse of him, right when he was acting out—that couldn't be a coincidence. It had to be fate, right?

She'd have to figure that out. She wasn't walking away, though.

Not until she knew for certain that he was getting help. If that boy was hers, the chip on his shoulder could be hereditary.

There was no way any progeny of hers was going to end up like her.

Not while she had a breath left in her body.

"MRS. BARBOUR IS on line two, Mr. Paulson."

Not again. "Thanks, Gina." He waited for the door to close behind his administrative assistant.

Loosening his tie enough to release the top button, Sherman Paulson pondered the blinking button on his phone console for several seconds.

As campaign manager for a couple of up-and-coming voices vying for careers in California politics, he was used to problem solving. Exceled at it, actually.

"Mrs. Barbour? Sherman Paulson here." As he

usually did when faced with adversity, he feigned a cheerful tone.

"I've got Kent in my office again, Mr. Paulson." His son's principal did not sound at all happy.

Pinching his nose between his eyebrows, Sherman asked, "What has he done this time?" Kent had promised, when Sherman had dropped him off that morning, that there'd be no more trouble.

"He pushed another student into a wall," the school principal said. "The other boy has a bump on his head."

"Did you ask him what the other boy did first?"

"I know what he did." Mrs. Paulson's tone didn't change. "The boy cut in front of him in line. Your son didn't use his words, Mr. Paulson. He didn't try to resolve the situation in a healthy manner. He went straight into attack mode."

Sherman wished like hell he couldn't picture exactly what Mrs. Barbour meant.

"We're willing to work with you, sir. We understand the difficulty of your situation and we sympathize, wholeheartedly…"

Yada, yada, yada, she might as well have been saying. In the two years since his wife's sudden and unexpected death due to a drunk driver, Sherman was accustomed to hearing similar sympathetic sentiments. And wasn't sure what any of them meant in real life where pain was a burning hell that never let up.

"…but my hands are tied on this one," the woman said, her tone changing, empathy losing out to authority. "I'm afraid that I've had to suspend Kent for the next week."

"But…" What in the hell was he going to do with the boy? He had to work. Had appointments and power lunches, schmoozing calls to make, and only six months to make miracles happen if he wanted a hope in hell of winning the position he sought as a state senate campaign manager. A job that paid far more than his current position working for local politicians.

"I'm sorry, sir, but policies are policies. Kent was the first one to make physical contact and the other boy has a visible wound as a result. I have no choice but to suspend him."

Sherman wouldn't have his job for a day if he accepted "no" at face value. "I understand your policies and support them completely," he began. "I'm not asking or expecting you to make an exception in our case." He continued the soothing litany he'd learned to employ in situations like this. "I understand that Kent has to be removed from his normal classroom for the requisite number of days…"

Deal with the problem at hand, he reminded himself, his steel-like mental control serving him, as well, as always. One step at a time.

"But I don't think a week's vacation from school is the reward my son needs at the moment," he continued, homing in on the meat of the problem because it was the only way to find a workable solution. "Is there someplace else there he can sit for the five days he's earned of solitary confinement?" he asked. "A guidance counselor's office or…"

Your *office*, he was thinking. He had a goal in mind.

Keep his son at school.

And safe.

In an environment where he couldn't possibly get into any more trouble. At least for a few days.

"Well…"

"Just a little desk someplace where he won't have anything to distract him from the schoolwork he's there to do. If he gets to leave school, he's going to view this as a win."

Sherman might not know how to control Kent's personality change since his mother's tragic death, but he knew his son well enough to know that Kent wanted out of school more than just about anything else on earth.

Other than knowing that the drunk who'd killed his mother was paying for the crime. They just had to find the guy first.

Sherman was working on that, too. When he could. As he could. However he could. But Kent, in his ten-year-old way, didn't yet understand that a political science degree didn't give Sherman the tools to find a killer who'd eluded the police. He had to identify him first, and that was something no one had been able to do as of yet.

All they knew was that he'd been driving a stolen car. And there'd been an almost-empty fifth of whiskey in the vehicle.

The pause on the line had grown in the space of Sherman's mental wandering.

Big mistake—allowing his mind to wander in the middle of a negotiation.

A bid for help and support.

The principal sighed, relaxing Sherman's spine just a tad.

"All right, Mr. Paulson. Starting Monday, for one week, I'll see that Kent gets his education from here, in our office, but I don't think for one second that his time with me is going to solve his problems."

Of course it wasn't. She was just a step.

To provide the way to get to the next step.

Or, in this case, to give him time to figure out what in the hell the next step would be.

CHAPTER TWO

WHILE SHE HAD a joint degree in fashion merchandising and design, Talia still had more than a year of work left on her degree in psychology. She was due to graduate in December and was determined to make that happen. She'd thought maybe she'd teach someday, if she could find a school system that would hire an ex-stripper, but somehow her life had once again redefined itself. Without any conscious direction on her part, she'd become someone new. A collage expert.

The idea had come to her after spending time with some of the residents at the Lemonade Stand, the domestic violence shelter her little sister had lived at the previous year.

Inspired by the notion that she might be able to help some of the women who'd befriended Tatum, she'd designed a program that used collage as a means of self-expression. To her surprise she'd discovered that the same skill that served her well in the fashion industry—an ability to see past the clothes on a body to the person they reflected—was an asset for collage reading, as well. Through her collage work, she'd been hoping to help women find their value within rather than relying on their outer beauty to give them their sense of worth. If victims could let go of their negative self-images and replace them with visuals of things that spoke to them, things that made them feel good, things that they liked, perhaps that would help them on their way to starting a new life. Her hope was that once the women realized their inner beauty they would gain the confidence to express themselves and make positive outward choices. Her work jibed with the Lemonade Stand's philosophy to give battered women a sense of their value to counteract the damage abuse had done to their psyches.

And somehow, the program had branched out. She was working with kids now, too. Test-running the concept in a total of six elementary schools. Her initial plan had been to present a variation of her Lemonade Stand workshop to high-school girls, with the idea to help them love their inner selves so they didn't give in to the pressure to feel that their value came from how they looked. So that they could make fashion and life choices that expressed their personalities rather than their sexuality. Such a class might have saved her life in high school.

And could have helped Tatum, too.

But the school board wanted her to start on a smaller scale, with both girls and boys, in elementary-level art classes. She'd been thrilled to win that much support and knew that a reference from her new sister-in-law, Sedona Malone, who was a well-respected lawyer in their community, had gone a long way to making this happen.

Collages were glimpses into the soul of those who made them. Or at least glimpses into their lives, their perspectives.

So what would a collage Kent made look like?

At an isolated desk against the far wall in the outer area of the principal's office, the little kid from that morning sat up straight with attitude emanating out of every pore of his body. Talia glanced at the woman by her side, Carina Forsythe, the art teacher in whose classes she'd been working all day.

"That's him," she said, having told the woman about the disturbing scene she'd witnessed that morning, wondering if maybe she could help. As a professional.

The boy might not even be her Kent. All day she'd wondered, going back and forth in her mind with certainty that he was, and then with just as much certainty that the chance of him having been in the hallway at the exact moment that she'd been wondering about him was little more than nil.

"Kent Paulson." Carina's young brow furrowed as she identified the student. Talia noticed the little details of those lines on the woman's forehead. Focused on them as her lungs squeezed the air out of her body.

He *was* her boy...her *son*.

She'd found him.

No one could know.

"...should have seen him a couple of years ago. He was everyone's favorite—not that we really have favorites—it's just that he was precocious, smart and so polite, too. But after his mother was killed..."

His adopted mother.

Talia had no idea if Kent knew that Brooke wasn't his biological mother.

Oh, my God. My son!

She glanced at the boy again. And couldn't look away. Was it possible that an invisible umbilical cord ran between them? One that hadn't been severed when she'd picked up that pen ten years ago and signed her name, severing her rights to her own flesh and blood?

She tried to speak but her throat wouldn't work.

"Anyway, you'd said you wanted to work with troubled kids, and I think it sounds like a good idea. Mrs. B.'s in her office. Why don't you go talk to her?"

"I...will..." The dryness in her throat choked her, and she coughed. Until she started to choke. Carina led her to a nearby drinking fountain. She sipped. Coughed some more.

And was finally able to suck air into her too-tight lungs.

When she could, she thanked the other woman.

Said something about not knowing what the coughing fit was about. Assured the art teacher that she was fine. Waited for Carina to continue about her day. Waited for the lump in her throat to dissipate enough for her to pull off the pretense of her life. And then, careful to avoid another glance at the child sitting along the far wall, she opened the door to the principal's office.

She wasn't a mother. She'd just grown a baby once.

"So? How'd it go?" Sixteen-year-old Tatum Malone climbed out of the driver's seat of their sister-in-law's Mustang, addressing Talia.

You'd never know by looking at her that the beautiful, vivacious blonde teenager had been a resident at a shelter for victims of domestic violence the previous year.

Talia, who was standing in the driveway of Sedona Malone's beach house, smiled as she greeted her baby sister, avoiding the hug with which Tatum usually greeted her family members. She never had been a touchy-feely person, always having to keep a barrier up. But now, after the choices she'd made, it was as if she couldn't let her family get too close to her. Or maybe it was that she was afraid that once they saw the woman she'd become, they'd withdraw. And if she was all-in with them, their rejection would be too much to bear.

That was Talia. Always holding something back just in case.

"It went fine," she said, pulling out her key as she headed up the back steps to the deck and the French doors that allowed her to sit at the kitchen table and watch the sun set over the beach just yards away. "The kids were great," she continued as she let them into the borrowed beach house, dropping her keys on the counter and heading to get sodas for both of them. "You should have seen some of the collages they made. I could spend a year analyzing them."

"Cool," Tatum said, sliding her slim, jeans-clad body into a seat at the table. "But that's not what I was talking about." Those intense gray-blue eyes pinned Talia and, not for the first time in the year she'd been back, Talia felt completely off-kilter. As though her almost ten-year age advantage over Tatum had disappeared and she was the younger of the two.

"Does Tanner know you're here?" Talia asked, sending a bold and piercing look back.

"Of course. I've got Sedona's car, don't I?"

Tatum could've had her own car, if she'd wanted it. But for now, she was sticking close to home—to Tanner and to Sedona, the lawyer who'd seen through Tatum's confused attempt to get help the year before, and ended up marrying their big brother.

"He pretty much asked me to come," Tatum

said, her look steady, "or he would have if I hadn't already said I was coming."

Still not completely used to having someone on her side, most particularly not someone she actually loved, Talia nodded.

"I saw him," she said, her fingers curling the edges of the place mat in front of her. Picking up her can, she took a long drink of cola, pretended that it had some magical strengthening power and said, "He's little. Like Thomas. Smaller boned than Tanner."

"Is he short like Thomas, too, or tall like you and me and Tanner?"

"I don't know. He's a lot shorter than I am, but he's only ten. How do I know how tall a ten-year-old is supposed to be?"

This was Tatum's nephew they were talking about. And family meant everything to Tatum. Talia understood. It was just taking some getting used to, this whole support system thing. She'd been alone in a rough world for a long time.

"Did you talk to him?"

Talia shook her head. "He's in trouble, Tay," she said. Instincts told her to keep the bad stuff a secret from her little sister, wanting her to only see the good in the world. But they'd all learned how much damage those kinds of secrets, that kind of protection, could do. Most particularly where Tatum was concerned.

Tatum's eyes shadowed, and her pretty blond hair fell around her shoulders. "What kind of trouble?" Her voice had softened.

"I'm not sure," Talia said.

Kent was supposed to have had the perfect fairytale life. That was why she'd given him up. To protect him from any chance that he'd grow up the way she had.

Then she and Tatum had found out on the internet that Kent's adopted mother had been killed in an accident. By a drunk driver in a stolen vehicle. He'd fled the scene on foot and there'd been no identifying fingerprints on the car or on the nearly empty bottle they'd found inside it.

Tanner was all for Talia approaching Kent's father, introducing herself and proposing some kind of arrangement that would allow her to see her son now and then. Tatum understood why Talia couldn't even think about doing that.

"He's been suspended from class for the next week."

"What? Why? It's kinda hard to get suspended from the fourth grade."

"No idea. But I didn't just walk away."

"I never thought you would."

Tatum's grin made her belly flop. She hated that. And loved it, too. All she'd ever wanted was a loving home and family of her own. Before she'd figured out that an open heart hurt too much.

Still, here she was, giving it all another chance. The family part, not the loving-home-of-her-own part. A permanent chance. She wasn't going back to a world that didn't see her as a human being. That only saw her as a body others could use for their pleasure. She'd failed Tanner. And worse, she'd been absent when Tatum had needed her most. Her little sister had paid a heavy price for Talia's easy way out.

Talia would spend the rest of her life paying off that debt.

The decision wasn't negotiable. But neither did it make the implementation easy. Or in any way comfortable.

"I talked to the principal," Talia said.

"Mrs. Barbour?" Tatum's frown was cute, scrunching up her nose in a way that reminded Talia of a time when Tatum had been about three and had walked by the bathroom after someone had just been in there. She'd walked around the house with her nose scrunched up for half an hour after that. When Talia had asked her what she was doing, she'd said she was keeping the bad smell out. She'd been too young to realize that it had only been a temporary thing.

"She was in charge of a spring fling production that involved all the area elementary schools when I was in sixth grade," Tatum said. "We called her Mrs. B."

"They still do," Talia said. "I asked if I could try some collage making with him. She said he was going to be spending the next week in her office and as far as she was concerned I could see him every day."

"So, you're planning to work with him all five days, right?" Tatum's voice was chipper, and her smile hit bone-deep.

"I think so. Yeah."

"Are you nervous?"

"What do you think?"

"I think you're going to spend the entire weekend pretending that you don't care and that this is really nothing more than making sure he's okay."

"It isn't. And how can I care for a child I've never known?"

"You knew him for nine long months. And never stopped loving him…"

Talia couldn't go there. Not now.

Not ever.

CHAPTER THREE

SHERMAN HAD TICKETS to a basketball game in LA on Friday night. He was sitting in a box with a man who he believed would support his candidate for the county auditor seat, most particularly after Sherman finished explaining to him how his candidate played into what the moneyed gentleman wanted most.

Sherman didn't really have an opinion on the man's politics. That wasn't part of his job. Showing the man how he could help Sherman's candidate—one of the campaigns Sherman and his team were currently managing—was what he cared most about at the moment.

Apart from his son, of course.

He'd planned to surprise Kent with the tickets and the trip to the city—with an overnight stay in a hotel—when he'd picked him up from school on Friday. He'd known about the game since Tuesday—the first day he'd received a call from Mrs. Barbour that week. He'd hardly been able to reward the boy then.

And not any of the days between then and Friday, either.

But Kent had promised to have a good day at school on Friday. And Sherman had been going to use the tickets as a reward.

He could hardly reward being suspended from class.

Instead, he dropped Kent off at home with his favorite sitters, the childless couple next door who spoiled him rotten, and headed into the city by himself.

FINDING KENT HADN'T been difficult. His adoption had provided for the eventuality. If either party wanted to seek out the other, contact information could be passed through the agency.

Because Kent was a minor, his contact information had been that of his father. And had included a sentence about his mother being deceased. Talia had found out a few more details on the internet. But very few.

She'd come back from the agency with a name. Knew he was in Santa Raquel. And from his address had found out what school he'd most likely attend. Finding his classroom hadn't been that difficult once she'd been in the school. The fourth grades were all clustered together.

Seeing him had been so easy.

And had upended her in a way being sold by her husband to his friends hadn't even done.

She'd given birth to someone else's child. That

was how she looked at her pregnancy and the adoption. She'd been growing a child for someone else to love and cherish because they couldn't grow one for themselves.

She'd had it all worked out.

Until she saw that little boy strutting his preppy stuff down the hall on Friday.

Friday nights were set aside for online study. Three of her five classes that semester were online. And if she was going to be ready to graduate by December, she had to adhere to her schedule.

Weekends were for work. By the time she drove to LA, worked an eight-hour shift at the high-end retail store at the Beverly Center, a mall in Beverly Hills, and drove back, the day was pretty much done.

Her schedule was tight. She couldn't afford to be flexible.

So she sat diligently at her computer Friday night. Tried to focus. And kept seeing a little face in place of the text on the screen.

Picking up her laptop she moved from the spare bedroom she was using for an office out to the kitchen table. There were no lights on the private beach, but she knew it was out there. That the ocean beckoned beyond.

A child needs to be touched, to be held, to be nurtured. Scientific studies show that a baby

that is not held often or at all is far more prone
to exhibiting signs of antisocial personality dis-
order or sociopathic tendencies.

She read the paragraph three times.
She'd given him up so he'd have a great mother to
see him through all of the difficult times of growing up.
He didn't have a mother anymore.

A child needs boundaries. He will test them.
He is doing so, not to have them moved, but to
assure himself that they don't.

Was Kent testing his boundaries?

In part, he finds his security in unmoving
boundaries, in the things he can count on.

A kid should be able to count on his mother. On
having her be a boundary that didn't change. Just
always there.
Unlike the woman who'd given birth to Tanner,
Thomas, Talia and Tatum.
Where had Kent's mother been driving to, or
coming from, that night she'd been killed? Why
had she been alone in the car?
Careful. The inner voice that had decided to show
up a little late in her life was speaking loud and clear

suddenly. She couldn't cross the boundary she was standing behind. She wouldn't. Because she'd be hurting someone other than herself.

She'd looked up her son to assure herself he was okay.

She was going to work with him the following week for the same reason.

Anything beyond that was clearly out of her jurisdiction and not her business.

Tonight, child development was her business.

For the rest of the night, she stuck to it.

Mostly.

"No, Dad, I don't want to go putt some balls and get ice cream."

The knife in Sherman's hand was in danger of losing its blob of butter as it stilled, suspended over the toast he'd been buttering Saturday morning. "What do you mean you don't want to go? It's already planned," he explained patiently.

The grief counselor had told him to be patient. Two years ago.

"I thought you'd like the surprise," he added.

"I don't." Kent sat at the table, already dressed in jeans, a button-down shirt and a sweater—green today—with his hands in his lap. Awaiting the cold cereal and toast Sherman was in the process of getting for him.

The butter dropped from his knife to the toast,

catching the side of his hand, as well. Sherman spread quickly, dropped the toast to the counter and licked the side of his hand.

He poured milk. Added a spoon to the bowl of Kent's latest choice in sugared cereal, took that and the toast to the table, a smile on his face. "Why not?"

"Where's your cereal?"

"I'm not having any this morning." He'd pulled off at a twenty-four-hour diner on his way home from the city and wasn't hungry.

"What time did you get home?"

"Sometime after midnight."

"Way after midnight. I got up at 2:00 a.m. to pee and Ben and Sandy were still here, sleeping in the recliners."

The love seat portion of the leather sectional he and Brooke had purchased the year before she...

Yes, well, he was glad that Ben and Sandy made use of the love seat.

"I was with a client."

"I don't care if you're out screwing someone, Dad."

Anger burst through him. He very carefully took the space between stimulus and response, to make certain that, for his son's sake, he didn't say something he'd regret.

Then he sat. Crossed his hands. Leaned over. And looked his son square in the eyeballs. "There are many things wrong with that comment," he said slowly, but with no doubt to his seriousness. "First, *screwing* is an inappropriate way to describe any relationship I might have with a woman. Second, if I was *making love* with a woman it would be absolutely none of your business. And third, I was with a sixty-year-old man at a basketball game and then we went to a restaurant, where I had a glass of sparkling water and he had a whiskey sour while we discussed Sadie Bishop's county auditor campaign, after which I got in the BMW and drove home, stopping only for a plate of greasy scrambled eggs, hash browns and toast. I have done nothing to deserve your disrespect."

Kent chewed. Crunching his cereal as if he was set to win a contest. His throat bulged when he swallowed.

"Yes, sir," he said then. "You're right. On all three counts. I'm sorry."

"Apology accepted."

Kent crunched some more. And Sherman sought to understand the boy.

Patience was the key. He was certain of that. He just wished he knew what to say sometimes, while he was waiting for patience to work its magic.

"So…how about that trip to the driving range?" he asked, back to his cheery self, when no other words presented themselves. Clark Vanderpohl and his son were meeting them at the course in less than an hour.

"Uh-uh."

Patience.

"Why not?" His tone was right on cue. Easy and nonthreatening.

"You're only taking me because you have business to do," he said.

"That's not true, son." He was completely sure about that.

"So we're not meeting someone who has something to do with one of your precious campaigns?"

Kent's tone wasn't easy. Or in any way upbeat or even particularly kind. But then, he was only ten.

Sherman was the adult here. Didn't matter how much he hurt, too, he had to maintain the order in their lives.

"I didn't say that," he said after giving himself the few seconds pause he needed to choose his response.

"Ha! See, I knew it." Kent slurped his milk.

Brooke would have said something about that. Sherman started to. But pulled himself back.

"What I said," Sherman continued, his tone as even as ever, "was that I'm not just taking you because I have business to do. It's the complete opposite, in fact. I invited Mr. Vanderpohl and his son to join us because I'd already planned to take you to the driving range, as I promised last weekend, and I wasn't going to disappoint you."

Kent came first. He always had.

"Cole's going to be there?" Kent's face lit up as he mentioned the banker's son.

"Yes."

"Cool!" Picking up his bowl, Kent put it to his lips, emptied it, licked the spoon and then very carefully wiped his mouth with his napkin, put the spoon in the bowl and carried the ensemble over to the sink.

Some moments he was still pretty much a perfect kid.

HER PALMS WERE SWEATING. Tanner had said she'd be fine. She'd believed him. He was wrong.

Making a beeline for the teacher's lounge, Talia made it to the bathroom in time to throw up. And then sat there shaking. She must have the flu.

Her forehead was cool to her touch.

But she definitely felt off.

Emotionally, she was a rock. Could count the number of times she'd cried since she was five.

Maybe it was something she ate.

Did that make you shake?

She could call someone. Sedona.

Pulling out her cell phone she pictured her new sister-in-law in her legal office, all capable and smart, answering her phone. Asking Talia questions that she wouldn't want to answer.

No, calling wasn't a good idea.

Kent Paulson, Sherman Paulson's son, was sitting in the principal's office, working on his assignments for the week. She was permitted to work with him at any time over the next hour.

The hour was ticking past.

He didn't need her.

This was about her. Because she wanted to meet him.

No, that wasn't right. She just needed to make sure he was okay.

And if he wasn't, she'd do what she could to see that he got the help he needed. From someone else.

As if his artwork was somehow going to give her a glimpse into his little-boy soul and she'd magically know what he needed?

Or maybe she'd know something instinctively because of who he was?

Did a woman still get maternal instincts when she gave up her baby for adoption?

Her stomach roiled and she almost puked again.

God, what was the matter with her? Nothing scared her.

Nothing.

Except maybe when Tatum had been missing. She'd been scared then.

Because she loved that kid.

She didn't love Kent. She couldn't. She didn't even know him.

He wasn't hers to love.

It was just going to be art.

Pictures in old magazines that she'd thought would be suited to a ten-year-old kid. Okay, magazines that Tatum and Sedona and Tanner had gone with her to buy Sunday night when she'd stopped by their place on the way home from work.

But still, just some pictures. He might not even cooperate.

Or like her.

So, fine. If he didn't like her, that was fine. He didn't have to like her.

He just had to pick some damned pictures so she could be sure he was fine.

She gagged again. But didn't have any stomach contents to lose.

This was ridiculous.

With a good long look at herself in the mirror, Talia bent, rinsed her mouth, pulled a stick of gum out of her mouth and opened the door.

Maybe he'd like her if she gave him a stick of her gum?

CHAPTER FOUR

THE FIRST TIME he'd seen Brooke, Sherman had been walking across campus, mentally rehearsing the debate he was about to win. She'd been in the middle of the lush green quad, in shorts and a tank top, lying on a blanket reading a book.

He'd stumbled. And damned near missed the competition that had ultimately, four years and many debates later, won him a scholarship to graduate school.

A lot had happened between then and now. Running into her at a concert on campus. Being inseparable for the remainder of their four years of undergraduate studies. Convincing her to put her marketing skills to work in his field and joining him as he signed on with one of the nation's top campaign management firms.

Years of miscarriages. Thousands of dollars spent on failed in vitro attempts.

Seeing Kent for the first time, less than an hour after his birth. They'd decided, long before he was born, to wait until his tenth birthday to tell him he was adopted. They'd wanted him to have grown to take their loving him for granted, to feel a part of them and to make the telling part of the celebration. They were going to tell him about his birth. And about how long they'd waited for him to come into their lives.

If he were the boy's biological father, would he know what to do with him? How to reach him? Help him? Was there some "fatherly" instinct that he was missing?

He and Brooke had talked it over a lot before his birth. The whole time they'd been preparing his nursery. Their ability to instinctively know what was right for their child even though they didn't birth him. Like knowing that he shouldn't know he was adopted. They'd made considered choices, based on weighing all sides of the situation.

Until he was ten, they'd decided not to tell anyone he was adopted. There were a few who knew, of course. People they worked with. But anyone who hadn't seen them in a while, anyone new to them, just assumed that they'd had him biologically. Kent was all theirs. That was all that mattered. Sherman had no family close enough to know that Brooke hadn't been pregnant. No one who would care one way or the other about his son's biological parentage.

Brooke was really the driving force behind the decision. She'd been adopted. To a couple who'd had a biological child a couple of years later. They made such a big deal of finally having a biological daughter. They told everyone about their miracle. By the time she was a teenager she'd been consumed with the need to find her own biological connection—filled with a need to be someone's miracle.

Her adopted parents had seemed almost relieved to have her do so, as though they were all right with being done with her. Or so it had seemed to the teenage Brooke. They'd continued to support her, both financially and otherwise, after her birth mother had refused to meet her.

Sherman had met them a few times, but with them in New York and him and Brooke in California, the visits had been infrequent. They'd appeared to him to love their daughters equally. But after she'd died, he'd never heard from them again.

Regardless of the fact that Brooke had never told them that Kent wasn't her biological child. Bottom line to them, he supposed, was that he wasn't theirs.

With Brooke gone, with Kent being so emotionally vulnerable all of a sudden, he hadn't known what to do regarding his adoptive status. Logic told him the boy would have to know at some point. You just didn't keep something like that from a person for their whole life. Shortly before Kent's tenth birthday he'd talked to Kent's therapist, Neil Jordon, about telling the boy the truth about his parentage, and had been quite relieved when Dr. Jordon had adamantly advised against breaking the news to him anytime in the near future. Kent was in no state to have his security, his foundation, further rocked.

Of course the fact that Dr. Jordon thought it would have been far easier on all of them to make the adoption a part of their family story from the beginning hadn't been as welcome a pronouncement.

It was lunchtime on Monday. Or rather, sixty minutes past the lunch hour, but the time that he and Brooke had set aside as sacred. Even if one or the other could only spare fifteen minutes, or five, out of a busy day, assuming they were both in the office, they used to meet at 1:30 p.m. every single day. If neither of them had had a lunch appointment, they'd share whatever they'd brought from home to eat. Sometimes, they'd just fill each other in on the fact that they'd catch up at home that night. More than once they'd locked his office door and made love.

Occasionally, they'd fought.

That last day, the fatal day, they'd fought. She'd made plans to have dinner in north LA with a nationally known reporter, Alan Klasky, from a not-so-reputable online news source—part of a plan the marketing team had come up with for damage control for a candidate who'd been caught on film at a strip club. The plan was to promise the rag exclusives from their office for the remainder of the campaign.

Brooke hadn't been fond of the plan. Sherman

had hated it, preferring to handle the blow they'd been dealt by the man's penchant for lap dances by flooding the press with the candidate's good deeds, of which there were hundreds. By getting good family press for him. From reputable sources.

Marketing had preferred to get in bed with a group that wasn't going to go away. They gave in to the blackmail.

Brooke was the bait. Chosen by their CEO because of her professionalism, her intelligence, her ability to create on a dime and because she was female.

She'd been honored by the recognition. Felt herself up to the task.

Sherman watched the fifteen minutes tick by that he still set aside, every single day that he was in the office, to close his office door and give his heart, mind and soul over to the woman he'd vowed to love forever.

Even though he'd stopped making love to her more than a year before her death.

It was a fine line between honor, decency, integrity—and justification. A line upon which he had to balance every single day of his life.

"Hi."

In the end, that was all there was. One word. No grand introduction. Nothing at all remarkable.

The little boy looked up at her, and Talia's throat

closed as she recognized not only the blue-gray eyes studying her, but their intensity even more. He was a few years older than Tatum had been when Talia had left home, but that look was very similar.

"Hi," he said, turning back to the workbook in front of him, the neat rows of pencil-written numbers in the three-digit multiplication problems hc'd been solving.

"I'm Ms. Malone."

The words won her another of those glances. He nodded.

Looking around for a chair, Talia prayed that she wouldn't throw up again.

Snagging a chair and pulling it close enough to reach his desk, she sat down. Kent pulled back, his eyebrows drawing together and up.

"I'm going to be working with you all week," she said, wishing she'd taken Mrs. Barbour's offer to introduce them, after all. The principal had been busy. And she'd wanted the moment to herself.

"What, you're, like, my monitor or something?" Belligerence, or derision, entered his tone as he gave a half scoff. As though he was too cool for words.

Or too old to need a babysitter.

"No." *I'm your mother.* The words flew, unwelcome and without permission into her brain. "I'm working with the sixth-grade art classes and have an hour break each day, and since everyone else here already has jobs to do, I'll be spending my break time with you."

"Got stuck with me, you mean."

"That's funny, and here I was thinking you were going to figure you were being stuck with me."

That gave him pause. And then, "So, what, you're just going to sit there and watch me do my math?"

He eyed the thick satchel she'd set on the floor by her feet. And sounded as if he kind of hoped she had more in store for him.

He was bored. She figured that out quickly enough.

"Nope. I'm here to work, not babysit," she said, wondering where the words were coming from. Surprised by the ease with which they slid off her tongue. The battered women hadn't been such a leap for her, but she was still a bit stiff with the kids. Until she pretended they were all little Tatums. Or until they got going on their collages and then she got so engrossed in reading their picture messages, in helping them compose those messages, express themselves, that she forgot to worry about anything else.

But this was...a ten-year-old boy who just happened to have shared her belly for nine months.

Oh, God. She was going to throw up again.

"What, you brought papers to grade?" he asked, his nose scrunched as he glanced at her bag again and then frowned at her.

He wasn't rejecting her presence beside him. Didn't seem to dislike her being there.

"No," she said, reaching down to her bag, thinking about putting her head between her knees while she was at it.

There was a trash can not far off. There if she needed it.

She wasn't going to need it.

"We're going to do an art project," she said instead, and pulled out the stack of magazines. A motorcycle and car one. Travel. Surfing. Boating. Sports—but not the famous one with pictures of girls. *Home and Garden.* Tatum had laughed at that one, but Talia would bet a week's groceries that Kent would use it. Maybe he'd home in on some brownies on a plate or a basketball hoop in a backyard display…

"What about my math and sentences for English?" There was no sign of the tough guy as Kent glanced down into her open satchel to see colored papers, markers, glue and a couple of plastic containers of assorted embellishments. She had his attention.

"What you don't finish at school today you have to do as homework," she told him.

"Cool." Closing his book, he turned to her with eagerness in his smile. And Talia had the strangest urge to give him a hug.

MONDAY'S DINNER PRETTY much summed up Sherman's day.

He'd had errands to run—a case of flyers to drop off at a candidate's office, shirts and pants to pick up from the cleaners, and they were out of toothpaste—after picking Kent up from school and was still in his creased gray pants, white button-down and gray-and-white silk tie as his son dropped into his seat at the kitchen table and announced that he was starving.

"You never did tell me how school went today," Sherman said as he dumped salad from a bag, tossed it with the chicken nuggets he'd just pulled from the oven, added some dressing and put it on plates for him and Kent.

"You never asked."

The boy had dropped his book bag by the door and sat in his pants, button-down shirt and sweater vest, his hand supporting his head, looking grumpy.

"Yes, I did. When you got in the car." And his phone had rung. He'd taken the call and…

"Fine. School was fine. Okay?"

His son's first day of in-school suspension and all he had to say was *fine*?

"What did you do?"

"Sat."

"Did you go to the cafeteria to eat your lunch?" Sherman, as he'd been instructed, had packed sandwiches. He'd added celery sticks and a couple of Kent's favorite cookies, too.

"No."

He frowned. "What about your juice?"

"Someone got it for me."

He nodded. Okay. So maybe this was good. Kent was seeing that if he misbehaved, he'd be taken out of society. Such as it was.

Brooke wouldn't be happy with their son missing lunch with his friends. Hell, *he* wasn't happy about it. Kent had been alienated enough from the regular kids, as he called them now, when his mother was killed.

Before the accident, Kent had been such a great kid. That person was still there inside him. Sherman knew it. And the counselor Kent was seeing seemed to think so, too. Somehow they just had to get through the anger stage of the grief process.

"Did Mrs. Barbour have anything special for you to do?" He put a plate of salad in front of his son.

"Nope."

"Did your teachers come in and give you assignments?" Retrieving foil-wrapped bread from the oven, he dropped it on the table along with some peanut butter and a knife.

"Nope."

He sat. Opened his napkin on his lap. Picked up his fork. "You just sat there all day and did nothing?"

Not at all what he'd envisioned when he'd asked for his son to spend the week in the principal's office.

"No." Kent was attacking his salad as if it was a banana split.

"You did schoolwork, then?"

"Duh, Dad, it's school."

The disrespect hurt as much as it irritated. He let it slide. Took a bite of salad. Missing the days when Brooke used to make it with fresh lettuce, cutting up cucumber and onion and celery and broccoli while he grilled fresh chicken for the top.

"So how'd you know what to do?" he asked, chewing.

Kent pushed salad onto his fork with his thumb. "Mrs. Barbour gave me a list."

Sherman picked up a piece of bread he didn't want, touching his son's wrist and motioning with the bread, then used it to push food onto his fork. "You just said she didn't have anything for you to do," he said.

"I said she didn't have anything *special* for me to do. It's all just regular stuff that we always do." The boy picked up a piece of lettuce with his fingers and popped it into his mouth.

Biting back the retort that sprang to his tongue, Sherman took a bite of salad and hoped he didn't get indigestion.

"Did you get it all done?" he asked a moment

or two later. Were they at least going to get to skip homework that night and go straight for the basketball game he wanted to watch? Kent loved basketball—or, really, any sport—and so far, they still bonded over their teams.

"No."

He stopped chewing. "No?"

"No."

Picking up a piece of bread, Kent used it to shove a huge bite of salad onto his fork the way Sherman always urged him to.

And now Sherman was worried. Why would the boy purposely do something to please him? Why start following the rules at that exact moment?

"Why not?" he asked. If Kent thought he was going to stop doing his schoolwork altogether, things were going to get a hell of a lot harder on him. While the boy had been acting out a lot, so far he'd maintained excellent grades. And so Sherman had been more willing to go along with the counselor's recommendation and give Kent some slack on some of the rest of it.

Because Dr. Jordon had recommended a less severe course of action, and because Sherman understood Kent's anger and had a hard time finding it within himself to be hard on the boy. He'd rather die for him than hurt him.

Kent shrugged. "I got extra to do," he said. And

dunked his bread into his chocolate milk, dripping chocolate on the table as he slurped the mess between his lips.

CHAPTER FIVE

"WHAT ARE WE going to do with this?" Kent frowned as he studied his partially completed collection of photos and moved a motorcycle up to a corner of the board—farther away from the center of his life, she noted silently.

"Why do we have to do something with it?" Talia prevaricated—something she was really good at. Better than giving direct answers, for sure.

"I dunno." He shrugged. "Just seems like we should."

Shoulds and have-tos seemed to carry weight with the boy. If for no other reason than so he could break the rules. And yet...

"I mean, why do all the work if it's for nothing?"

"Just for fun."

"You don't go to school to have fun," he said, as though she'd never been a student.

Every day for three days he'd been sitting at his desk when she arrived, dressed in pants— sometimes jeans but always a clean and new-looking pair—and a shirt and sweater or sweater vest. She'd never seen him in tennis shoes.

"There's nothing wrong with enjoying learning," she said, watching as he swapped the positions of a backyard grill and a video game character. He had an eye for shape and color. And she itched to intervene, to make suggestions, to take part.

But she couldn't.

This was his story. His expression. The collage was possibly going to be her only insight into the person who was her son.

She was there to facilitate only. Just like giving birth to him. She hadn't been a participant in his life. Not since Tanner had had her baby's father arrested and Talia had made the decision to give him up for adoption. Her role was facilitator.

Still, as he bent over his collage, she longed to touch his hair. To smooth the little piece that wanted to curl just above his ear. Was that why his father kept Kent's hair so short? Because it had a tendency to curl?

Talia's hair was straight. And blond. Nothing like Kent's. Kent's hair came from Rex. The high- school teacher who'd gone to jail for having sex with his student.

"What do you think should go here?" The boy turned to look at her.

He had Tatum's eyes. A grayer version of Talia's blue ones.

"I think you should decide," she told him. "This is

your time to make all the decisions. To use whatever pictures you want to use from these magazines."

She'd already learned to qualify her statements with him. The day before he'd tried to get away with cutting out letters to form swear words for the middle of his collage.

"What if I want to use a picture that isn't in the magazine?"

For a second she froze. Did ten-year-old boys look at dirty pictures? Was that what he was implying?

"What picture?"

He reached for his notebook, thumbed through some papers in the back of it, fumbled around in a plastic pocket and pulled out a photo.

"This one," he said.

Oddly, it was a picture of him. Dressed very similar to the way he was now. Obviously a school photo. Maybe a year or two old.

What kid carried around a picture of himself tucked in his notebook?

"Sure, you can use it," she said, while her mind wrapped itself around the newest piece of the puzzle she so desperately wanted to see complete. To know that it was a good picture. A healthy one. The picture she needed to have with her as she traversed the roads of her solitary life.

He dropped the picture in a space he'd left after she'd made him remove the curse words. "You never said what's going to happen to this."

Why did it matter so much?

"What do you want to happen to it?" she asked.

"Doesn't matter to me."

She wished she could believe that. Because she wanted to keep it more than just about anything. To hang it in her home. To have it to look at for the rest of her days.

"I'll need to keep it for a week or two," she said. Her program trial included written reports from her on every collage made, to show the board of education what she gleaned from the collages and how that information, that insight, could be used to help the kids. "But after that it's up to you."

The collages she was having the kids make in class were on sixteen-by-eleven-inch pieces of poster board. Kent's was on a full-size piece of poster board.

Picking up the scissors, Kent reached for a magazine. "I guess I could take it home. I mean, if we have to do something with it," he said.

His tough-guy armor had some definite chinks.

"I'll make sure you get it back, then," she told him. Wondering if it was against professional ethics if she took a photo of Kent's finished work to have blown up and framed for her wall.

SHERMAN TOOK KENT into LA for a basketball game Thursday night. The tickets were a gift from one of his clients, the seats located in a private suite with a full buffet spread. Kent was grinning and talking the entire way there, throwing out statistics and asking Sherman's opinion on scores and strategies. A banker and his family were supposed to be there, as well. One that Sherman was counting on for a sizable contribution. But when their passes got them on the elevator and then into the suite, it turned out that they were sharing the box with just the banker and his twelve-year-old daughter, who knew absolutely nothing about basketball. And who seemed to think entirely in rapid-fire questions.

Sherman tried to involve Kent in the conversation. To ask his opinion on answers to some of the more thoughtful questions, but his son was having none of it. Five minutes into the game, or the constant chatter depending upon one's perspective, Kent got up, helped himself to a plate of finger food and reseated himself in the farthest corner of the booth away from the rest of them, planting his face at the glass separating them from the rest of the stadium.

Sherman called out to him a few times. All but once Kent appeared not to hear. And Sherman, who had business to tend to, couldn't call his son to task. He probably wouldn't have even if he could. He didn't blame Kent for being disappointed.

"Quite the game, huh?" he asked as soon as the two of them were alone in their car, pulling out of the parking garage. Their team had won in the last seconds of the game with a three-point shot from midcourt.

"You wouldn't know," Kent practically spat. "You hardly saw any of it." In his jeans and team jersey, Kent looked about as cute as any little guy ever had, but Sherman didn't figure his son would want to hear him say so.

"I saw all of it," he said now. "I just didn't get to listen to as much of it as you did." Their suite had had the announcers' voices piped in.

"Yeah, well, you could've told me it was going to be business."

He'd hoped it was going to be a couple of families spending an enjoyable evening, with the dads having a chance to spend some relaxation time together before discussing business over lunch Friday.

At least his lunch appointment for the next day was still on.

"What about that spread, though?" he asked, pulling onto the highway that would take them to their home over an hour down the road, way past Kent's bedtime. The boy was going to be tired in the morning, not that Sherman was all that worried about it, considering his son was only going to be sitting in the principal's office all day. "Chicken nuggets, mozzarella sticks, brownies, chocolate chip cookies..."

There'd been healthy foods, too, but he named Kent's favorites.

"I had carrot sticks," the boy said. He had, too. Kent had always loved carrots. Even as a baby. His favorite baby food had been jarred carrots.

"You also had two brownies, a plate of nuggets and some cheese sticks," Sherman told him. If Kent thought his father was ignoring him, he needed to know that wasn't the case.

"So?" Arms folded, the boy looked out his window.

"So...I was just talking about the spread. You liked it."

"Whatever."

God, he hated that word. Wished it had never been invented. If he had a dollar for every time he came up against that word in a week, he'd be a damned millionaire. Damned because the word was a reminder, every single time, that he was failing his son.

No matter how hard he tried. He just hadn't found the way to get it right yet. To make Kent's world right.

But he would. Sooner or later, they were going to beat this thing.

And be happy together again.

FRIDAY WAS GLUE DAY. She'd covered the board with a tacky substance on Monday night as she'd prepared it to take to Kent on Tuesday. Enough to hold pictures in place temporarily, but allowing for removal and switching positions without damaging the photos. Each day she'd carefully covered and carried the board back and forth from the trunk of her car—which she'd cleared to allow the collage to lie flat—to the principal's office. Each day her son had seemed more eager, watching for her as she'd come around the corner. Each day since the first, he'd used up every second allotted to them, searching out pictures, cutting and, later, as she'd shown him, tearing them into the shape he wanted and placing them on the board.

Friday, when she'd turned the corner into the office, he'd been grinning and rubbing his hands together.

She'd dressed up that day. Working at a department store required that she have expensive-looking professional clothes and while she spent most of her time in jeans these days, she had a decent wardrobe.

Emphasis being on *decent*. The slinky leggings and revealing tops she used to wear were packed away under her bed.

"Wow, you look pretty!" Kent said, and then ducked his head.

"Why, thank you," Talia said, acting as though she'd heard the same from every kid she'd passed in the hallway. "I've got an appointment this afternoon," she told him, not bothering to mention that the appointment was him.

She'd worn the black slacks, black-and-white silk

shirt and black-and-white tweed and silk jacket to honor their last meeting.

Today she would say goodbye to her son. And she would be fine.

If anything came of the collage, if she studied it and felt certain that Kent was crying out for help in some way, she'd approach Mrs. Barbour. Or Kent's teacher. Someone.

"You don't have to leave early, do ya?" Kent raised his arms up so she could place the board on his desk.

"No." If she had her way, she wouldn't leave at all.

But Talia knew she wasn't going to have her way this time. She'd given up that right knowingly, of her own accord, ten years before.

She handed him the glue. Showed him how to best apply it so as not to damage the magazine photos. "Be sure you're positive of your positioning before you glue," she told him. "Once they're set, we can't get them back off or change them around anymore."

She'd been positive when she'd given this child away that it had been the best thing for him.

Some thought she'd taken the easy way out. Well, Rex had. He'd wanted her to have his son, for them to have that between them while he rotted away in jail. But she couldn't do that to her boy. It hadn't been easy giving up her baby.

It had been the hardest thing she'd ever done. Way

harder than taking off her clothes and walking onto stage for the first time, wearing only a couple of pasties, a G-string and stiletto heels. Though she'd wanted to die that night, too.

Giving up Kent had been the hardest thing she'd ever done until today. Saying goodbye a second time, after spending a whole week's worth of sessions alone with him, in their little glass room in full view of the principal's desk and that of her secretary, too, was going to knock the breath out of her permanently.

"I can't decide if I should put the gun here, or the microscope."

That gun bothered her. It was innocuous enough. A toy cap gun. When there'd been other, much more deadly choices. He'd picked a toy.

And he was a smart boy. Smart enough to know that if he'd cut an Uzi out of a magazine someone might have asked why.

She wanted to pick the microscope. To advise him that maybe the gun didn't really go with the rest of the poster. But she couldn't color his story with her own brush.

Besides, it was with other boy things—a computer, a tablet, the microscope…

"It'll show up better here, don't you think?" He was frowning, his lips pursed as he pondered his dilemma. None of her students to date had taken the project so seriously. Not even the adult ones who knew that there was a purpose to the activity.

Then again, she'd never spent one-on-one time with any of them, either.

"I think you're right—it has more prominence," she said as much as she could. "But only because of the grouping around it," she finished. "Change anything in the group and you could change the prominence. Put the gun on top and it would have prominence. Put it below and it might still steal the show." He had it pointed upward, and the shape of it drew the eye.

After some deliberation he set it aside. "I'll come back to that part," he said, and picked up a birthday cake. It had six candles. He pasted it on a picnic table that was already glued to the board.

The rest of their time together flew by in kind. Kent's independent work was amazing for a kid his age. At least Talia thought so. And yet, he involved her in every step of the process, as well. He knew his own mind, but he also asked for her opinion.

All in all, without studying his collage or knowing that he'd been expelled from class, she'd say that his parents had done about the best job parents could hope to do raising a child.

Or a mother would hope that someone else would do when raising her child.

"What do you think?" Her son held up the top edges of his poster.

His work with her was done.

She had to blink. Pretended to need to scratch her nose.

"I think you've got the makings of a talented artist." They weren't any of the words raging through her. They were the ones she could say.

And they were the truth.

Her son might not have her hair. Or her nose. But he had her artistic ability, and then some.

He nodded. "I like it."

"Good."

Oh, my God. This was it.

"How soon can I have it back?" He was looking at her. She couldn't just sit there and stare at him. Or cry.

"Within the week," she told him.

"Cool."

Talia stood. There was no other choice. She collected her things just as she'd done the other four days she'd been there. Packed them into her bag.

Kent helped her cover the poster board, his smaller fingers brushing her hand, and she almost lost it. And then a look of horror crossed his face.

Because he somehow knew that he'd touched a fraud? A woman who was far too dirty to even breathe the same air he breathed?

Boys his age had to stay as far away as possible from the type of woman she'd been.

But she wasn't that woman anymore. By choice. It had been her actions that got her away from that life.

"You aren't going to show anyone else, are you?"

His question finally registered.

"I can't promise that, Kent," she told him. She gave him one thing she'd always promised herself she'd give to everyone. Her honesty. For the most part she'd kept that promise. "I can promise you that I won't show any other students, though. And it's not going to be hung on display."

His features relaxed. "Okay, then. No kids."

Why didn't he want anyone else to see his collage?

The questions attacked her, as they'd been doing all week, and she wondered if she was up to this task. This time. Could she even hope to give Kent's collage a fair read?

Not that it really mattered in the end. He was being cared for by professionals. Mrs. Barbour had told her that Kent saw a counselor on a regular basis. And his teachers and father were watching out for him, too.

Her little collage experiment was just a school art exercise at this point.

Her bag was on her shoulder. His poster under her arm. And Kent had his math book open. "Okay, then," she said, turning toward the door. "See ya."

"Yeah, see ya."

Talia let herself out. She made it to her car.

And then she fell apart.

CHAPTER SIX

SHERMAN DIDN'T MAKE Kent go to bed early. He'd told his son on his tenth birthday that he could stay up until ten from then on if he wanted to. But the boy still held to his nine o'clock bedtime anytime that they were home.

He got himself up at six in the morning, too. Brooke used to wake him every day. Sherman had taken over for her right after the accident, but every morning Kent had already been on his way to the bathroom to brush his teeth and comb his hair before getting dressed for school. But he still presented himself at his son's bedroom door every day. To say good-morning.

On Saturday at 6:05, Kent was still asleep. With his heart in his throat, Sherman stood frozen until he saw the soft rise and fall of his son's chest. And realized that he was falling back into the debilitating habit that had practically suffocated him—and his son, too—after Brooke's death. He'd attended a grief counseling group, but it had been Dr. Jordon, Kent's counselor, who helped him see that he was in a state of almost-constant panic—fearing that he was going to lose Kent, too.

Kent was healthy. Robust. Perfectly fine. He wasn't going to lose him. What he was going to do was take advantage of his boy's sleeping in and get some work done on the computer.

Noncampaign work.

For two years he'd been surfing the internet for any mention of anyone who'd gone missing around the time of Brooke's death. Or of anyone spotted around the neighborhood where the car her killer had been driving had been stolen. He was active on social networks. Trolled Facebook pages of anyone who said they were from that area. Same for Twitter. YouTube and Tumblr, too, in case someone posted a video or photo he might recognize from the crash scene.

The police had done what they could. They'd retrieved the surveillance cameras from a convenience store in the stolen car's neighborhood. They'd talked to folks who lived within a half-mile radius of the crime scene. The guy had been driving the wrong way down the freeway on a very deserted stretch of California highway.

Law enforcement was convinced that the crash had been the result of drunk driving, period.

Sherman wasn't so sure. More paranoia? Maybe. But the stretch of road Brooke had been on had been long and straight—the crash happening in the middle of the stretch where someone could have seen cars for a long distance in both directions. Even if he'd been drunk surely she'd have seen him in enough time to at least swerve. But she hadn't done so.

The man she'd been meeting in the city that night—Alan Klasky—had said Brooke had only had one glass of wine and had ordered coffee to go for the ride home. Investigators had determined that she'd been holding the half-empty cup when she'd been hit head-on. Something about the splatter of the coffee on the air bag—her right wrist and her face had been a clear indication that the cup had been upright. She hadn't fallen asleep. Couldn't have or the cup would have fallen out of her grasp. Or tipped, at the very least.

He ran over the details in his mind. Arranging and rearranging had become a habit for him, too. Always looking for another angle, for anything they missed. He wasn't sure why he couldn't let it go.

Brooke had been killed in a car accident by a drunk driver who'd stolen a car. His wife was gone. Kent's mother was gone. The only thing left was making whoever had done this pay for what they'd done.

Important, yes. But enough to hang the rest of his life on? Or to occupy so much of his time and brain power?

He'd probably be better served using that energy

to figure out his son. But then, he struggled with everything he knew about Kent, and about grief and kids going through grief, and kids who lost their mothers, and boys' relationships with their mothers, and ten-year-olds in fourth grade on an almost hourly basis, too.

Wonder was that he got anything else done.

Must be like Brooke had always said—laughingly in the beginning and then, later, not—he was the master of multitasking. He worked on a campaign and his mind also germinated other issues at the same time.

He slept and seemed to work out solutions to problems, she'd once said to him. She'd begun to take offense at the way he always seemed to have plans for them, to know what they should do in any given situation. She'd begun to feel as if she was losing herself little by little to him.

Shaking his head, Sherman moved from one social networking site to another and swore when his computer froze up on him.

His time on the case was limited by the fact that he didn't ever work on it when Kent was awake. Brooke's death had changed their son. Clearly, he wasn't recovering as well as they'd all hoped. Wasn't adjusting at all as Dr. Jordon had first predicted he would. Sherman wasn't going to make matters worse by bringing up evidence in the case for his precocious son to grind in that busy mind of his.

While the cursor turned over and over on his screen as the web page loaded, he moved to the computer on the next wall in the office he and Brooke used to share and he and Kent now shared. Using his mom's computer had been important to the boy.

Signing on, he opened the internet browser, typed what he wanted and, while he waited for the screen to open, perused the list of recently accessed folders that had flashed on the screen when he'd put his cursor in the search bar. He'd pulled off all of Brooke's files, storing them on an external hard drive in his room, before he'd turned the computer over to Kent.

Mostly it was school stuff. Kent regularly showed Sherman his computer work. Making everything accessible to his dad had been one of the prerequisites of his son's having his own computer. There were dangers out there that Kent might not be aware of. And he'd readily agreed to Sherman's rules.

Sherman didn't exercise his right to search very often. It wasn't as if Kent had a lot of time at the computer without Sherman present in the room. But when he saw a folder he didn't recognize—triq3tra—he investigated. The folder was three-deep in last year's math folder. He'd never have found it if it hadn't been in the recently used list. Heart beating uncomfortably, he clicked on it, hoping to God he and Kent didn't have worse problems than he thought.

The file was password protected.

No matter what he tried, Sherman couldn't open it.

TALIA WAS IN the shower Saturday morning, trying not to worry about the fact that she hadn't even started her homework for the coming week and was working eight-hour shifts at the mall in Beverly Hills both Saturday and Sunday. She'd always been a night owl, even before her previous profession. And she had no social life—completely her choice. She knew she'd get the work done.

She just preferred to keep to her schedule.

"Tal?"

At first she thought she'd imagined the voice. Her inner self calling her to task, no doubt.

"Talia?"

"Oh!" Through the glass door of the master bathroom shower, Talia saw Tatum round the corner. She turned her back and instinctively covered herself, then realized what an idiotic thing that was to do.

"Sorry," Tatum said, sitting on the stool in the separate room across from the shower. "But it's not like I haven't seen it all before," she said.

When Tatum was small, more often than not she'd showered with Talia. Someone had to help the little girl bathe, make sure that she got the soap out of her hair.

"I'm not used to have someone walking around my house while I'm showering," Talia said.

She didn't want her sister to see the body that had rocked the stage more nights than she could count. She knew she'd get over it in time—time took care of everything, didn't it?—but right now, her naked body shamed her. Illogical though that was.

"Sorry," Tatum said again. "You're usually heading out the door by eight. It's five to, and when I saw your car but you didn't answer my knock, I got worried."

And Tatum, like Sedona and Tanner, had a key to the place. At Talia's insistence, not theirs. She wanted her little sister to have a place to hang out, or hide out, at any time for any reason. "I was up late last night," she said, finishing her shower and reaching for a towel at the same time she shut off the water.

"Doing homework?" Her sister's voice came through the open door. Talia could see her denim-clad knees bobbing up and down.

Tatum knew her schedule.

"No."

"You spent the night with his collage, didn't you?"

An adult might have been too polite to ask. Tanner would have been too cautious around her to push.

"Yep."

As Talia wrapped a towel around her body and another one around her head, Tatum left her perch on the stool and followed her to the bedroom. "And?"

All of Talia's underwear was still pretty much the unmentionable kind. She just couldn't afford to replace them and had no intention of anyone seeing them.

"Pick me out something to wear, would you?" she asked, pointing to the walk-in closet opposite the regular closet on the far side of the room. Her stuff would have fit easily in her regular closet, but she'd never had a walk-in before. She liked getting dressed in it. It was like a private dressing room.

At the moment, it gave her the privacy to grab a thong and a scrap of lace with underwire and get them on before pulling on a robe and heading back into the bathroom to semidry her hair. Just enough to get it up in a twist. Any more than that would dry it out.

"How often do you wash your hair?" Tatum asked, coming in to sit on the counter and watch as Talia expertly flipped the long blond strands up and around her hand. Hooker's hair, she thought, knowing full well that it had made her a lot of money over the years. She should cut it. Dye it.

But she'd always loved her hair. Even as a little kid.

"Three times a week," she said.

"I only do two." Tatum picked up her can of hairspray, read the label. "Otherwise, it gets too dry."

"Have you been using the hydrating conditioner I gave you?"

"Yeah. And the detangler, too."

"It's only been a couple of months. Give it time. Your hair will be soft as a baby's by summer."

She liked to dress before applying her makeup—so as not to smear anything on her clothes. But Tatum was sitting there. Watching her.

"I wish I could do that as quickly as you," she said, watching at Talia applied a coat of face cream to her skin, topped it with foundation and then began applying three shades of eye shadow, liner and mascara to her eyes. All to have the end result look as if she wasn't wearing much makeup at all.

And she didn't want Tatum to ever be as quick as she was at the artifice. Going from lap dance back to the stage in five minutes hadn't left her with much time for touching up her makeup. Leaving a bedroom where she'd just been slapped in the face by her husband, to go out and meet his guests, hadn't left much time for covering up, either.

But she'd managed.

"How about getting me some coffee?" she asked as she added a bit of blush to finish.

"Sure, mocha or dark roast?" She and Tatum had shopped together for the little cups of coffee that went with Sedona's one-cup machine. She'd said she didn't need it at Tanner's house as they'd never just drink one cup of coffee there.

"Dark roast."

As soon as Tatum slid off the counter, Talia threw on the light purple blouse and beige silk-lined pants her sister had chosen for her. Before she was in the wedged sandals Tatum had also chosen, her sister was back, placing a cup of coffee on the bathroom counter.

"Wear this," she said, pulling her favorite pendant out of Talia's jewelry box. It was an inch-long hand, decorated with colorful little stones, and on a fairly short gold chain. Tatum found the matching earrings and laid them out, as well.

The sisters had ordered the ensemble off a home shopping television network to commemorate the first time Tatum spent the night with her in the beach house. Tatum had picked a piece, too. Talia was still paying them both off.

"You never told me why you're here," Talia said as she gave herself one last glance in the mirror.

"I just wanted to see you," Tatum said. Then added, "I'm on my way to the Stand for a session and…I'd hoped you'd stop by last night…"

Oh, God, she was failing her little sister again. "You should have called," she said, not bothering to hide the sorrow on her face as she faced the beautiful young woman Tatum had become. "I'd have been there in a heartbeat if I'd known you needed me."

"Chill, big sis," Tatum said, touching Talia's wrist

lightly. "It wasn't me I was concerned about. It's you. And I didn't call because I didn't want to bother you, but I worried about you all night. Yesterday was your last day with Kent."

"Yeah, but you don't need to worry. I'm fine."

"That's why you spent the night with his collage?"

Talia meant to brush past her sister, down the hall and out the door. She was going to be late for work if she didn't get a move on. Instead, she stood there helplessly, her eyes filling with tears.

"He's..." She shook her head. "No, never mind. I'm fine."

"You can see him again, Tal," Tatum said, following her through the house and out the door, double-checking that Talia had locked it.

"No."

"It was in your adoption agreement. You can contact his father and at least ask if—"

"No." Talia was okay now, her purse in hand on her way to work. Where expensive clothes and good jewelry were the only things she'd have to worry about. That and trying to help women whose bodies weren't perfect look good.

"Just...think about it, okay?" Tatum asked, standing in between Talia and the driver's-side car door.

"It would be a selfish thing to do." She said out loud what she'd been telling herself all night long.

She had to contact someone, though. The more

she'd studied Kent's finished product, without the boy there to distract her, the more things she'd seen that concerned her.

He hadn't been overt, of course. He was too smart for that. But somehow those bad words had made it from the trash to his poster. Not the exact letters, of course. These were much smaller. And partially hidden. He'd used letters as borders on a number of pictures and she'd thought him creative. Until she'd seen the ones she'd prohibited earlier in the week. He must have pieced them together from magazines at home and slipped them onto the collage without her noticing.

"Not if you're doing it for me," Tatum said. "And him. Did you ever think that maybe he'd like to know he has an aunt? Or maybe I could be a friend to him now that his mom's gone? Kind of like a big sister."

There were things she should say. A right way to handle this. Talia stood silently.

"Well, anyway, just think about it," Tatum said, stepping back from the door.

Talia nodded. Tatum backed up a few more steps.

"I love you, Tal." Her sweet voice carried across the driveway.

"I love you, too, Baby Tay." She wanted more than anything to make things right with Tatum.

Needed to do so if she was ever going to be right with her soul.

Tatum's frown turned into a huge grin, and Talia figured she'd done okay. This time.

CHAPTER SEVEN

SHERMAN PACED. BECAUSE what he wanted to do was haul his son out of bed, into the office and stand there while Kent opened the restricted file folder on his mother's computer.

His computer.

Dr. Jordon had told him the key to reaching Kent was patience. If he came on strong, the boy was just going to clam up, get defensive. Kent was pushing Sherman away. He needed to know that he was loved, no matter how much he acted out. He was testing Sherman, to see if he could make Sherman leave him, too.

Or some such thing.

It made sense. Sherman got it, logically. And he was beside himself with worry, disappointment and a bit of anger, too, as he stood there locked out of a computer in his own home, and waited.

As it turned out, Kent slept until eight. In spite of the vacuuming Sherman had done. And in spite of the number of times he'd let the screen door slam shut behind him after spotting a weed in the juniper tree bed from the living-room window, or checking on the mail in case he'd missed it the night before, or making sure the hose was wound up.

Maybe he'd wanted to let the door slam a number of times to get his son up and out of bed. That was possible, too.

Sherman had a bowl of sugared cereal sitting on the counter, ready for milk, and pushed the button down on the toaster to cook the bread he'd had waiting there.

He poured milk over his own oat cereal and joined Kent at the table. He talked about their plans to go to the batting cages later that afternoon. About a game they were going to watch that night. He asked his son if hot dogs sounded good for dinner.

He made it until Kent came out of his room in jeans that were too pristine to belong to a little boy and a game-day jersey tucked into them before calling his son into the office.

"Log on for me," he said, pointing to Kent's computer.

Without hesitating, the boy did just that. And then plopped down into his chair.

"Show me what's new," Sherman said next.

Kent took him through a couple of new homework folders. Showed him a new level he'd reached on a downloaded video game. A cartoon game where he had to figure out increasingly difficult puzzles to move from one level to the next. Nothing to do with death, dying or killing. The boy was not allowed to do any online gaming at all. Sherman wasn't chancing what he might come across or be asked to do during the game chats. But Kent didn't seem to mind.

Leaning forward in his own chair, which he'd pulled over, Sherman followed Kent's explanations, praising him where praise had been earned. And slowly started to crumble a bit inside.

Kent wasn't going to show him the folder. He knew it as surely as he knew he was sitting there. The boy had just accessed the folder that week, though Sherman had been able to ascertain earlier by clicking on its properties that it had existed for almost a year.

"That's it," Kent finally said, dropping back in the chair that was too big for him. His head was resting against the back of the chair, which meant that his back nearly covered the seat of it.

"You sure?" Sherman asked. He'd have crossed his fingers behind his back if he'd been his son's age.

"Yeah."

"You haven't done anything else on this computer this week."

"Nope."

"Nothing at all?"

"Nope."

Kent's heel tapped on the floor, his expression placid.

"You know what happens if I find out you're lying to me." Just checking. Or reminding.

"I lose my right to my own computer. I have to do homework on the laptop that's offline and empty of all games."

"Right." He waited. Giving Kent the chance to think on it and come clean.

The boy had to know he was going to bust him. He knew the folder was there. And he'd also know that Sherman knew something. He'd never grilled him before.

And maybe he should have.

Or...

Maybe he should leave Kent to his privacy. The idea was tempting. It couldn't be a permanent condition. He was going to have to know what was going on. But maybe he should speak with Dr. Jordon first. Maybe he'd like a good, relaxing weekend with his son before they got up Monday morning and had to slay dragons again.

Yeah, maybe. He could keep an eye on Kent all weekend. Make sure that the boy didn't access whatever was in the troubling folder.

Or maybe he should give Kent time alone in the office and wait for him to think it was safe to open the folder. Maybe he should bust him then, with the evidence on the screen…

Duplicity had never been his way. He wasn't usually a coward, either.

And since when did he need a psychologist telling him how to discipline his son?

He amended that last thought. He'd needed it since Brooke's death, of course. But no matter how much Kent was struggling…

"I can't abide lying in this house, Kent," he said aloud. There was no attack here. Nothing to push Kent into defensive mode. There was only impenetrable fact.

"I'm not lying." His son looked him straight in the eye.

And left Sherman no choice but to lean forward, take the boy's mouse and find the incriminating folder. Kent, still leaning back as though he hadn't a care in the world, watched him. Sherman clicked to open the folder and got the password protection screen.

"Open it," he told his son.

Sitting up, Kent did so, quickly enough that even though he was watching, Sherman didn't catch the password. Clearly, it was one they'd never used before. He'd tried everything he could think of while his son slept in.

The folder opened, and Sherman blinked. "There's nothing there."

"I know."

Could Kent have come across some elaborate program that allowed him to erase the contents of a folder upon opening it with some password keystroke?

There was no other way the boy could have emptied that folder. Unless he'd done it earlier that week and that was why he'd accessed it.

But then why leave it there at all, if he was going to empty it?

"What was in there?"

"Nothing."

"The folder's been there almost a year."

"Yeah."

If he wasn't mistaken his son was hiding a grin. But not a fun one. No, his eyes took on almost a sly look. A knowing look. If a ten-year-old could manage such a thing.

"Did you create it?" Kent seemed willing to answer anything, so he was going to ask everything he could think of.

"Yes."

"Why?"

"To see if you were really checking up on me like you said you were going to do. I created a password-protected folder just to see if you'd find it and ask me about it. It took you almost a year. Good going, Dad."

Sherman sat back, his fingers on either side of his

chin. He'd shaved in a hurry. Missed some spots. He ran a hand through his hair. He wore his longer than Kent's now that Brooke was gone. She'd liked it short. He liked it more casual and...

"You were testing me," he said to the boy, just to clarify.

"Yeah."

"How'd I do?" Had Kent wanted him to find the folder? Or just the opposite? Had he needed to know his father trusted him enough not to look?

Kent shrugged. "Not bad," he said. "Took you a while to find it, but you grilled me as soon as you did."

As if that was a good thing?

"You did just find it this morning, right?" For the first time since the inquisition had begun, Kent showed a sign of...fear?

"Yes." He sat there, taking it in, finding no concrete thoughts. "How often have you accessed it?"

"I dunno. Maybe eight times."

"I guess I've been a little lax, huh?"

"Nah. You did fine, Dad. Can we go to the batting cages now?"

"What did we agree to at breakfast?"

"I'd clean my room and help with the bathroom first."

"Right, and have we done that?"

"Nooo." Kent's grin was all little-boy then, and it struck Sherman's heart clear through. "I was just hoping you were feeling bad enough that we could skip the cleaning part."

"You want to live in a pigsty?"

"No."

"You got money to pay a cleaning lady?"

The boy's sigh was long. "No, Dad. You know I don't."

"Guess that means it's up to us to get the cleaning done, doesn't it?" Sherman stood, both hands on his son's shoulders as Kent did, too. "At least you got out of vacuuming this week."

Kent threw another killer grin over his shoulder. "Why do you think I stayed in bed?" he asked. "I waited until I heard it in every room before I got up."

Sherman's burst of laughter surprised the hell out of him.

SHE COULD LEAVE a written report with Mrs. Barbour and walk away. Professionally, anyway.

Doing so would be appropriate.

Late Sunday night, after stopping after work to see her family—adamantly avoiding any mention of Kent Paulson—and then finishing the last of her online homework, Talia pulled a jacket on over her sweats, took her laptop out to the deck on the back of her borrowed beach cottage and sat down with the ocean she could hear but not see.

She saw a couple of lights bobbing in the far distance. Ships out to sea? There was nothing but blackness where she knew the beach to be—the stretch of space between her deck and the water.

It fit her, this little cottage. Alone, she didn't need a lot of space. And yet, she never truly felt lonely here. How could you when all of life was spread before you just by sitting on your back deck?

Maybe someday she'd actually be able to afford a place like this. And not have to rely on handouts from the family she'd let down so badly.

As she sat there, not yet opening the laptop, Talia stared out into the darkness and replayed a scene from earlier that day. She'd just finished ringing up a fifteen-hundred-dollar sale—a couple of outfits with the highest quality costume jewelry embellishments—when the store's manager approached her.

"Have you got a minute?" Mirabelle had asked.

"Of course." Even if you didn't, you found one when the head boss sought you out.

"You've been working here for well over a year now," the savvy, middle-aged woman said, as though Talia didn't know the length of her employment.

"Yes."

"Since your first month you've been one of our top earning associates."

She nodded. Helping people look good wasn't all that tough. Getting them to spend their money on looking good hadn't been her doing. That was human nature coming into play. Their own, not hers.

"While finishing up a four-year college degree in three years."

"Yes, ma'am."

"I hear that you're in school again, adding psychology to your major?"

"That's right." Though her original employment had been granted partially on the basis of her performance in the fashion area of study, surely the store wouldn't have a problem with her continued education. She had her fashion merchandising degree with a dual in fashion design. And her work wasn't suffering.

"What's the starting salary for fashion design grads who are psychology students in California these days?" Mirabelle, decked out to the nines in a red suit with black trim, gave her an assessing look.

As far as she knew she'd have to have a doctorate in psychology to actually work in the field of psychology. She was only going for a master's degree. She told the woman a little bit about her collage program—starting with the experience with collage that she'd received as part of her fashion design degree. And then she admitted that, so far, her collage work was all done on a volunteer basis.

The older woman nodded. Talia held her gaze. She needed this job. The store paid the highest sales commission by far. With only two days a week to work, Talia had to make those hours count.

"Good," Mirabelle said after several seconds, a

small smile forming on her face. "I'd like to offer you an opportunity to do far better than that," she said. "I have an opening for a full-time buyer for women's fashions and accessories. You'd have full purchasing privilege in all of the best houses around the world. I'll pay your travel expenses and a small salary. In addition, you'll get a percentage of each of your items that sell in our store."

Mirabelle named an amount she could expect to make that astounded her.

"I..." She was tempted. She could buy a beach cottage. Be able to help her family if they ever had need...

She'd get to travel the world without selling her soul. She'd have respectability.

And she'd be spending a good part of her life traveling. She knew what being a buyer meant. Her nights would be largely spent in hotel rooms. Far away.

"What would the small salary be?"

"Twenty thousand a year. But if you do half as well as the woman you're replacing you'll make more than I've just told you to expect."

After her items arrived and starting selling, of course.

Twenty thousand was less than she'd made at eighteen.

But the commission was more than she could hope to make anytime in the near future.

Still, she'd be gone most of the time. Away.

Mirabelle had given her two months to think about the offer. The position wouldn't be available for another three months.

She had time to weigh the pros and cons. But her gut was telling her that she couldn't take the job. She wasn't going anywhere until Tatum had graduated from high school and was settled in college. And then she still wasn't leaving. She'd learned that in her life family came first, and for her, because of her past, that meant that she had to be where they were. In case they needed her.

So that they knew she was there for them.

She opened her laptop. Opened a blank word processing document and started to type.

About a little boy who was hiding things. Who had thoughts about violence. And a gentle heart. A boy who was angry, and who loved to read and have family picnics. Who wanted to lash out and liked puppies. A boy who was smart enough to keep his true feelings hidden, talented enough to mask his feelings with an artistic presentation, tender enough to see the value in doing the project at all and young enough to put his frustrations right there for all to see. If they looked.

She was telling the story that she saw when she looked at Kent Paulson's collage. She might be right. Or not. She could be reading him spot-on, or be a bit off the mark.

But she knew she wasn't completely off. Talia had a special talent for interpreting people's collage work. Her instructors in college had seen it. The psychologist who supervised her master's thesis work, a project involving the use of collage in assessing children, saw it.

She finished the report. Sent it to Sedona's home printer. Only one light bobbed on the ocean now. Didn't mean it was the only boat out there. Inevitably there were others. But it looked like the only one. Looked starkly alone.

Like her. She wasn't alone. She had family who loved her. Really and truly loved her. They'd have to really love her to see the real her in spite of her past.

Yet as she sat there, contemplating the report she would deliver in the morning, she had never felt so starkly alone.

For one week, she'd almost felt like a mother. From a distance. On the outside looking in. But still...

And now, she'd see Mrs. Barbour in the morning and then just be Talia again. A woman who'd given up her son for adoption seconds after his birth.

Not if you're doing it for me. And him.

Tatum's words had been playing in her head all weekend. Her little sister wanted to meet her nephew. Her only nephew as far as any of them knew. Tatum needed family almost as bad as Talia did.

And what about Kent? She'd abandoned him

once. Was it right or wrong to do so again? He'd seemed to like her.

Maybe he'd just liked her art project.

His "see ya" hadn't sounded particularly…anything. Just polite. It certainly hadn't seemed to faze the boy that they were never going to see each other again.

If ten-year-olds even thought that way. She had. But then, she'd been an adult at five.

What if he thought she'd still be around the school? That he'd be seeing her just like he saw all of his other former teachers?

Was she really thinking about seeing him again?

Could she keep pretending she wasn't looking for a way?

But it had to be for the right reasons. She had to do it for others. Not just for herself. Not to give her a sense of self-worth or because it felt good in the moment.

The thought was followed by another. She wasn't in a position to determine what was best for Kent.

She should just let it be. Deliver her report to the principal and leave well enough alone.

Unless she really believed she could help him.

What if he looked her up as an adult and she found out that he'd suffered something she could have prevented?

She had a plan. Not that she'd told anyone. But she knew about a program that might help Kent Paulson.

If she dared take this any further.

If she dared... Because she might get hurt? Or because someone else might?

The truthful answer to that was both.

One o'clock passed. Then two. Talia sat on the back porch, watching the bobbing light become two again. And then three. Ships passing in the night.

She held her coat close, shivering. Because she couldn't do anything else. She was frozen on the precipice of making a new life with better choices, or remaining in the old one in a new city with the same old mistakes.

How did she trust herself to know the difference?

She'd thought, when she'd run away at sixteen, and then again at eighteen, that she was doing the right thing. Not all women grew up innocent. Not all were mother material...

She sat there until her mind quieted and there was only resolution left. She stood, just before three, and went inside to go to bed. She would have to get up in a few hours, but she knew what she was going to do when she did.

CHAPTER EIGHT

By TEN O'CLOCK Monday morning Sherman had already chaired a couple of productive meetings. His staff was scurrying about the office, making things happen. He'd suffused the air with a positive energy that would make him a mint if he could sell it.

And every time the phone rang his stomach lurched. Kent was back in class today. They'd had a fairly decent weekend. If you didn't count the rudeness at the table when he'd taken him to meet the representative of an animal rights coalition for lunch on Sunday. He'd thought Kent would enjoy hearing about the animals. Had even contemplated the idea of adopting a pet, if Kent asked him.

But his son had put on the headphones to the video game Sherman hadn't even known he'd brought along and ignored every attempt he made to quietly get Kent to put the thing away.

At eleven, when Gina stuck her head into his office, announcing that Kent's principal was on the phone, he was almost relieved to get it over with. The principal had mentioned a private school to him a couple of times, a place where troubled boys went. He was not sending Kent to one of those places.

But he might have to find an alternative. A private school that he could afford. So that Kent could get himself kicked out of there, too?

"This is Sherman," he said into the phone, his eyes closed as though he could block what was coming.

"I'm sorry to bother you…" Sherman leaned as far back as his chair would go, throwing an ankle up over his knee, as Mrs. Barbour rattled on about another teacher, one he hadn't yet heard of, who'd come to her about Kent. Eyes still closed to the rest of the world, he let her prattle on, knowing that somehow they were going to get through this.

What doesn't kill you makes you stronger. His old man's words to him before he'd left with his army unit for the overseas mission that had killed him. *Remember that, son.* His father's last words to him.

"I've read the report, Mr. Paulson, and I think it would be in Kent's best interest if you at least met with her."

Wait. What? Foot landing on the ground with a thud, he sat up. Opened his eyes and said, "Why does she want to meet with me?" An art teacher had found signs of anger in Kent's work. Unfortunately, this wasn't groundbreaking news to him.

"She'd like to tell you that herself, sir."

"Who is this woman?"

"Her name's Talia Malone."

"And you said she took time out of her day to work with my son every day last week?"

"Yes, sir. Her collage program, which is also part of her master's thesis, has been tentatively approved by the school board and she was in our building, anyway. I didn't feel there was any harm in giving Kent an opportunity for some one-on-one time with her. You told me you trusted me to make appropriate decisions for him during school hours and—"

"Yes, yes…" he cut in. "I'm…grateful for all that you're doing. And of course I'll meet with anyone who thinks they can help Kent. I'm sorry. I thought… I expected…"

"You thought I was calling because Kent was in trouble again. I understand." Mrs. Barbour's soft tone reminded him of his mother. Anita Paulson had remarried a couple of years after his father passed away. Another military man. Sherman had been in high school then. Unwilling to be uprooted yet again by military life. His mother had reluctantly allowed him to stay with a friend's family while he finished high school. From there it had been college. And Brooke. His mother, on the other hand, had lived in four different states and was currently in Belgium where her husband, a full colonel now, was serving his last term before retirement. She'd seen Kent a handful of times. Brief visits that always ended with promises for more time soon.

Mrs. Barbour was listing off times when this Talia Malone would be available to meet with him.

"Whatever works best for her," he said, not making note of any of them. Didn't matter to him when it was. As long as it happened. "As soon as possible, whatever's best for her," he amended. If he had something on the calendar he'd switch it.

"Tomorrow, then? Just after lunch? Which would be one o'clock. I can give you the conference room down the hall for as long as you need it," she said, all business as usual.

Grabbing a pen, Sherman took down the pertinent details. An appointment for a new lease on life.

That was right up his alley.

TALIA DIDN'T HUG a water fountain for comfort. She didn't throw up. She also didn't tell anyone, most particularly Tatum, that she was meeting her biological son's father that Tuesday afternoon. She dressed in conservative black pants, a white blouse and her tweed blazer, twisted her hair back into a bun, glued the wayward tendrils down with professional-quality freeze spray and walked into that meeting with her big-girl panties firmly in place.

She hadn't set out to do any of this. Had only wanted a glimpse of her son, to assure herself he was fine before she went on with her life and left him to his. She'd needed the closure of the life she was leaving behind.

But he'd been in trouble, and she'd been able to help. Not as his mother. As the person she was becoming in her new life—the professional Talia.

She had to finish what she'd started. Professionally.

Talia Malone, woman, mother, didn't factor into the meeting. And somehow that made it possible for her to walk through that door with some composure.

Sherman Paulson was taller than her five foot seven by a good six inches. He'd been sitting on the far side of the empty conference table, his hands folded loosely in front of him, but stood as she came through the door five minutes early with her arms full.

She'd expected to have time to set up an easel.

"Let me help with that," he said, reaching for the most cumbersome item she carried —the poster board held to her side by her left upper arm.

"No!" The harshness in her voice embarrassed her. "I'm sorry," she said quickly, dropping her satchel, her purse and her keys in a heap on the table as she rescued the poster board from under her arm. Looking for the easel Mrs. Barbour had told her would be in the corner of the room, she retrieved it and set it up on her side of the conference table.

Crazy, but it felt safer that way. Felt as if Kent was still a little bit hers. Instead of all his. Even if for a few seconds.

With the board still covered, she arranged it on the easel and then sat down.

He took his seat, as well.

"I'm Talia Malone," she said. "I'm assuming you're Kent's dad?"

"Sherman Paulson, yes," he said, holding his hand out across the table. She had to take it. His grip was firm. Warm. The fact that she noticed confused her a bit.

Other than the dark hair—a little more casual than Kent's, a little longer—he didn't look anything like his son. But then, he wouldn't.

"Thank you for meeting with me." Based on the light beige dress shirt, rolled at the cuffs, the navy-and-beige tie and navy dress pants, he was coming from work.

"I'm eager to hear what you have to say," he said, meeting her gaze directly. "It's no secret that Kent's struggling. We've tried, and are trying, all of the conventional methods—private counseling, extra attention at school and home. All kinds of behavioral theories have been put into practice…" He spread his hands open on the table, and out of nowhere she had the idea that this man was gentle.

Not just on the surface but all the way through.

"Needless to say, I'm open to suggestion at this point. Mrs. Barbour said that you know of a program that might help?"

She felt as if she was in the middle of a snowball that had just been hurtled down a very steep hill.

"I'd like to back up a minute if I could," she said,

and then felt guilty for taking more of his time than necessary.

She was a volunteer, not yet a professional in any sense. What did she know?

Unless… The thought had occurred to her several times over the weekend only to be brushed aside, but…was it possible she could see so much in Kent's collage not just because of her artistic ability but because she'd been endowed with a mother's instinct when he was born? Surely the nine months he'd lived inside her, feeling the very beat of her heart, could have bonded them in some spiritual way.

"Unless you're in a hurry," she amended. And then what?

She had things to tell him. Things she really thought he needed to know. And…she was hoping to glean whatever information she could from him to help her sleep peacefully without her son in her life. To help her let him go. Once again.

"I canceled this afternoon's appointments," he said. "I meant it when I said I'm open to anything that might help my son. He comes first."

He got a gold star for that.

"Okay, well, first let me tell you a bit about my program." She described collaging in general, and then added, "Children, in their innocence, go for pictures that speak to them on a level that's sometimes deeper than they even understand. My theory is that oftentimes with their collaging, they're subconsciously telling their own stories. It's been long understood that certain colors specify different characteristics about a person. Color also speaks to emotions that individuals are feeling. What I do is put all of that together to come up with a three-dimensional profile of the child through his or her collage work."

He was studying her, clearly listening intently. His brown eyes had hints of amber that seemed to pierce right through her. And she faltered.

Could he see her duplicity?

Tatum had asked her to meet with him, but she'd meant by going through the adoption agency so he'd know who she was.

She'd considered the idea. Nonstop for months actually. But she couldn't do it. Not because she thought he'd reject her. But because she was deathly afraid that if either of them knew who she was—and what she'd been—she'd bring more harm than good to an already struggling tragedy-stricken family.

In short, they didn't need an ex-stripper to deal with. That was a burden she'd brought on herself and she was going to do all she could to make certain that it didn't reflect on anyone else in her life. Her thoughts flew about a hundred miles per second.

"I'm sorry. Did I lose you?" she asked when Kent's father remained silent.

"Not at all. I'm processing." His sincerity was

evident. "I'm assuming that's my son's collage sitting there." He motioned to the easel.

"Yes."

"I'm wondering what's there. And, quite frankly, I'm a little nervous to find out."

"Well, I have to tell you…my reading of collages…my program…I intended it for older subjects. High-school girls were my target, but the Santa Raquel school board wanted to trial the pilot in elementary-school art classes and so I reworked the focus of my thesis. Personally, I think they were probably thinking that if it turned out to be a bunch of hooey, there wouldn't be any loss. The kids would still have had a fun project for art class." Talia looked out the window behind him. She couldn't believe she'd just told him that.

"So it's still in the trial stage?" His quirked brow was more curious than derisive.

"Yes."

"You're telling me you have no concrete evidence or statistics to prove that you know what you're talking about or that any of this is accurate."

She could tell him about the women at the Lemonade Stand. The counselor there who'd worked side by side with her over the past year had been amazed at the results. But she wouldn't. Their business was not hers to tell.

"Yes," she said instead, after a long enough pause to consider her response.

If he walked out now, she'd lose this chance to help Kent. How could she possibly go to the adoption agency, come into their lives in a normal way, after seeing Kent's father in this venue? Her last chance for making that choice ended when she asked Mrs. Barbour for this meeting.

"But you obviously believe in the concept."

"I'm hoping to turn it into a career." Even if it took several years of working in sales while she took her program to schools for free.

He nodded. "What you've said makes sense. You have my interest. But I guess I'll know better after I see my son's work. And hear your interpretation."

That was her cue. She was too busy letting out a huge sigh of relief—silently, of course—over the fact that he wasn't ending their meeting to dive right in.

Her heart opened just a bit to him, too. She was grateful that he loved her son enough to be willing to consider all avenues to get him the help he needed. To put Kent first in his life.

It was more than she'd done.

CHAPTER NINE

SHAME WASN'T SOMETHING that Sherman felt often. He generally looked before he leaped, considered his response before replying, his choices before acting.

But sitting in the conference room of his son's elementary school Tuesday afternoon, he was filled with shame.

"Keep in mind that Kent had to work with the magazines I brought him," she was saying as she turned toward the easel.

Desire shot through him like hot lead every time he looked at the woman who was there to help Kent.

"The project could possibly have been more revealing if he'd been able to browse more than eight magazines."

He'd had a beautiful woman in his bed before. Brooke had won her hometown beauty pageant back in Kansas. So it wasn't just the slender blonde's looks that were doing things to him. It wasn't the way she held her head—though he did find her posture captivating. Something about her voice drew him, but it wasn't just that, either. It wasn't even how much his approval seemed to matter to her.

"I'm going to give you a couple of minutes to study the board yourself," she said, her fingers reaching up to loosen the taped brown paper from one corner.

Just watching her take the tape off a corner of the board with her long, graceful fingers had him shifting uncomfortably in his seat.

"You can come over here," she invited, moving to the next corner.

He told himself he was just nervous about seeing the poster, about getting this unexpected glimpse into his son's psyche instead of trying to bore his way through the thick wall of stone his son had built around himself.

He stood. She reached for the third corner. He rounded the table. She removed the paper. Took a step back.

Sherman watched her. It was much easier to do that than think about the real task before him.

"Go ahead," she told him. "Have a look. I'm sure that with your knowledge of your son and his life you'll find some significance I missed. My hope is that when we put your observances together with what I see, you'll come away with some new insight that helps you help him."

She wasn't coming on to him. Or even seeming to notice him as anything other than a means to helping his son. She didn't smile into his eyes. Or smile at all.

"I'm just going to leave you alone for a few minutes," she said. "Would you like some coffee or a bottle of water?"

"Water would be great, thanks," he said. Cold enough to tamp the unexpected, inappropriate and completely unwelcome urge to ask her out. Kiss her. Take her to bed.

The energy seemed to leave the room as the door shut behind her. Sherman dropped down to the chair she'd vacated.

He noted the silver flathead screws holding the silver easel secure. He noted that the edge of the poster was slightly bent on one corner.

And then he raised his gaze to the collage that promised a glimpse inside his son's soul.

SHE GAVE HIM ten minutes. Or rather, gave herself ten minutes to get back on track and do the right thing. To help her son, not herself.

And then, armed with two bottles of water, she opened the door to Kent's father.

He stood as she entered the room, met her gaze, and the ten minutes worth of composure she'd gained disappeared instantly. An hour's worth, a week's worth, wouldn't have been enough to remain immune to the brightness she saw in Sherman Paulson's eyes, the stiffness in his jaw. The raw emotion that emanated from him.

And met an answering well of confusion, fear and anguish inside her.

She was the professional here. She had to establish and maintain a degree of distance. Of calm capability.

She reached over the table to set his water down in front of him and then sat in the chair she'd vacated earlier. Opened her notebook and turned to the poster.

"I'm going to start by telling you what I see," she said. "I don't want there to be any doubt in your mind that my impressions were any way swayed by yours."

She slid a tablet and paper over to him. "If at any time while I'm speaking, you have something to add, information that either adds or detracts validity from my interpretation, please jot it down. When I've finished, I'd like to turn the floor over to you. Once you've added any insights you might have, we'll determine whether we can come to see the full picture."

"You said you had a possible solution..."

"I have an idea to present to you, a possibility that might help, but we're getting ahead of ourselves. If I'm way off, my solution won't be viable, so to discuss it now would be a moot point."

She wasn't going to make an offer she couldn't follow through on and if Kent didn't fit the profile she saw, then she couldn't recommend him for the program she thought would help him. She wasn't going to mention the women's shelter to Kent's father at all if there was no cause.

The programs at the Stand were too sensitive— and critical.

For the next half hour she led Sherman Paulson through her interpretation of Kent's story. There was the little boy who still liked stuffed animals. He'd chosen a stuffed pickle for his picnic. A stuffed basketball in another section. A stuffed computer for the most alarming part of his collage. She discussed food favorites. Hot dogs and, oddly for a ten-year-old boy, salad. The types of television shows he liked—family sitcoms.

Sherman made notes.

His favorite sport was basketball, though he liked athletics in general.

"The organization here is really quite remarkable," she stopped to tell him. "Most of the kids I've worked with, even the adults, collect their photos and then put them on the board either with no fore-thought or planning at all, or with shape and maybe color in mind. Kent not only put a lot of thought into the colors and shapes he was using, but he also grouped his pictures in categories, almost as though he was purposely trying to say something with his work."

Sherman's brow rose. He scribbled a note on his pad.

"In some ways his groupings made reading his story easier." Her voice grew more confident with every word, every sentence. She was no longer Kent's mother, a stripper or even Talia Malone. She was on a mission, a conduit doing a job separate and apart from herself or her life.

It had been that way the first time she'd helped a classmate in college in Vegas do a collage. She'd felt as if she'd finally stepped off the stage forever and into real life. Her professor had told her she had a gift.

An odd concept for a girl who'd thought her only gift had been her looks, her sexuality.

"There are school time, home time and what I've labeled in my notes as free time groupings. There are day and night groupings, too. And summer and winter. He organized his collage by time. By how he spends his time, where he spends his time."

Sherman wrote.

"Over here is where things start to get more serious," she said, moving to the part of the poster that had been hardest for her to analyze—and yet was the section she'd been most curious about since the beginning stages of the project. From the first day Kent had kept certain photos separate from the rest. And he'd glued these photos on last.

"He's got the stuffed computer, the squirt gun, the cap gun, a sharp winged action figure…" The list went on and on. Some of the photos were big, some tiny. If you didn't look closely you'd be likely to miss a few of them. Some were fully exposed, others had only a small portion showing, peeking out from underneath other photos. "And there are three cars," she said, pointing out the upside down one, the one inside a random bicycle wheel and the third, almost completely covered by the stuffed computer. He'd done a kind of hidden picture motif with that one.

"A lot of these pictures could represent toys that he has now, has had in the past, or wants, but I don't think so.

"I've discovered in most of the people I've worked with that generally when you're exposing a like or a want, you couch it in something that will keep it safe. Say over here on the grass. Or maybe with the pickle on the table. You'd expect to see something in the bedroom out out. Or see the basketball hoop over here with the rest of the toys…"

She spoke for another ten minutes and then said, "The real tell to me here is the color choices. I'd say that Kent's favorite color is green."

She could have asked him during their week together. She purposely hadn't done so.

"This is all highly subjective, of course, but if you do a color search on the internet, I think you'll find that there is an overall consensus about a lot of what I'm about to point out to you. Over most of this collage, Kent is displaying negative emotion, mostly anger."

Sherman started to say something, but made more notes instead.

"Except for here." She pointed to the stuffed basketball, the picnic with the big green pickle, the outdoor grill and a bicycle. "These all have some brown, either in the border, the background or in the picture itself. Brown stands for security. For being grounded. You'd think that his depictions of family—" she pointed to pictures cut out from ads depicting a mother and father and at least one child "—would include brown, but as you can see, it's not there. Anywhere."

Sherman leaned across the table, studying the collage, as though if he looked hard enough he'd find some brown.

Talia's heart lurched as she saw herself over the weekend doing the exact same thing. A parent desperate to know that his or *her* child felt safe? Knew he was okay?

"You see green in things that he likes—around this basketball rim, in the relish he colored on the hot dog at the picnic and the border he put on that little piece of garden over there. That's what tells me his favorite color is green."

Sherman met her gaze and nodded, and she could almost feel the energy surging through her. The man might not know it but they were mother and father, connecting over their son.

No! Wait. They weren't connecting, and Kent wasn't her son. The man was just unusually attractive to her. Which was pretty incredible in itself as she'd learned to look past and through men a long time ago. Anything remotely having to do with sex was pretty much at the bottom of her list of priorities now.

At least for the moment. Sara, the counselor at the Lemonade Stand who'd facilitated her collage program, had told her over a friendly cup of coffee one night that Talia would most likely experience a full realm of normal human emotions again.

When she was ready.

"But you see," she pretty much blurted, "the rest of this poster is dominated by deep reds, black and some dull yellow."

"Colors of the rainbow," Sherman said. And Talia felt sorry for him. Because she'd grasped for hope, too.

"Colors of anger. Of violence. Lashing out. And—" she pointed to the pale yellow "—illness of some kind."

Not physical, though. She'd bet her life on that one. Not in Kent's case. "The yellow surrounds the computer," she said. "There's some kind of issue there."

Sherman wrote some more, his pen sliding lightly across the paper.

"And then we have the lighter red and the purple," she finished softly. "These colors represent peace, love, nurturing."

She shouldn't have looked at him then. Her words stuck in a throat gone suddenly dry.

"You could think that your son has just used all of the colors of the rainbow," she said slowly, with a thickness not natural to her. "But look where the lighter reds and purple are…"

One place. Around a vase of flowers. And the stuffed, green-bordered basketball.

"Kent obviously feels or has felt a healthy kind of love. It lives and breathes in him."

Sherman's eyes were bright again, and Talia turned back to the poster. "But it's very clear to me that anger is the dominant force in his life right now. Look at all three of the cars. They're all black."

Pen hit paper across the table again. Watching, Talia said, "I understand that your wife…Kent's mother…was killed in a car accident." When Sherman looked up and nodded, she held his gaze and continued, "That would explain one black car. I think the fact that there are three is an indication that a lot of his anger somehow stems from that incident. Or maybe he just saw three cars that spoke to him about his anger."

Could be he just liked black cars, too, her gaze

tried to tell him. But her words couldn't. Because she didn't think it was true. They'd have some green on them, if he liked them, based on the rest of his work.

Her palms were sweating.

Could be she'd taken on more than she could handle. "Mr. Paulson—"

"Call me Sherman," he said. And added, "Please."

She nodded. Took a sip of water. And then another, holding the cap to the water bottle in her hand like some kind of talisman that would ensure her involvement would turn out for Kent's good.

Putting down his pen, Sherman also picked up his bottle of water. "So is it my turn?" he asked, his expression dead serious, but not the least bit defensive.

Talia nodded.

And tried so hard to find a level of detachment in spite of her need to soak up every morsel he was about to give her.

CHAPTER TEN

SHERMAN WASN'T HIS usual self. He couldn't find the composure that normally saw him through life—the good and the bad. Sitting in that conference room with Talia Malone, there was no even keel.

"First," he said, relying on his notes to help him choose what he had to say, "what you said about Kent giving us messages…" He read what he'd written. "It fits with what his psychologist says. He thinks that Kent's anger and acting out is his attempt to express something—obviously anger for one thing—that he can't express in a healthy way. For whatever reason."

Her accuracy excited him. Or something about her did. Maybe just the idea that at the end of this exercise was a possible solution. A way to help his son.

"I'd suggest that you take whatever you get from this meeting today to Kent's counselor," she said.

He already intended to do so.

"Except for the collage," she added. "I promised I'd get it back to him by the end of the week. But you can ask him for it. Or take a picture of it here to email to his counselor."

"Dr. Jordon," Sherman told her. "His therapist is Dr. Neil Jordon." He wanted to tell her everything he could think of. Give it all to her.

"You might discuss with him whether or not Kent should know that you've shown him the collage," she said now, frowning. "Keeping secrets, even when you think you're doing it for someone's good, is sometimes far more harmful than telling would have been. It's a matter of trust."

When he found himself interested in whether there was more to her emphasis on trust than what met the eye, something personal maybe, Sherman looked again to his notes. His allowing Talia Malone to distract him from his purpose—even for a second—had to be a defense mechanism. An attempt to distance himself enough to give Kent the best of him, not merely an emotional reaction.

"I'll certainly speak to Dr. Jordon about it," he said now.

She nodded. Took a sip of her water. And turned those remarkable wide blue eyes on him. That look could really suck a man in.

"And most likely Kent, too," he continued. "We have an open-door policy at our house. I'm not in the habit of keeping secrets from my son, not that I tell him all of my adult stuff, of course—that would be inappropriate."

What in the hell?

Years of practice, a lifetime of practice, of choosing his responses carefully so that he didn't blurt out words that weren't meant to be said, gone, just like that?

He coughed. Ignored the heat rising up his neck and said, "I make it clear I expect that same honesty from him," he finished, choosing to ignore the middle part of his spiel.

"That's good," Talia Malone said. And then she added, "I have to tell you…it's important." Her lips snapped shut. Had she said something she regretted, as well?

No, it was Kent. That was all. The kid was just so damned…compelling. He drew you in until you felt his pain and would do pretty much anything to ease that pain. So it wasn't just Sherman. She must be feeling it, too.

His notes were in focus again. "The time management thing," he said, trying to find his business mind-set—the one he never had a problem using when he was with clients, either in the office or outside it. "It makes total sense that Kent would approach this project from a time-oriented standpoint." Another validation that this woman's work could very well be accurate. Relief was a heady thing. But he couldn't get ahead of himself. Another lesson he'd learned young that had seen him through some pretty atrocious times.

"Brooke and I...Brooke, Kent's mother..." He had to pause then. Not because he chose to, but because he still couldn't bring himself to talk about her.

Unresolved issues, the social worker who ran his grief counseling class had said. Maybe from the way she died. From the suddenness. A need to know why. Or who. She'd said only he could know what those issues were.

His only issue right now was getting help for his son.

"We've always had...and now *I* have this calendar on the refrigerator. We kept...*I* keep our appointments on it, mine and Kent's, and schedule in the time for chores, too. Every Sunday night we sit down at the kitchen table and make a list of everything we need or want to do that week. We go over everything. And then put it on the calendar, which then goes back up on the fridge. That way if something comes up, we can look at the calendar and know exactly where we can slot it in, or move something else if need be."

Her gaze had shadowed. Prompting him to blurt, "It's the way we keep control of our lives," he said. "We get so much more done, have more time for fun and are generally more successful and thus happy and at peace, because we're able to choose what we want to do with our time rather than just have our time taken up putting out fires."

"Yet, fires happen sometimes," she said softly with a glance at the collage on the easel next to her.

Pursing his lips he went back to his notes.

"How did you arrive at the conclusion that Kent likes old family sitcoms?" He hadn't seen evidence of a single one of the shows that they watched together. Or that Kent had watched with Brooke. And still watched on occasion.

Turning to the board, Ms. Malone touched first one clipping and then another. "These pictures all feature the types of families you find on old sitcoms. Every single one of them has a smiling mother, a dad in the background, sometimes facing the camera with a smile, sometimes turned sideways, and at least one kid. If you look, in every one of these it appears that the mother is doing something to please the kid. Each one seems to me to represent the family sitcom formula of an earlier day. A more simple time."

"Kent didn't live back then." He was being difficult. And there was no reason for it. He wanted her help. Had a pretty good idea he *needed* her help, though heaven help him, he couldn't explain why she'd been able to breach walls that no one else, including a professional therapist, had been able to breach.

But then, that was the point of her particular program, wasn't it?

"No, but there are plenty of cable stations that

play reruns," she said. "And as I said from the beginning, I'm not necessarily right. I'm only here to give you my impressions and I've just told you what I based those on."

Falling back in his chair, Sherman twirled his pen between two fingers and said, "Your impressions are right."

SHE HAD TO get out of there. She was in too deep. Falling fast. Heady and needing time to assimilate. Her interpretation was spot-on.

She'd sensed that it was. But her instincts had been known to let her down. In a big way.

And...

She liked Kent's father. Loved how much he loved her son.

She'd done what she'd come to do. Ascertained that the boy was fine. Well loved. Well cared for.

It was time for her to bow out.

"Kent's mother used to watch all of those old shows with him," Sherman Paulson was saying.

He couldn't be "Sherman" to her. That would make it personal.

She needed to like this guy professionally. So that she could be sure that she was reading him right, where Kent was concerned.

Giving herself a mental shake at the internal confusion she was causing herself, she listened to him talk about the woman who'd mothered her son when she'd chosen not to do so.

"From the time he was a baby, she'd sit with him and watch old reruns. Or have them playing in the background while we cleaned or did other things. She was a big believer in the theory that we're shaped by the television we watch. She insisted that those shows would instill good family values in Kent."

Wow. She hadn't dared hope for Kent's home life to be this good. She'd made the right choice, giving him up.

Relief flooded her. And some sadness, too.

"My wife was a walking mother machine," Kent's father said, his gaze somewhat distant now. "Everything she did was done with forethought. I'm the same way. It's one of the things that drew us together, our desire to think first and avoid making choices that we'd regret."

The exact opposite of her.

"She applied the philosophy to parenting, and it worked wonders."

Shaking his head, he said, "When I hear myself talking it's no wonder Kent's angry. Look what he lost."

Something welled up from inside her, causing her to blurt out, "I see what he has. By your own admission you're continuing to live your lives in the same manner, right down to the calendar, providing

Kent with the stability, the security, the assurance that even through tragedy life goes on. Every child needs that."

No, no. She was getting personal again.

His gaze was searching, and she couldn't withhold what he was looking for.

"Look at his collage, Sherman." *Mr. Paulson.* "He's saying how important all of these things are to him. Look at the colors. Look where there's green. Or light red. Or purple."

On the depictions of family. The food. The basketball. The picture of the bedroom.

"He doesn't own, nor has he ever expressed desire, for a single one of those toys."

They were back to the crux of their problem.

"He's understandably angry," she said now, grasping at straws rather than gleaning anything from Kent's personal expression. "He lost a fabulous mother." She wanted to believe that was all this was.

"It's been two years. He should be through the first stages of grief by now. Especially as young as he is. Kids are more resilient, I'm told."

"I'm concerned about the guns," she told him. "And the concentration of black. My concern means nothing," she hastened to assure him as soon as her words were out of her mouth. "I'm not a professional therapist or even a social worker. But I'd feel better if you'd at least talk to his therapist."

He didn't need her. Didn't need her help. He'd just

needed a way for Kent's therapist to get past Kent's walls. She'd just given it to them.

"You think he's prone to doing something violent? Like maybe hurting others?"

"No. Not at all. He chose a cap gun. A squirt gun. I think he's telling us that his anger is raging inside. But by the amount of dark red on this collage, I don't think it's going to go away anytime soon. Not by itself. From what little I've been told, he had an episode the week before last that required discipline. I just don't want it to get out of hand."

"It's already out of hand." His words fell ominously between them. Sherman sat forward, put both elbows on the table and faced her. "It wasn't one incident two weeks ago. It was four. In one week. A boy cut in line in class, and he shoved him so hard the kid hit his head against the wall. But this has been going on, escalating, for the entire school year. We've tried just about everything, and every time I think we're onto something or might have it licked, he gets into more trouble."

She remembered the day she'd overheard Kent in the hallway, mouthing off to his teacher. Not that she could tell Sherman Paulson that she'd been spying on his son. Because she certainly couldn't tell him why she'd been spying.

But she'd noticed something then—Kent had exhibited no fear of being in trouble.

"He didn't seem all that upset to be spending last week in the principal's office," she said.

"The more whatever this is escalates, the more he seems not to care about other things, either."

"But he cooperated fully with me. Without any attitude at all."

"Confusing as hell, isn't it?" he said, shaking his head. "Maybe now you can understand why I'm so eager to hear what you have to suggest—a hundred times more eager, crossing the line to desperate— now that I've seen your work."

He smiled. Not a flirtatious or even a charming smile. It was a plea for whatever help she could give him.

She could have no more to do with Sherman Paulson. He wasn't her problem. And there was absolutely, unequivocally, no room for a man in her life.

At least not for a very long time.

His smile faded. "You said you had an idea?"

If she went forward with this, if she entered into any more of a relationship with either of the Paulson men without coming clean, she would be making a big mistake. A potentially catastrophic one where her own heart was concerned. If they ever found out the truth about who she was, they'd never trust her again.

But if she came clean…if she told Sherman Paulson who she was, would he be as apt to trust her now? Would he change his mind about the faith he'd placed in her where Kent's collage was concerned?

And if he discounted all that they'd done here, all that he'd discovered, if she didn't give him the option she had for Kent, her son could suffer.

This was more than just a week's expulsion. The kid was on a course to severely hurt his life.

God, she'd made a mess.

"I have an idea."

She wasn't like him. She didn't take enough time to consider her responses. She reacted.

CHAPTER ELEVEN

"HEY, WHAT DO you say we have a fire?" Speaking over his shoulder to the kitchen table as he finished up the last of the dishes, Sherman made the suggestion lightly.

He didn't want to come on too strong. Or let his excitement make him misstep. They might finally have an answer that would suit Kent. If he could get his son to buy in to the idea.

Without that critical agreement, they would be right back where they started. At least Kent had managed to mind his manners and stay out of trouble at school so far this week.

His son slurped his soup, picked up the bowl and drank out of it, then burped out loud without excusing himself.

"I've got homework," he mumbled, reaching for a math book that was sitting beside him on the table. Per their schedule, Kent had made dinner that night. Peanut butter and jelly sandwiches and canned spaghetti. Dinner was his responsibility one night a week. And that was the night Sherman did the dishes alone.

"I know. After that. Instead of television." There'd been a picnic on that collage. And several smaller items that, while not really picnic items, had graced the outdoor meals he and Brooke used to have with Kent on cool winter nights. Like a near-exact replica of the stool that Brooke used to sit on when she roasted marshmallows.

And a butane lighter—theirs had been blue as had the one in his collage. There had also been a clothesline that Talia Malone had thought spoke of family and motherhood—Sherman was surprised Kent even remembered the clothesline they used to have. It had been there when they'd bought the house, and Sherman had removed it when they'd put down the pavers and the grill and the butane fireplace.

He'd tried so hard to keep things the same after Brooke's death, but they hadn't had a fire since then. He hadn't even realized it until now.

"So what do you say?" he asked, drying his hands on a paper towel, tossing it into the trash can and taking his place at the table.

"Is someone else coming over?" Kent glared at him.

"Of course not."

The boy answered a decimal division problem correctly and turned the completed page over to the work on the other side.

"So what do you say? A fire sound good?"

"We don't have any wood," he mumbled to the eraser on his pencil.

"I got some."

Kent sat up straighter. Looked like a normal kid as he perused Sherman's face. "You did?"

"Yes." Why was that so hard to believe? He'd forgotten about fires. He didn't have anything against them.

Kent went back to his work. Sherman watched him complete every problem on the page correctly. "So what do you say?" he asked when the homework was done.

"I don't care. Whatever."

He'd take it.

With a grin.

TANNER SAT AT one end of the dinner table on Tuesday night, Sedona at the other, with Tatum and Talia facing each other between them. Her big brother had a thing for family gatherings at the family table—once upon a time she had, too. And was glad he was finally living the life he so rightly deserved.

"So…" Tatum didn't quite grin at her, but she wiggled in her seat as though she could hardly contain herself. At least she'd waited until they'd finished eating the baked chicken and rice that she and Sedona had prepared.

It wasn't Tatum that Talia responded to, though, as she said, "I…" Then she stopped. Tanner wouldn't ask. Not anymore. Not since his overprotectiveness had driven her away. But she needed him to ask.

"Obviously you have something important to talk about or you wouldn't have made a point of making sure we'd all be here for dinner tonight," Tatum persisted.

"Okay."

"It's about Kent, isn't it?"

"Indirectly."

Tanner and Sedona were watching them like a tennis match. Talia could see them out of the corners of her eyes.

Sherman Paulson had been more eager than she could have hoped. And he'd been attracted to her, too.

The first was good—but only if it wasn't because of the second. In her life, it always was.

Or had been.

"Do you need help with something?" Tanner's quiet voice was like a warm breeze from the past, settling something within her.

She glanced at Sedona, saw her beautiful, compassionate smile, noticed Tatum's concerned gaze and then focused back on Tanner. He was just sitting there. Waiting. She could talk. Or not.

She wasn't good at talking. Never had been.

"I can't do this," she said, scooting back from the table. "I can't talk about it." To him. She couldn't leave the more recent past behind where he was concerned. And she needed him so badly.

Tanner's hand on her arm, gentle and not the least bit firm, stalled her departure from the table. "Don't give up on us, sis. I know it's hard. Please, stay."

He was only asking for what she wanted, too.

"Pretend you're ten again," Sedona said. She'd changed out of her work duds—a silk suit and pumps—into the jeans and blouse she always wore around the farm and out into the vineyards to help Tanner with their highly sought after crop.

Ten-year-old Talia hadn't worried about disappointing her big brother. She hadn't thought it possible back then.

She was there because she wanted to be. Because this was the life she'd chosen. She couldn't let herself down again.

Taking a deep breath, she said, "I met Kent's father. At school. Professionally. I might see Kent again. I don't intend to tell either of them who I am. I wanted to discuss my choice with you."

Tanner's expression didn't change. With his wrists resting on the table on either side of his dirty plate, he just sat there patiently.

Only the people in that room, and the workers at the adoption agency, knew of Talia's relationship to Kent. Her secret was safe. And necessary.

"I really don't think I'm taking the easy way out," she said. "That little boy needs help, Tanner. Far more than I even realized. I was right about his anger issues and his disregard for authority. What I didn't know is that he hasn't gone a full week without disciplinary action since school started last fall. I just couldn't chance prejudicing his father against my assessment because of who I am. My work is valid and…I really think it could be critical in this case."

Tatum jumped up. Started clearing away plates.

Tanner didn't seem to notice. "Okay."

Her mouth actually dropped open. When she realized it, she closed it. And then took a sip from the glass of the wine Tanner and Sedona had produced the previous fall—the first of their own brand that actually got labeled and shared.

"That's it?" she asked. "Before I ever saw him you said you thought I should just introduce myself to his father and try to make arrangements for visitation."

"I didn't tell you to do anything of the kind. I told you I thought it was completely appropriate for you to introduce yourself if you wanted to. And that you needed to be very sure of your reasons if you attempted to see him without introducing yourself first. Because once you met him under any other circumstances you could be sentencing yourself to a life without your son and I know how much that's going to hurt you."

Well, yeah, technically that was what he'd said.

"If I screw up this time, it's going to be completely my own doing, huh?"

"You aren't going to screw up, sis. I know that."

Talia shook her head. Why did life have to be so damned hard?

"You know what I want from all of this?" he asked, leaning on the table toward her, holding her gaze until it was just the two of them in the room.

Talia shook her head. But maintained eye contact with him.

"I want you to learn to trust yourself, to start to see who we all see when we look at you." His response made it hard for her to breathe. "And I want to somehow be able to make it up to you for letting you down."

He'd said something similar before. A few times. She'd thought he'd just been saying it to get her home. To make her feel better.

Tanner hadn't let her down. It had been the other way around. Mostly.

Talia's eyes landed on Sedona's hands on the table. They were soft, feminine hands. Tender hands. Not calloused from years of swinging on a pole.

The only dirt in Sedona's life was out in the vineyard, nurturing very expensive grapes.

"I have to do everything I can for him. He's desperate." She finally forced words that sounded unnatural even to her own ears. And as Tatum quietly cleaned the kitchen, with intermittent glimpses over to the table, letting Talia know that she was following every bit of the conversation, Talia gave them a replay of the day—minus the closeness she'd felt to the man who'd adopted her son.

"Right, so I told him about the Lemonade Stand." She held her breath, ready for recrimination.

"Good," Tanner said. "If anyone can help him, Sara can." The counselor had helped bring Tatum back to them. As far as Tanner was concerned the woman was a Malone family guardian angel.

Somehow, he believed in such things.

"He won't really be with Sara," Tatum said. "He'll be in that group with the other boys his age."

"The anger management group," Sedona added. "He'll be playing board games, learning to be competitive in a healthy manner. And learning how to talk about his feelings with others, too, of course. They're planning a few outings for the boys later in the spring, I think."

Sedona would know. She worked at the Stand as legal counsel for abuse victims. She'd represented Tatum. That was how Tanner and Sedona had met.

"It's a good idea, sending him to the Stand," Tanner agreed with a nod.

"I spoke to Lila before I met with Kent's dad." Lila McDaniels, the Stand's managing director, had to approve any nonresidents receiving the Stand's services. It was unusual, a nonresident taking part in resident activities, but it wasn't unheard of.

Most particularly in the physical therapy department. Under special circumstances patients could be approved and then the Stand benefitted from the money charged for services that were free to victims.

"When's he going to start?" Tatum piped up.

"I don't know yet." Talia's gaze bounced from one to the other of them. She'd been alone so long... "Sherman's going to talk to Kent and then get back to me."

Did she sound as desperate as she felt? As out of control? She stood up. "Well, I've got homework to do and an art class to prepare for tomorrow," she said, longing for the chair that sat empty on the back deck of Sedona's little beach cottage.

Tatum grabbed a box of cards. "Sure you don't want to stay and play?"

"I'm sure." Maybe someday. When she was more comfortable in her new skin.

Grabbing her bag, Talia made a beeline for the door, down the steps and out to the driveway where she'd left her old car. She had the driver's door open before she realized she wasn't alone.

"Hey, you okay?" Sedona grabbed the top of the slightly dented, faded red door. Her thick, wavy hair added a bit of drama to her fine-boned, fair-skinned features in the moonlight. She'd have made a mint on stage, Talia thought, and then hated herself for thinking it.

"Yeah. Fine." She wondered who'd sent the other woman, Tanner or Tatum. Maybe both.

"You know that you could end up getting badly hurt here." Sedona was always honest. It was one of the qualities Talia admired most about her.

"I know. I stand to lose no matter what." Amazing how easy she found it to talk to this woman. "I'm basically kissing goodbye to any chance I have of ever being a part of my son's life as his birth mother."

"For now, at least, yeah."

"I couldn't risk telling Sherman who I was and having him shut the door on the chance to see that Kent gets the help he needs."

"I understand."

"I don't think he'd have been as open to listening to me if he'd known who I was. He probably wouldn't have even met with me, not with Kent in his current fragile state, but even if he had, he wouldn't have seen me as just another professional. He'd have had his defenses up and—"

The touch of a hand on hers stilled her words.

"I agree, Talia," Sedona said, that soft smile making her more beautiful than ever. Talia was so glad Tanner had found this woman. He deserved every inch of her goodness.

"I just worry about you," her sister-in-law continued. "The more you see this little boy, the more of your heart he's going to take."

"I know."

"Forgive me for saying so, but you don't have a lot extra to lose. You're just a baby when it comes to loving, Tal. You're only now learning how to open your heart to the goodness of others. I don't want to see you clam up again…"

Talia felt the prick of tears and blinked them away.

"I can't turn my back on him a second time," she said. "And an ex-stripper as a birth mother isn't going to do him any good. The kid has sitcom ideals and he's already lost so much. But as a collage expert and his connection to a great program, I really think I can help him."

"You've thought this through."

"Yeah."

"And it still doesn't make me feel any better about the heartache you're walking into."

"My son's heart is hurting, too."

"He has his father…"

"And I have all of the love that you and Tatum and Tanner give me," she said. "It's going to have to be enough."

"Just do me a favor."

"What?"

"You come talk to me, or someone, if you get in too deep."

She nodded. But knew from experience that when you were in that deep, you didn't see it.

"Don't shut me out, Tal, please? If I get worried and come to you? You'll let me in?"

A quip about Sedona owning the house she lived in and thereby having the right to come in at any time was on the tip of Talia's tongue.

She held it there. Nodded. And when her sister-in-law let go of the car door, she climbed in, shut the door and drove away.

Before she started to do something really stupid like cry.

CHAPTER TWELVE

"HERE, TRY THIS." Sherman put a pinch of powdery coffee creamer in his son's hand. "Throw it above the flame, and stand back," he said, ready to grab the boy's arm if he stumbled or got too close to the fire.

Kent shot his little hand above the flame and was rewarded with some sparkly flashes. "Cool!" The look he turned on Sherman was one he hadn't been sure he'd ever see again—it was as if he was actually looking up to him again. "What else have you got?"

Sherman had taken a few minutes to collect a bucket full of stuff before coming out to the fire with Kent that night.

Their first fire without Brooke. He'd needed it to be special. And different.

He needed Kent amenable to him when he worked up the courage to talk to his son about the program he wanted him to participate in. He had until the morning when he'd told Ms. Malone he'd call and let her know whether or not to make the arrangements.

Pulling out his next sample, he handed it over to Kent. "Table salt," he said as Kent tossed the crystals.

"Orange flame, way cool!"

"Water softener salt," he said with the next pass off.

"Purple!"

"Epsom salt."

"Wow, I've never seen white flame. Let's do that one again," Kent said as he tossed the substance into the fire. So they did.

But the boy wasn't done. "What else?" He turned, looking at Sherman's bucket as if it was Santa's sack.

"Laundry detergent." He handed over the sample.

This time Kent surprised him. He held the powdered chemical and said, "What color is it going to be?"

He was testing him.

Thank God it was a test he could pass. "Light green flame," he said. And was rewarded with an impressed glance from his recalcitrant son.

They went through other chemicals. Other colors. And then Sherman said, "Sugar. I'll throw this one."

Kent stood back without being asked and waited. Sherman tossed the sugar and watched his son as little tiny sparks flew around the fire.

"Like a sparkler," Kent said, watching. "Hey, maybe we can make our own homemade sparklers," he said next, standing beside him in their backyard under the stars.

"I've never done it, or heard of anyone doing it, but we can look it up on the internet," he agreed.

"Then we wouldn't have to wait until the Fourth of July."

With a pang, Sherman remembered that he'd taken Kent to a professional baseball game with a client on the Fourth last year. They'd seen fireworks there and he'd called it good.

"Now for the flour," he said, not wanting to ruin the moment with regrets. "Stand back."

Kent obeyed immediately, anticipation in every line of his body as Sherman filled his palm with flour and threw it above the flame.

He quickly grabbed Kent's arm, shielding the boy as the flash flame shot up in front of them.

"Do it again!"

Sherman did.

And Kent laughed out loud.

As it turned out, Sherman didn't get around to asking Kent about Ms. Malone's program until he was tucking his son into bed a couple of hours later. They'd stayed out by the fire for a while. They'd tossed on some copper that made multicolors. And then, thinking of his son's collage, of the fact that his son opened up when he was being artistic, he'd had another idea. He'd run into the kitchen, emptied a bottle of beer into the sink and then dropped it into the fire. With their outdoor barbecue tools, he'd helped his son pull at the glass as it softened, until they'd made what they both decided was a slightly off-kilter ship.

Their ship in the night.

At least they were on the same one.

"You had a good day at school today," Sherman said as he looked at that brown-bottle ship on his son's dresser, right where Kent had put it when they'd come in the house.

"It was okay."

It was great! The boy hadn't been in trouble.

"I met Ms. Malone today."

"My art teacher? What about her?"

"She's not the regular art teacher." Sherman wasn't sure why it was important to him that Kent understood that. "She's a collage specialist."

"I know. She told me." He was lying on his back, his head on his pillow, sweet and clean and inno-cent-looking as he stared up at Sherman. Sherman sat on the side of the bed.

"So she showed me the collage."

"It's dumb. Just a bunch of glued magazine pic-tures."

"I didn't think it was dumb. I thought it was pretty amazing."

"Yeah, right, Dad. You have to say that."

Okay, so this was going nowhere fast. He had to

change tactics before something besides household chemicals blew up in front of him.

"She knows you've had some trouble."

"Duh, Dad. I was suspended from school last week. That's why she was there. Of course she knows."

"So she told me she has a program that she thinks might help you."

"I don't need help."

There'd been nothing in Kent's collage against the doctor, but there also hadn't been one thing that indicated any outside help in the boy's life. And, clearly, Kent wasn't opening up to the man.

"If it works out well, you might be able to skip some of your meetings with Dr. Jordon."

"For real?" Kent's sudden seriousness told Sherman that even if Kent didn't agree to sessions at the shelter, it was time to get him out of his current counseling sessions. Even though Dr. Jordon was Kent's second one-on-one therapist and came with the highest recommendations.

"For real."

"Okay."

That was it? He'd been worried for over eight hours for an easy okay?

"For real," he quoted his son.

"Yeah," Kent said, yawning. "I like Ms. Malone." With those words the boy turned on his side and closed his eyes.

Sherman waited until Kent's breathing steadied into an obvious indication of sleep, then bent over, kissed him on the head, tucked his covers around his shoulders and wished him a very quiet good-night.

TALIA WAS STILL on the back porch, head back and eyes closed, almost dozing with the ocean waves in the distance, when her cell phone rang. Tatum had a habit of calling her before bed. Not every night. But often.

"Hey, Baby Tay, I'm fine," she said, picking up the phone from the table beside her without opening her eyes.

A very male cough responded, and she sat straight up. "I'm sorry, Ms. Malone, is this a bad time?"

Pulling her phone from her ear, she looked at the screen, recognizing the number, though she'd only officially had it since that afternoon. Sherman Paulson.

Almost as though she'd conjured him up. She'd just been thinking about him…

About his son.

"No, Mr. Paulson. I'm sorry. I thought you were someone else."

"Baby Tay."

She couldn't tell if he was laughing at her or not.

"My little sister. She calls me to say good-night."

"And that's how you say good-night? Telling her you're fine?"

He was sharp. She'd hand him that.

He was also her connection to her son. To helping her son. He was the man who'd clearly give his life for Kent.

"She's a worrywart."

"You called her Baby and said she's your little sister…" His words were innocuous but his tone sounded just a tiny bit flirty.

And she was just a tiny bit flattered. For a brief second.

"She's sixteen and Baby Tay is her nickname."

"So why is she worried about you?"

It wasn't a professional question. So she couldn't answer.

"I'm sorry. I overstepped and made you uncomfortable."

She didn't want him apologizing to her any more than she wanted him flirting with her. And she wanted both.

"It's fine. I'm… Did you talk to Kent?"

"I did. And he said okay."

"Good." Oh, my God! She was going to see him again for sure! She got to help him! And she would be able to keep track of how he was doing. Her heart pounding, she stepped off the deck and walked in the sand that led down to the ocean.

"He likes you."

Her toe caught in the sand. But she kept walking. The water wasn't far off. It was chilly, but she had a sudden urge to feel the water on her feet. Pulling her hoodie close, she kept on.

"I like him, too," she said softly. "More than that, I really think this program is going to help him."

"It's all young boys, you said."

"Yeah, there are currently four of them. The group meets every day. The more often Kent can join them, the better. We want him to feel as much a part of things as the other boys."

Amazing how comforting the beach was to her, even in the dark of night. The constant sound of the waves crashing was her company.

"I wish I could just take every afternoon off from work, but while my schedule is flexible, sometimes I can't help being late. Mrs. Barbour has been good enough to watch him for me until I can get to school."

He stopped. And then said, "I'll see if I can arrange transportation for the days I can't get him there."

Step. Step. Step.

"I can take him if you'd like." Speak without thinking it through. That was her way. "I hold sessions there three afternoons a week, anyway."

She told him very little about herself. And had to keep it that way.

"I can't ask you to…"

Step. Step. Stumble. Step. "You aren't asking, I'm offering." Talia felt as much as heard the change in her voice. The throatiness. It came naturally. When she was talking to a man and wanted to manipulate him into giving her what she wanted.

A necessary skill for a stripper if she was going to make good money.

"He likes you."

"So you said." Step. Step. Step. She couldn't let it go to her head.

Step. Step. Step. Or her heart.

"No, I mean, I'm going to have to be in your debt and accept your offer because he really likes you. You have no idea how refreshing that is in his life these days. I firmly believe that if anyone has a chance at getting him to buy into this with full commitment, you do."

Step and... She dipped her toe into the frigid ocean. "So I'll take him," she said. "And you aren't in my debt."

Quite the opposite. Not that he could ever know that.

"How soon can we start?"

"You'll need to go down and have an interview with Lila. She'll run a background check on you. As soon as that's cleared, we'll be ready to go. The group meets from four until five Monday through Friday."

"I'll go in tomorrow morning," he said. And something cracked. Loudly.

"What was that?"

"A bottle."

"What?"

"I'm outside by the fire Kent and I built tonight, melting a beer bottle. I put it too close to the middle of the fire and it burst."

She pictured him sitting alone by a backyard fire. Maybe he'd changed from his work clothes to jeans. Or sweats.

How far away was he? A mile or two? More?

Waves lapped gently against her toes, numbing them, as the night air chilled her skin.

Inside, Talia was burning up.

Sherman started to talk about a ship in the night and the look on their son's face when he'd seen copper change flame to colors. He thought he was only talking about his son. Not theirs.

And Talia, sitting in the sand, had tears on her cheeks.

CHAPTER THIRTEEN

SHERMAN LIKED LILA MCDANIELS, the managing director of the Lemonade Stand, on sight. Somewhere in her fifties, the woman could have passed for nondescript with her brown linen suit and mostly gray hair back in a bun, but the depth of caring shining from her eyes filled her office with life.

She wasn't overly friendly. To the contrary, she was all business as she put him through the ropes, asking what he considered to be completely private questions about his past relationships, his current relationships, about his home life growing up and his current home life. She asked about his career history. And asked him to tell her about his son. He answered every one of her questions without hesitation. He'd strip naked and crawl on hot coals if it would help Kent.

And on Wednesday afternoon, after getting a call from Ms. McDaniels saying he'd passed his background check, he left work again to drive Kent to his first meeting with Sara Havens, the therapist who facilitated the anger management session for young boys at the Lemonade Stand.

He'd told Kent the boys were his age, give or take a year. And that there were four of them.

"I get it, Dad," Kent said, staring out the passenger window, preventing Sherman from seeing his expression. "It's another grief thing, and I don't need it, but it's better than talking to stupid Dr. Jordon."

"You know, if you'd clean up your act in class, you could be done with all of this."

"Whatever."

"And no, it's not so much about grief," Sherman said. He'd met Sara Havens that morning, as well. She'd suggested that he let her introduce Kent to the group, and Sherman had been relieved to abdicate the job to her. At the same time, he wasn't sending his son in there without at least some kind of preparation. "The boys, three of the four, are currently living at this place."

"It's an orphanage?"

"No. It's a shelter for people who've been physically hurt by a family member. Most of these boys have mothers who've been beaten up by their husbands or brothers or someone close like that."

Not anything he'd choose to expose his ten-year-old to. In a perfect world. But Kent's world was far from perfect these days. And if he didn't straighten up, he was heading for far worse life lessons.

He glanced over and saw the boy staring at him. "Were the boys hit, too, Dad?"

In his preppy green pants and green-and-beige

sweater with his white short-sleeved shirt showing at the neck, Kent looked like his mother's little
darling. Sweet. Innocent. The complete antithesis
of a troublemaker.

"I don't know. Probably some of them."

"Why do I need to go there? You never hit Mom
or me."

"No, but someone hit Mom's car and hurt her and
maybe you can help these boys know how to feel
about that." Whoa, man. He was really winging it
here. But life was often better if you were thinking
of others instead of yourself, right?

Kent didn't say a word for a couple of blocks.
And then asked, "Is Ms. Malone going to be there?"

"I don't know. Maybe not today. But this group…
it meets every day after school. And she's going to
be driving you here."

The ten-minute drive from Kent's school to the
Lemonade Stand had passed quickly.

His son's mouth dropped open. "I have to go
every day?"

Shrugging, Sherman said, "Let's just give it the
rest of this week and then talk about it, okay?"

"Whatever."

He parked the car. "Kent?"

The boy didn't answer.

"You said you'd give this a try."

"Yeah, before." He said the last word with disgust.

"Before what?"

"Before you were just using it as a day care so you don't have to come get me at school. How come Ms. Malone can't just take me home? I don't need a babysitter."

Taking his keys out of the ignition, Sherman waited for the instant flare of anger to pass before saying, "That's unfair, Kent. We've talked about these accusations of yours."

"Sorry." He didn't really sound it, but the belligerence was gone from his voice.

And that was good enough for Sherman. "Look at me."

He waited. Eventually, Kent turned his blue eyes up his way. "I am not trying to get rid of you." His tone was deadly serious. "I could enter you in any number of after-school programs, and still might, if my work schedule requires it. I have to make enough money to pay our bills and put money in your college fund, too."

"'Kay." The boy reached for the door handle.

"Kent?"

He looked back.

"Those boys in there, they're all hurting. They aren't lucky enough to be able to stay home in their own rooms. I need your word that, no matter what, you'll use your words, not force, if any of them cause any problems for you."

He nodded.

"I mean it."

"I know. I'll be good."

For once, he sounded as if he meant it. And Sherman wondered what kind of spell this Ms. Malone had spun over the Paulson men.

TALIA WAS ADDING more collage classes at the Stand. She'd still be doing her regular three afternoons a week, but she was now going to be working with the younger girls in residence. Her adult classes were moving to two nights a week, Tuesdays and Thursdays at seven. It would mean more of a homework crunch. And a couple of very long days, as Tuesday and Thursday mornings were also when she had to drive into LA for the two classes she couldn't take online. But long hours were nothing new to her.

And nothing she couldn't handle.

Keeping busy was better than being idle. It left no time to dwell on what couldn't be, what once was, what had been, what might have been...

She was just leaving Lila's office on Wednesday, having purposely hung around just in case she'd run into Kent and Sherman Paulson, when she ran into them heading toward the door.

"Ms. Malone!" Kent saw her before his father did, leading Talia to immediately jump to the conclusion that he'd been looking for her.

Because she'd been so desperate to see him and hoping that he'd be glad to see her, too.

"Hi, Kent!" She'd purposely dressed in new black

jeans, a white blouse and short black sweater in case she ran into them. Because she felt confident in them, yet they were still conservative. "How'd it go?" She focused on the boy.

"Great!" he said with a grin.

At which she couldn't help sneaking a glance at Sherman. The man was staring at her. Intently. She could read a huge thank-you in his gaze.

And, she was afraid, something more. She looked away.

"So we're on for tomorrow, then? I'll pick you up from school at three-thirty?" His group didn't start until four.

"Yep." Kent didn't offer any details of what had transpired over the past hour. Details she desperately needed.

But they weren't hers to own.

"We're going to Barry's. You wanna come?" the boy asked, naming a well-known burger place not far from the beach, as she walked with them toward the door.

"Oh, I—"

"Please," Sherman said just when she was going to use the fact that his father would want some time with him as her excuse to beg off. "Buying you dinner every night for the next year would be the least we could do," he said.

"Cool! Can we, Dad?"

"No!" Talia was quick to say, and some of the joy

went out of her son's expression. "But I'll come tonight, how's that?"

"Great!" he said, skipping out the door as Sherman held it open, his brown eyes gazing at her as he waited for her to follow his son past his body and out the door.

"I, uh, my car's not—"

"Ride with us and I'll bring you back here afterward," he said, still holding open the door. She was close enough to smell a faint hint of whatever musky scent he'd put on that day.

His scent did something to womanly parts of her that had been deadened to a man's touch by the time she was eighteen. Her best choice in that second was to get away from the scent as quickly as possible. So she passed through the door. And then had no other viable choice but to continue on to the silver BMW and climb in the front-passenger door that her son held open for her.

KENT LIKED CHEESE but not on his burgers. He was a fan of French fries. And didn't ever drink soda, mostly because he'd never been allowed to do so. He ordered orange drink. But only after his father told him he couldn't have a chocolate shake. He put his napkin in his lap, covered his mouth and excused himself the one time he burped, and spoke with better elocution than she'd had at twenty.

As Talia sat beside him—his choice—and across

from his father, in the hard plastic booth, she knew a strange kind of peace. She'd done the right thing, giving him up.

She also found out that Kent's dad was a bigwig at a campaign management company. She'd heard of one of his candidates. Sherman took Kent to all kinds of expensive and exciting places, introduced him to people Talia might have met in the dark hallways they didn't let their public see, and he didn't like cheese on his burgers.

They drove back to the Stand, and she jumped out, leaning down to tell Kent, buckled into the backseat, that she'd see him the next afternoon.

She was okay. Fine. And then she caught the look in Sherman's eyes as her gaze brushed by him on the way out.

He looked...hungry. "Here's my card," he told her, handing her a business card. "Feel free to stop by anytime and I'll show you around."

He'd made the offer at dinner, when Kent had told her about the cool room at his dad's office that had photo equipment and a full wall of different colored paper. A small in-house printer for some of their more basic jobs that required computer-generated art only.

She nodded. He glanced at the cleavage she purposely wasn't showing, but which just might have been visible due to her bent-over position.

He wished her good-night.

She nodded again.

And hated herself for liking that look in Kent's father's eyes.

CHAPTER FOURTEEN

SHERMAN DIDN'T SEE Talia Malone again that week. Or the Monday of the following week. She picked his son up from school each day. He knew she drove an old beater, which his son thought was way cool and that he'd suggested to her that Sherman and Kent should maybe fix it up together in their garage.

Funny that, because the only thing Sherman knew about fixing cars besides basic lightbulb changes and battery jumps was which garage to take his to.

He knew that Talia had a college degree in something Kent couldn't quite remember and that she was going for another degree, too. He knew she lived alone. And that she had a small place on the beach. She had no pets but had always wanted a dog—at which point in the conversation Kent had slid in the idea that he and Sherman should get one.

He'd actually been thinking about that idea himself. Brooke had been allergic to animal hair so they'd never been able to have a pet.

Each day when Sherman picked up Kent from the Lemonade Stand he looked for Talia. She was nowhere to be found in the main portion of the building that he was allowed to be in. Even on the nights when he went early and waited in an alcove halfway down one of the two main hallways. Or when he waited in the other hallway the next night.

He thought about her every single day—at the time she was picking up his son—but also anytime he saw a blonde woman with long tanned legs, or just a blonde woman, or any woman, or really just anytime at all. At first he'd figured that his obsession with her had been a product of his intense gratitude for what she'd done for his son.

In a week's time, Kent had had two episodes at school and one at home. Not great, but a definite improvement.

Sherman figured that, over time, Talia's consumption of his thoughts would fade. It didn't.

He was about at the point of calling her up and asking her out on an actual date—a first since he'd married Brooke—thinking that maybe if he spent a normal evening with her he'd somehow dispel the mystique with which she held him in thrall.

And then, out of the blue, on Wednesday morning, a week and a day after he'd first met her, Gina buzzed him to tell him that Talia Malone was in the office asking to see him.

On any other occasion he might have had Gina show his guest to the conference room across the hall, or into his private office. Instead, he was at the door before he'd made a conscious decision to stand.

As if the woman would somehow fade away if he didn't get to her in thirty seconds.

"Talia, come in," he invited, and wondered if Gina had heard the eagerness in his voice.

"I'm sorry to bother you," she said, barely looking around as she came in, as though she didn't want to impinge on his private life.

God, she'd been in the shower with him, in bed with him, every day for a week. It didn't get much more private than that.

"It's not a bother. What can I do for you?"

"I was going to call, but you said that you were sure there was some extra paper that I could have for the kids at the Stand, and I was hoping I could just pop in and someone could give it to me without actually having to bother you."

She was long-legged and gorgeous, the blonde in every man's dreams, carried herself with a sexy confidence that had nothing to do with the way she was dressed. And her manner seemed almost...demure. As if she was just a tad bit unsure of herself.

While he stood there gaping, trying to come up with an appropriate response, she said, "I told them they didn't need to disturb you, but as soon as I gave my name, they brought me back here."

"I told reception that you were going to be picking up Kent every afternoon and that if you ever called you were to be put through immediately. No matter what. They simply applied the order to your physical appearance."

He smiled. Crossed to his desk. Motioned for her to have a seat in one of the two mahogany-and-leather chairs in front of him.

She didn't sit, but rather stayed standing, clutching the large satchel slung over her shoulder. It was cloth and emblazoned with the name of an exclusive high-end clothing store at the Beverly Center.

"I really was just hoping I could hit you up for a donation of some different colored and textured papers," she said. "Different weights, too, if you have them. The Lemonade Stand does business almost exclusively by donation. I'm working with the girls on texturing and design collages, a kind of fashion thing, and I remembered what you'd said about the paper room."

And he'd told her anytime she'd needed anything to come by. He remembered. He owed her far more than as much paper as she could use. Besides, the firm got it at cost and it would be a write-off, which they always needed.

"Of course," he told her, scrambling for a reason to sit and visit with her before he walked her down the hall.

In jeans again, sandals that showed her prettily painted red toes, a solid-colored, tight-fitting T-shirt and a short white jacket, she could have walked off any of the fashion magazines she likely had her girls cut up for their collages. He felt decidedly plain in his brown pants, striped shirt and boring brown tie. They weren't new. Or ironed, either.

"Have you got a minute?" he asked when no one moved toward the door. "I'd like to talk to you about Kent."

She'd taken a very obvious liking to his son, and for the first time in his life, Sherman used him to get something for himself.

Five more minutes of this woman's time.

"I've got about fifteen, actually," she said, sliding into the chair he'd indicated, more than sitting on it. At least as far as his overactive imagination could ascertain. "I'm teaching an art class at Osborne in forty-five." One of the other elementary schools in their district.

"Kent said you take classes at UCLA." He only had fifteen minutes of her time and that was as good as he could do?

"That's right. I'll have my master's in psychology by December."

"You don't look old enough to have your master's degree." He'd have put her at twenty-three tops. And only because her eyes had stories to tell.

"I'm twenty-seven." She offered nothing else.

He wanted more. Like what her undergraduate degree was in—the one his son couldn't remember.

He thought about what he wanted to say.

"You said you wanted to talk about Kent?" she asked, frowning. "Is there a problem?"

"No. Exactly the opposite, in fact. I don't know what it is with you that's different from everyone else who's tried to help him, but he responds to you. And I'm eternally grateful."

"Maybe it's just that I'm not a counselor or his teacher. I'm just an art person with a little psychology training and some theories."

"Your art and theories are the only things that seem to have reached him."

She smiled, but the look was distant, and he found that odd.

"So he's not giving you any problems?" he asked, since it was all he could come up with regarding the one topic she seemed to want to talk about—his son.

"None. But then I'm only with him ten minutes a day."

"He's on time?"

"Yes." Her words were detached, but that look in her eyes... The intensity was back again.

And he had to know what went on in that brain of hers. That heart of hers. What was she thinking? Feeling? Was it anything like the fire raging through him?

Sexually, and...in every way.

"He's agreed to continue with the program," he said, and realized he had a valid reason to speak with her after all. "If you'd rather not continue driving him, I've arranged to have the wife of one of the guys here in my office pick him up. Kent knows her and—"

"Has he indicated that he doesn't want to ride with me?" He knew at least some of what she was feeling now. Her distress was obvious.

And so incredibly sweet.

"No, no. To the contrary, I think he'd move in with you if you'd let him." He was joking. Completely. But the idea of him and Kent living with this kind, delectable woman…

"I just don't want to put you out."

"It's no bother, really," she said quickly, both hands on the strap of her bag now as she shook the hair back away from her face. The strands ended at her breasts, and he couldn't help noticing as they moved, too. "I'm—" she licked her lower lip "—going that way, anyway, three of the days, and it's not that far from where I live."

"Kent says you have a cottage on the beach."

"It belongs to my sister-in-law." She was so careful about having her story straight, about making sure no one thought she was something she was not. He liked that about her, too.

"I…like Kent, too," she said now, her smile cutting off his breathing space. "He…in some ways he reminds me of myself as a child."

"Oh?" Sitting forward, he felt like a cat in front

of a can of tuna, ready to pounce on the good stuff. "How so?"

"I never quite felt like I fit in with the other kids, either," she said. But she didn't look at him. And he knew there was more.

And that he wanted to know what it was.

"Why is that?"

Her shrug was a definite blow-off. And the clock was ticking. He needed more time. "Kent doesn't have a mother, I didn't have a father," was all she said as she stood.

Another small piece of her to file away in his memory bank. Another set of questions he wanted to ask.

He headed for the door. "So, for now, we'll stick with the status quo as far the driving?" he asked.

"I'd like that, yes." So careful. With everything.

She walked beside him down the hall, her shoulders just a couple of inches below his. Just enough to fit comfortably under his arm were he to wrap it around her.

A couple of his associates looked up as they passed opened office doors. He saw some raised eyebrows. A smile.

"I know it's only been a week, but do you think the program's going to be good for Kent?" she asked him.

"It's already good for him. Not only have there been less instances of aggression and belligerence this week, he's been more…his old self in between times. More like the funny, eager little guy he used to be."

Her gaze softened, and he added, "Don't get me wrong, it's not a lot, but it's enough that I noticed."

"I'm glad." The words felt like so much more.

"He's made a friend there. A kid named Jason. You know him?"

"No, but I think I know his mother. I can ask around if you'd like."

"No." They'd reached the door to the printing room, and getting the keys in his pocket, Sherman unlocked it. "I want him to be free to do this on his own for now," he said. "Dr. Jordon said it's important for him to find his own way, to feel as though he has as much control over his life as a ten-year-old can have."

"That sounds right."

So did she. So right. In so many ways.

Maybe it had just been too long since he'd been on a date. Or had any intimate contact with a woman. Maybe he'd just hit the point in his healing that he was ready. For whatever reason, Sherman didn't take time to figure out the best course of action as she chose her paper, gave him effusive thanks for something that cost him nothing and turned to go.

"I have box seats for the symphony next week. Would you like to go?"

"When?" The word was out almost before he'd finished speaking.

"Wednesday night. It's a Broadway pops show."

"I'd… What about Kent?"

"The next-door neighbors, a married couple who never had kids, stay with him whenever I have to be gone. They're good with him. He likes them."

"Okay." Sherman didn't understand what caused the shadow that flashed over her expression as she said the word.

But he knew that he wanted to find out.

CHAPTER FIFTEEN

SHE WAS GOING to have to cancel the date. Talia knew it the second she agreed to go.

She hadn't meant to say yes. Couldn't believe she had. But standing there, in his office, high on the fact that he wanted her to continue driving his son—and on something else she couldn't define—she'd just jumped right in without thinking.

She couldn't go. There was no future for her in a relationship with Sherman Paulson.

Or probably any other guy she'd want to make a family with. What decent man was going to want an ex-stripper as the mother of his children?

One thing Talia had learned a long time ago was that she was not the type of girl one took home to Mom. Even before her blatant bad choices it had been that way. Before she'd ever understood what it meant to be considered a bad influence on the good and decent people of this world.

The first time she could remember a mother refusing to let her daughter play at Talia's house, she'd been six.

"I want to meet him." Tatum sat with her in the

dark Thursday night, having ridden back with her from the Lemonade Stand. She'd joined their collage session that evening, at Sara's behest.

While Tatum was as young as some of the girls in Talia's new afternoon collage class at the Stand, she was different, too. She wasn't a child of a victim. She'd been a victim. And had recently been struggling with the idea of dating again.

There was a boy in her school that she liked. Really liked. He'd asked her out. And Tatum, scared of giving up control of her mind and heart again, had said no.

Talia didn't have to ask who they were talking about as the two sisters sat together on Sedona's back deck, sipping iced tea.

"Did you call Tanner?" To let their brother know that she was spending the night and that Talia would take her to school in the morning.

"Yeah, while you were in the bathroom. I want to meet him, Tal."

Tatum was the most stubborn of the Malone children. Thank God. She'd been too stubborn to just accept the treatment she'd received at the hands of her ex-boyfriend. As young and hurt and confused as she'd been, she'd escaped to the Lemonade Stand. And refused to leave. At all cost.

She was Talia's hero. Not that her younger sister would ever believe that.

"I don't think that would be a good idea," she

said softly. Saying no to Tatum was not a feat she'd yet mastered. And probably wouldn't, either, unless it was a matter of health or safety. "It's killing *me*, Tay. And my heart's practically stone."

"Your heart is not stone! Don't say that."

She could feel Tatum's gaze, but didn't turn her head.

"I know it's hard," Tatum continued. "But life's hard, right? It's hard as hell knowing he's out there and that I can't see him," she said. "Besides, I don't want to just run into him by myself at the Stand. I want him to know that I'm your sister. I want to be able to talk to him. I can only do that if you introduce me. Come on, Tal, he's my nephew!"

And Talia understood the significance of the comment. The Malone children, all but Tanner having been sired by different pimps and dealers, had absolutely no family but one another. No aunts or uncles or cousins. No grandparents. They'd always just had Tanner. And now Tanner had Sedona.

"Kent can't know he's your nephew," she said.

"So? He doesn't know anything else about us, either. That doesn't make me care about him less. I just need to see him. To be able to picture him. To know what his voice sounds like." Tatum took a deep breath, loud enough for Talia to hear, and she braced herself. "I need you to know that you aren't alone, Tal. In the future, when you remember him, miss him, I want to be able to share the memory with you. For real."

Oh, God. What had she done to deserve this kid in her life? She couldn't believe she'd ever deserted her. But she was here now. And…

"If Tanner says it's okay, I'll take you with me when I pick him up from school tomorrow. I can swing by and get you first. You've got your regular session with Sara, anyway."

Tatum shot forward in her seat. "You mean it?"

"Yeah. But only if it's okay with Tanner. Talk to him," Talia said, hating that she was pawning off the bad-guy routine on her older brother, but not knowing what else to do.

"I did. He says it's fine!"

Shit. She hadn't expected that. "You've already talked to him about it?"

"Uh-huh. And Sedona, too. Last night. I'm worried about you."

"And they really agreed that you should meet him?"

"I'm not made of eggshells, Tal."

"I know."

"But sometimes I get the idea *you* are, you know?"

Yeah, well…

"I'm not, so stop driving yourself nuts. I'm fine. I've always been fine. And I always will be fine." If life had taught her nothing else, it had taught her that she was a survivor.

"So tell me about his father…"

"What?"

"I saw the look on your face when Sara mentioned *Sherman* picking up Kent. And I'm sorry, but when I was coming out of the craft room tonight, I heard her telling you that she'd heard you agreed to go to the symphony with him next week, that Kent had told her about it because it's, like, his dad's first date since his wife died and that it was about time. He'd been worried that his dad wasn't ever going to get over his mother's death."

Oh, God. The mess just kept getting bigger. As soon as Sara—who had permission from Sherman to discuss Kent's progress with her in case she had any input from what she'd read in his collage—had told her about Kent's positive reaction to their date, she'd known she had to go.

Kent wasn't looking for a mother for himself. He needed to watch his father heal to know that all would be well in his world.

At least according to Sara.

But there was a part of Talia that still wanted to cancel. If she went, she helped Kent.

But to go was suicide.

"You like him, don't you?"

"Who, Kent? He's my kid, Tay, of course I like him."

"I mean his father."

"There's no point to that."

"I didn't ask if there was a point. You like him."

"He's a nice guy."

"You *like him* like him."

"I like how much he loves Kent. He's the father we all dreamed about having when we were kids." At least she had.

"Tanner was a pretty cool stand-in," Tatum said slowly, and Talia envied Tatum the fact that she'd realized the support and love they'd had from their older brother far sooner than Talia had.

Of course, Tanner had cut his parenting teeth on Talia. And they'd been sharp.

"So, say he like likes you, too," Tatum said softly.

"There's no future in it, Tay, so don't get started."

"I don't see why not. Even if you were to get married and had to tell him that you'd given up a baby for adoption, there's no way he'd ever know that Kent was that baby…"

"Unless Kent wants to find me someday." She used to dream about the idea. Until she'd mucked up that reunion by being duplicitous now.

And it was just as well. What kid wanted to look up his birth mother only to find out she'd been a pole dancer on some of the most elite stages in Vegas? Or that she'd married a somewhat elderly Las Vegas wannabe kingpin who'd sold her off to his friends?

If not for Tanner coming to find her, if not for his intervention, she'd have been dead from that choice.

"By then they'd both love you so much that, while there'd be some rough waters, they'd understand and forgive you. And when the shock was over, think how happy Kent would be to know that the woman he loves like a mom is his real mom?"

"Brooke Paulson was his real mom." She couldn't forget that. Or let Tatum, with her head in the romantic clouds of youth, forget it, either.

And Sherman? How would he feel if he ever found out that Talia was Kent's biological mother? She'd have had a chance gaining his sympathy if she'd contacted them through the adoption agency.

But then he'd have known about her past. He'd never have been as open to her collage reading. Or her advice. And Kent would probably be permanently expelled from fourth grade at Santa Raquel Elementary by now. At least if you listened to what Sherman had to say about his son's behavior.

"Just do me a favor, will you?" Tatum asked.

Talia's stomach cramped. "What?"

"Just let yourself have fun for one night. Go out with him. If you like being with him, like it. And don't worry about anything. Just for one night?"

"What good would that do?"

"It would show you what it feels like to be happy, Tal. I'm afraid you never knew, or that you've forgotten."

Talia turned her head then, in spite of, or maybe because of, the moisture clouding her gaze. "When did you grow into such a wise young woman?" she asked. But she knew.

It had been while Talia was away.

NOT LONG AFTER Kent went to bed Thursday night, Sherman was on his computer, doing his habitual searches for anything having to do with Brooke's accident. Somewhere, someplace, there had to be a mention of someone who'd been affected by that night.

As always he typed in the date. Tonight he opened his search to all of California. In the past, he'd narrowed it to a one-mile radius of the crash, to just Santa Raquel, to every other city on the route between Brooke's dinner meeting and home, and broadened it as far as the entire continental United States.

Someone had run from the car that had killed his wife. He or she had to have been hurt.

He read through messages, chat room archives and boards for victims. It was more a form of therapy for him now; he didn't hold out much hope that he was actually going to solve his wife's death anymore.

It could have been something as simple and tragic as someone having fallen asleep at the wheel.

Except that the car was stolen.

And the driver had disappeared.

Two crimes to pay for right there. And that was

before you considered the woman who'd died all alone on the road that night.

And then there was that piece. The car that had hit Brooke had come from out of nowhere. There'd been no skid marks. No tire tracks on any shoulders in the road. Brooke had had no time to react. To swerve or slam on the brakes.

It baffled even the most experienced investigators.

Tonight Sherman was on the computer not just out of habit, but out of guilt, too. He'd failed Brooke somehow. Not by not finding her killer. But before the accident. He and his wife had somehow lost their way.

She'd told him a year before the accident that she didn't feel any sexual attraction for him anymore. He might have been poleaxed by the announcement if he hadn't been suffering from the same lack of desire. Frankly, he'd become more pumped by votes on a leader board than his wife's naked body.

Maybe if he'd been hungry for her body, she'd have felt desirable, too. Maybe she'd still have wanted to make love if he'd given her any reason to want him as a lover.

All water under the bridge, except that he was sitting there alone, completely on fire for a woman in a way he'd never been hungry for Brooke. Not even close.

Hence, the guilt.

Would his wife have been as eager to keep an appointment that went against their principles if she'd felt as if her husband really valued her at home?

He and Brooke had come together over similar mind-sets, plans, beliefs. They'd not only wanted the same things out of life, they'd wanted to get there the same way. Their ideas about the way to live day to day had been identical. They'd made a perfect pair. Everyone had said so.

And in bed they'd done fine. She'd only been his second lover. His second time at love, actually, having pretty much crashed and burned the first time his senior year in high school. He'd met Brooke a few months later, his freshman year at Cal State, and had been faithful to her ever since.

He'd just trained his passion—his focus—on other things. Winning elections. And Kent.

In the bedroom-turned-office where the computer was, he sat at the desk scrolling. Lit only by a small lamp on the desk that had been Brooke's, the room was quiet. Peaceful. He'd already turned off the rest of the lights in the house and made sure the house was secure.

Tomorrow was the anniversary of the car accident. Of Brooke's death. He and Kent had talked about it at dinner. Sherman had thought he should pick up Kent after school so they could visit the cemetery before dark. It was an hour's drive away.

Kent hadn't wanted to miss his session with his friends at the Stand.

And Sherman had given in without any fuss at all. Because he hadn't wanted to go. He'd been glad to see another sign that his son was moving on.

Was that wrong? He didn't want Kent to forget Brooke. Would never want that. But the boy was alive with an entire lifetime of opportunity before him if he could get to the other side of the issues that had been plaguing him.

He stopped. Moved the curser to reverse scroll on the page he'd been halfheartedly perusing.

A date. That and the words *stolen car* jumped out at him. He clicked and the link brought up a blog belonging to a woman named Tricia. A quick glance showed him that she blogged fairly regularly about a number of topics, but he didn't take the time to know why. Or who she was. What he did was read the post that she had just published.

Today is the anniversary of the last time I saw him.

I wouldn't give him the keys to my car. It was almost nine and I could tell he'd been smoking pot. He'd promised to meet someone in LA. He wouldn't tell me who. And when I hid the keys, he stormed out. He was so angry, as he had been so much of the time. But only for those last couple of years. Since the courts gave him to me and wouldn't let his father see him. He didn't understand it was for the best. Didn't know what his dad was into.

He had a good heart. In spite of the trouble he was in. I hope and pray every day that he straightened up his life. That he is out there somewhere, maybe with a wife, a little baby, and working. He'd have made a great teacher if he'd only stayed in college. Maybe he went back to college. As long as he's happy, I can live with the fact that he's still angry with me. Still refusing to come home.

I fear for him every day. And I remember how much he loved to surf. I pray for you, Eddie. I picture you surfing the waves with a grin on your face. If you ever need me, I am here for you.

Sherman couldn't leave the page. Her son had left on the exact date that Brooke had been killed. At night. It was as if this mother's pain was his own.

He scrolled down and found out that she'd been writing these blogs to her son Eddie for the two years he'd been gone. Just little things. Mostly telling him how and what she was doing. Every bit of it innocuous. Nothing personal. Until tonight's post. She was hurting beyond her ability to cope. He could feel it.

And then he saw where she was from. Santa

Barbara. And he started to shake as his mind flew down a crazy path.

The kid had been desperate to get to LA on the night Brooke had been killed. After dark. Desperate enough to steal a car?

He'd been high.

Could he have been speeding down the road toward LA at the same time Brooke was heading back up that road to Santa Raquel just one exit down the freeway from Santa Barbara?

There'd been no tire tracks crossing the median, but the collision had been head-on. Which only left the paved turnaround cutting through the median. Could someone have been waiting out there in the dark in a stolen car, hoping to meet someone? The car had come from somewhere. It wasn't up to him to know where and how. He just needed to find who.

And if it was Eddie?

He looked at the picture Tricia had posted of herself at the top of her blog. Dark-haired. Pretty. Somewhere in her late forties. And alone.

What would it do to her if her Eddie turned out to be Brooke's killer?

He wouldn't. Sherman was definitely just overreacting. Not taking the time to think, to choose his response.

But he picked up the phone anyway before he changed his mind and called the Santa Raquel precinct to leave a message for the detective he'd been told to talk to if he ever remembered anything else pertaining to the last time he'd talked to Brooke.

They'd never said so, but Sherman knew that they suspected foul play. Cars didn't just come from out of nowhere and kill a woman before she had a chance to even put on the brakes. The coroner had said that Brooke had been awake at the time of the crash. She should have responded.

The police thought Brooke had been a victim in the wrong place at the wrong time. Caught in the middle of something that had nothing to do with her.

And Sherman wondered if maybe this Eddie knew what that something was. If nothing else the detective could make a call to Tricia and find out if her son might have had any reason to be in the area where the car that had killed Brooke had been stolen.

CHAPTER SIXTEEN

TALIA'S PALMS WERE sweating again as she drove her old car into the strip mall parking lot. It looked innocuous enough. A hearing-aid shop. A hairdresser. A tax preparer.

And an adoption agency.

The Talbot Company, a private group that specialized in the placement of infants born to unwed teenage mothers. They not only found homes for the babies, but had counselors on staff who were assigned to each and every teenage mother, ensuring that she was ready and willing to give up her child. The agency was as much about the mother as about the baby.

Tanner had found the place for her.

Not only had her counselor been at the hospital when Kent had been born, been there when he'd been taken from her to be given to Brooke and Sherman Paulson, who'd been waiting just down the hall, but she'd visited Talia several times during the following year, as well, to make sure she was doing okay.

Her counselor, Lisette Swift, had helped her,

along with the agency's attorney, to form the agreement that had given her the right to know, at any time, the name and family name of her child, as long as she agreed to never contact her son without contacting his parents first. In the agreement, her son was to be given her contact information any time he requested it after the age of eighteen. And if he wanted it prior to his eighteenth birthday, the information could only be given to his adoptive parents. Until a time when her child made such a request, her contact information was not to be shared with his parents. She'd needed the anonymity. And also the hope for the future.

The last paragraph had allowed for either party to rescind their contact information at any time without having to inform the other party of their choice to do so.

In other words, if Sherman or Brooke Paulson had decided to keep Kent's information from her, they would simply have had to contact Talbot and complete the necessary paperwork. And she wouldn't have known unless she'd contacted the agency for the information.

Just as Sherman Paulson would not be told what she was doing early Wednesday morning that following week when she should have been signed in to her online class lecture.

Lisette was still there, ten years after she'd held Talia's hand while her baby had been taken from her and whisked out of the room before she could see him.

"Ms. Malone!" she greeted—exactly as she'd always addressed Talia—as though they'd been in touch over the years. She walked Talia back through a corridor she remembered as though she'd been there yesterday. The paint might be different. But that didn't play in her memories of the place.

Lisette's office was at the end of the hallway. She motioned Talia in and shut the door behind them before moving to the couch and coffee table similar to the ones where they'd always conducted their business.

"Thank you for seeing me." She wasn't a scared and heartbroken sixteen-year-old kid anymore. She was in control now.

"Of course. I got your message and have the paperwork ready." Looking from Talia's blond bun, over her navy dress slacks, navy formfitting tank and short jacket, Lisette smiled. "You look great."

"Thank you." She wished she felt great. "So do you." The dark-skinned woman looked exactly the same as Talia remembered her. Same beautiful creamy skin and compassionate brown eyes. She'd gained a few pounds but they looked good on her.

"I'm managing this place now," she said with a look around the office.

"Oh! I'm sorry. I guess I should have asked to

see a counselor. I just assumed, when they said you were still here…"

"No, darling, you should have done just what you did. I'm no longer counseling newcomers, but you're mine, girl! I wouldn't hand you off to someone else."

Something vital settled inside her. She wasn't alone.

And, on this score, never had been.

"I have your paperwork right here." Lisette opened a manila folder on the table. "When we're ready to sign, I'll call in a notary to witness it."

"I'm ready." She smiled. No point in wasting this woman's time. She had far more important things to spend her time on. Young girls who were in crisis…

"Not so fast, girl," Lisette said. "You're all grown-up and looking fine, but we need to talk a minute."

She had the right to do this. She was certain she did. And it had to happen. Before she went to the symphony that night.

Too many people stood to get hurt if she didn't.

"You realize that if you sign this paper, that baby you gave up will never be able to find you? Not ever?"

Pain sliced through her. "Yes, ma'am."

"Why would you do this, sweetie? You were so adamant that you wanted to have the possibility of future contact."

She and Tanner and Tatum had learned the hard

way the cost of keeping secrets. Sometimes it was unavoidable, but whenever possible...

"Because I've seen him, Lisette. And I feel absolutely certain that if he ever found out who I was he'd be devastated. He's... His birth mother was killed."

"I know." The other woman's voice was soft. And oddly comforting. Just as Talia remembered.

"I... After that time...I didn't prosper like I promised you I would," Talia said, her voice calm. Even. "I ended up stripping in Vegas. Doing pretty much everything you could imagine a stripper in Vegas might do. Other than the drugs and alcohol. That little boy doesn't ever need to know that's what he's come from. It's not a legacy I want to leave him. Which is why I gave him up in the first place."

"You gave that child up because you were sixteen, his father was going to prison and you wanted him to have a momma and daddy who could provide a stable life for him."

"I gave him up because I was the whore daughter of a whore," Talia said. No more secrets where the truth could be told.

"You loved his daddy. I saw it in your eyes, heard it in your voice and felt it in your heart."

She'd been a fool who couldn't discern that when men looked at her they saw a body, not a person. "I need to do this, Lisette. I've thought it through completely. I've talked to my brother about it. And this is what I need to do."

Kent was too vulnerable for her to chance the possibility that Sherman could someday find out that the woman who'd taught his son how to collage had been duplicitous.

"Does he know he's adopted?" Lisette didn't hand over the paper she held.

"I don't know."

"There've been no requests from the family since the day they named their baby and took the boy home. I wouldn't even have known about his mother's death if I hadn't heard about it on the news. Tragic accident, that."

She nodded. And itched to snatch the paper and get it done.

Tatum was involved now, too. If Sherman found out that Talia had deceived them and refused to allow her near Kent again, Tatum would suffer, too. She had to wipe out that possibility. To protect everyone.

"Some girls, I wouldn't hesitate to do this," Lisette said, "but you…I don't feel good about you severing all rights and possibilities."

"It's my choice, Lisette." And she'd made up her mind.

"The file will still be here."

"Sealed," Talia confirmed.

Without another word, Lisette pulled a cell phone

out of her dress pocket and in less than a minute a notary was in the room, witnessing Talia pick up the pen. Reading the words on the paper in front of her.

And signing her name.

She was giving away any chance she might have had to be Kent's biological mother. To ever acknowledge him as her son. To find the core-deep happiness she'd always craved. She was sentencing herself to a life of silent heartbreak.

If Kent or his father ever came looking for her, they'd find the record of his birth sealed from them.

Because it was best for him. And Tatum.

And past time for her to put both of them first.

"NOT THAT TIE, Dad, this one." Kent came up behind Sherman as he stood at the mirror above the double-sink vanity in the master bathroom knotting a black tie around the collar of the white shirt he'd worn with black pants to work that day. His jacket would cover the wrinkles.

Kent held up a striped, slightly newer tie. "This one's cooler," said the young man still wearing the sweater vest and jeans he'd worn to school and to the Lemonade Stand that day. Kent had definitely gotten his style from his mother.

"You sure you're okay with this?" he asked. And then clarified. "Me going out with Ms. Malone."

"Heck, yeah," the boy said with so much enthusiasm Sherman had to rebut.

"You understand it's only a date, right? A first date."

"Don't worry, Dad. Sara and the guys and I talked all about how our parents will likely date, how they *need* to date." He rolled his eyes while looking at himself in the mirror. "But that it doesn't mean they're going to rush off and get married."

But what if… "How would you feel about me getting married again someday?" he asked, testing those waters, too.

Kent shrugged. "Guess it depends on who to," he said. "I get to have the chocolate ice cream cup in the freezer tonight, right?" he said then.

"Yep."

"And you told Ben and Sandy?"

"Yep."

"Cool. Can I go watch Cartoon Network?"

It wasn't allowed and he knew it. "No."

"Can I watch anything?"

"Is your homework done?" They both knew it wasn't.

"You're no fun, you know that?"

"Sure I am," Sherman told him. "Who's taking you to a Lakers game Friday night?"

"Just you and me?"

No. But… "Cole Vanderpohl's going to be there." A client's son—but one who Kent genuinely liked.

"Then I say you're half-fun. Every once in a while."

The boy was gone before Sherman could form a comeback.

TALIA HAD BEEN to the symphony before. To shows whose ticket price was more than she paid in gas in a month. She knew how to behave. And how to dress. But those other times she'd been an escort to an older man who wanted to think he was the envy of those around him with a beautiful young blonde on his arm. This was a date, and she was nervous.

Hating the fact, she was tempted to slip back into her old persona, don the armor and lock away any and all emotion.

And she might have done so, weak as it would have been, if the second she'd seen Sherman Paulson step out of his car in the driveway, her body hadn't betrayed her.

As he climbed the two stairs to the back deck and took her hand, she went damp between her legs. They walked together to his car, and she was aware of how sensitive her nipples felt as they rubbed against the lace of her bra. She was wearing a black sheath dress she'd bought at a substantial discount the previous Sunday in anticipation of this night.

Mirabelle had been up to see her again, to give

her a bonus check for making sales associate of the month, and had reminded her that she had six weeks before she'd need an answer on the promotion.

Sherman smiled at her as he climbed into the driver's seat beside her.

He asked if she was comfortable. She assured him she was as he showed her the BMW's dual climate controls and how to adjust the temperature of her heated seat. By that time they'd reached the highway, and she wondered how in the hell she was going to make it all the way to LA without jumping the man.

Something was seriously wrong with her. She was all about taking control of her life and was losing control.

First Kent and now his father. The Paulson men were taking over what little bit of good sense she'd managed to find.

"Kent tells me he got to meet your little sister," Sherman said as he set the cruise control and glanced in her direction. His arm rested casually on the armrest between them. Where her arm had been.

"He did," she said now, trying not to rub her arm where it had touched his. Or to put it back.

"The one you called Baby Tay?"

"Yeah. Tatum." Ten minutes in the car with Kent had been all it took for Tatum to accept him as one of her own. Which awarded him a place in her heart. She'd managed to cajole Talia out of two more rides to the Stand since then. And had walked Kent to his meeting room that afternoon.

"Is she your only sibling?"

"No."

"How many do you have?"

"Three."

"All sisters?"

"No."

His brow was quirked as he looked at her. She wasn't comfortable answering questions about herself. None of the men she'd been with in the past had cared to find out anything about her. "I have two brothers," she said anyway. Because she liked him. And wanted the night to go well.

Because she wished, just for a few minutes, that she could do as her naive little sister had suggested and have some fun tonight. To know what it felt like to be truly happy.

Just for a few minutes.

CHAPTER SEVENTEEN

"YOU LOOK LIKE you're enjoying yourself." Tipping his glass of tonic water to hers, Sherman almost had to pinch himself as he stood with Talia Malone in the lobby of the symphony hall during intermission.

He'd texted Kent, who'd done all of his homework, eaten his ice cream and wanted permission to play a non-internet game on his computer. Permission Sherman had granted. Along with the right to stay up an extra half hour that night. Kent had gone three days without getting in trouble at school. Good behavior deserved a reward.

Sherman was having a hard time convincing himself that the woman standing there looking at him as though he was the only guy in the room wasn't his reward for good behavior.

It sure felt that way.

"I actually really like the symphony," she was saying, stepping to the side as a couple passed behind her. She moved with the grace of an angel. Every movement of her body was a work of art. "It kind of reminds me of the ocean, you know? Like it's filled with life and story if you just stop and pay attention. If you just allow yourself to feel it."

He stared. He couldn't help it. She was amazing.

"Sorry, I don't usually say such silly things…"

"No!" Was she kidding? "I find you refreshing beyond belief."

So much so that he couldn't bear the thought of dropping her off without asking her if she'd be interested in going out with him again.

They talked all the way home. About the symphony. About Kent. And the SAT scores that had just won Tatum entrance to pretty much any college she wanted to go to.

And then they were standing on her back deck, and the night was ending.

She'd grown quiet. More like the reserved woman he'd first met in the elementary-school conference room. He was attracted to that woman, too. That part of her. But preferred the part she'd shared with him that evening.

"Kent told Sara that this was your first date since your wife died," she said, walking to the railing on the deck, rather than through the door she'd already unlocked. She took hold of the railing as she faced the ocean.

Sherman joined her.

"It was."

"I hope it was okay for you."

If he told her how great the night had been for him she'd probably run for the hills. "It was."

"It was nice for me, too. Thank you."

Her words sounded like "good night." But she didn't go in.

Neither did she turn so he could kiss her, which was about all he'd seemed to be able to think about the past ten minutes or so of the drive. He was a randy schoolboy again, obsessing about whether or not he'd get to do it with her.

He'd held her hand on the way from the symphony to their car. But that was the only time he'd touched her. Something about her said that she wouldn't accept a man's touch lightly.

"I... The anniversary of Brooke's death was this past week." He didn't consider his words before speaking. And knew better.

"I'm sorry."

"I found this blog on the internet. It was written by a mother whose son left home that same night in anger, and she hasn't seen him since."

He'd reported the information, expecting to be told that he was imagining things that weren't there, expecting to be placated with a sympathetic tone. Instead, he'd received a call back that detectives were speaking with the woman. And looking for her son. For some reason, instead of kissing his date, he told Talia the story.

She glanced at him. "You might have done it,

Sherman! What if you helped them find the man who did this to you?"

Not to him. To Brooke. And Kent.

"Maybe. I thought I'd feel better if we found him. Now I'm not so sure. It doesn't bring her back."

"You always hear about families needing closure."

Maybe Kent did. Maybe, if investigating this Eddie kid could lead them to some new information, it would help his son. Maybe all he and Kent needed was another woman in their lives. Not to replace Brooke; to love them. And be loved.

Maybe he was losing his marbles. They'd had one date.

"It's late," she said, half turning.

"You don't look all that tired."

"I'm used to… I'm kind of a night owl," she said. "I love the ocean at night and find myself drawn out here when I probably should be resting."

She didn't want to go in.

He didn't want to go.

"You mind if I sit here for a few minutes and enjoy it with you?" He pointed to the pair of chairs behind them.

"Not at all." She sounded surprised. "I've got a bottle of my brother's wine in the fridge. Would you like half a glass? I know you're driving and it's late, but this is good stuff. Tanner doesn't actually share it much yet—I just snatched a bottle the other night when I was over there."

Actually, Tatum had snatched it for her, with Sedona egging her on. Just in case.

"I'd be honored." He wanted to follow her inside, too, while she poured it. To get a glimpse of her home, see another facet of her, another hint at who she was, but he didn't.

She didn't invite him.

Which just made him want it more.

IT HAD TO END. She knew that. But an extra hour wasn't going to hurt. Amazingly, she'd done what Tatum told her to do. She'd allowed herself to have fun.

So tomorrow, when the teenager asked, she could make her happy.

She seemed to be making Sherman Paulson happy, too. In spite of this being the time of year of the anniversary of his wife's death. Talia's heart went out to him.

"Wow!" he said after one sip of Tanner's wine. "That's good stuff."

Not exactly how a connoisseur might have said it, but she wasn't one, either, so she smiled. "I know. Tanner doesn't do anything halfway."

"Tanner. Tatum. Talia. What's your other brother's name?"

"Thomas." She'd seen him for the first time in

more than a decade the previous summer. They all had. He'd gotten married while they were all in New York together where he worked as a stockbroker. Talia had two sisters-in-law whom she really liked.

"Your mom obviously liked names that start with a *T*."

"My mother was an egocentric who liked the attention we got her." Oh, God. She didn't just say that. Putting down her wineglass, Talia froze. Hoping that he was going to let her statement pass.

She didn't talk about her past, her mother, to anyone. Ever. Had never even come close to a slip.

This man was not good for her. Not good at all.

And yet, she didn't want him to go.

"What about your dad? Didn't he have a say in your names?"

"Dads. There were four of them." She didn't need to answer him. She needed to keep her mouth shut.

Something was happening to her. The life she was supposed be getting in line was spinning out of control.

"Oh."

"Yeah."

"Do you see her much?"

"Not since I was sixteen. That's when Tanner got custody of us three younger kids." Something deep inside her was fighting to get out. Talia fought to keep it down where it belonged.

She was not going to let her new life be ruined.

"He's a lot older than you, then?"

"Seven years."

"He took custody of three younger siblings when he was twenty-three?"

"I told you he didn't do anything halfway." None of them did. Thomas had graduated from Harvard at the top of his class. Tatum was graduating at the top of hers. And Talia had made it to the top of the pole.

"Do you know where your mother is now?"

The ocean roared softly in the distance. Reminding her that she was more than Tammy Malone's daughter. More than a collection of skin and bones. She was a human being—just as much as anyone else.

And just because she'd made stupid choices didn't mean she wasn't smart.

"Dead."

She could feel him watching her in the darkness. And had the strangest urge to bury her face in his shoulder and let him hold her. Just hold her.

She had a feeling that if she asked him to, he would. Just hold her. A novelty in her world.

"I'm sorry."

Her mother had been willing to sell her for a fix. One fix was all she'd been worth. And still, Talia had cared about her.

"She's at peace now," was all she said. No one would ever understand her mixed emotions toward Tammy. She didn't understand them herself. She abhorred everything the woman had been. Abhorred what she'd done. Yet Tammy had been the only parent she'd ever known.

Thank God Talia had saved Kent from the same fate.

SHERMAN PUT HIS empty wineglass down on the small table between them.

"It's late, I should get going." Ben and Sandy didn't mind staying late. Ben, a website developer, worked from home, and Sandy, a nurse, worked weekends at a rehab center.

She nodded. He could see the shadow of her face in the darkness. Would this be it for them? One incredible evening?

"I'm…I… You don't need to worry that…my family… They're good people."

Of course they are were the first words that sprang to his lips. *They produced you.* But Sherman took his pause to consider what she'd said. And why.

"I don't think any less of you for what you've just told me." He spoke softly, slowly, needing her to hear the sincerity in his voice. In him. "To the contrary, you and your brothers and sister…it sounds like you had a tough time growing up and look at you now—a college graduate going for your master's. Your brother is a damned good vintner in a place where the competition is fierce. And from what Kent says, your little sister's pretty much perfect. *Smart* and *nice*, too, were his actual words."

"It's just… I don't… I've never…"

And with a rush of heat, he thought he understood. "You don't tell people about her."

"Right."

But she'd told him. And he couldn't help but draw a conclusion from that.

She liked him. More than a little. Maybe as much as he liked her.

His penis got hard in time with the softening of his heart. Could he really be this lucky? To find his perfect match at thirty-eight?

"My father was in the Gulf War." He needed her to know him at his worst. "I was thirteen when he deployed. I was on a city debate team—he'd signed me up so I'd have a positive outlet for my constant need to argue, he'd said—and had one competition standing in between me and a trip to Washington, DC, to compete before Supreme Court justices."

"Quite an accomplishment for a thirteen-year-old boy." He could hear a smile in her voice. And sex, too.

Another half glass of wine would be good.

"Yeah, well, I was pissed as hell at him for going. My last words to him as he left were to tell him that all he ever did was let me down and to not bother coming back on my account."

"Kids say things they don't mean."

He sat forward, knees spread, forearms resting on his knees, and stared at the darkness surrounding his shoes. "He was killed six weeks after he got over there. Drove his jeep over a land mine."

And Sherman, a teenage boy sobbing over his father's casket with words ringing in his head that he couldn't take back, had made a promise to the man he'd idolized, that he would spend the rest of his life not only watching his words, but also his attitude. He would never again let negative emotion control his actions. He would always look for the positive. Spread the positive. Make lemonade out of lemons, just like they said at the Lemonade Stand.

"I don't know what to say." Her soft voice was like a salve for the old wound.

"My words didn't kill him," Sherman said slowly. "But his death made me the man I am. And that's something I don't tell anyone."

He couldn't hear what her silence was saying to him.

"I'd like to see you again. Personally, I mean." Rubbing his hands slowly back and forth, he waited for her to seal his fate.

"I…"

She had doubts. He felt a "no" coming. He had one shot.

"I wasn't in love with my wife."

"I…"

She was looking at him, lovely in her black sheath

and shawl, though he was seeing more by memory in the darkness. He could smell the hint of flowers that filled the air around her.

"But I fear that after only two weeks and one date, I might be falling for you."

"No. Please. Don't do that."

"I'm fairly certain I don't have a say in the matter." Crazy. His whole life was based on carefully thought-out choices, answers, plans.

"It's just because I'm your first date in so long."

"You're my first date in so long because I haven't met anyone else who interested me. I'm thirty-eight years old, Talia. I'm way beyond acting rashly. I'm also not one to waste my time. If you're not interested, just say so and I'll be on my way. And hope that none of this will affect your willingness to help my son."

"Of course it won't. It's just…you don't know me."

"I have a feeling a lifetime with you wouldn't be enough to know you completely. You're like the ocean you love so much, with depths that I can only imagine, but would very much like to explore."

"I don't know what to—"

"Are you seeing someone?" He hadn't asked before. Hadn't really cared. Until it dawned on him that he might be too late.

"No. I just…"

She sat back with her glass in her hand, as though

she wasn't going anywhere soon. And as long as she was there, open to him being there, he wasn't going to leave.

"I'm not imagining that you're attracted to me." Guys knew these things.

"No."

He'd never met a more recalcitrant woman. And yet that attracted him, too.

"Does the fact that I have a son bother you?"

"No, of course not! I just—"

"I'm not asking for a commitment, Talia. Just a chance."

"I want a chance." The words were so soft he barely heard them. But the longing in them was clear.

Standing, Sherman placed a hand on either side of her chair, leaned over and kissed her. He'd been thinking just a quick touch, enough to speak of things yet to come. But when his lips touched hers, he almost lost his balance.

Her lips were full, soft, and they greeted him like a lost lover, caressing him with tenderness. He tasted her hunger. Heard her moan.

And had to leave.

Before he scooped her up and took her to bed.

CHAPTER EIGHTEEN

AS A TREAT to his son, who made it through the week with only two minor incidents, Sherman got a room in Beverly Hills Friday night after the Lakers game. Today—Saturday—he was taking his son to a movie premiere and hoped that Kent wouldn't cause too much of a fuss about having to dress up, eat finger food and sit with adults he didn't know while they watched what he hoped would be a drama he'd enjoy. Something about a guy lost at sea. The film was rated G so he figured if it was suitable for kids, Kent would find something of interest in it.

He'd taken the premiere tickets from the stash of perks at the firm with the express purpose of getting to know the producer, a man who'd openly expressed views similar to those held by one of Sherman's candidates. He was hoping for a sizable donation as his candidate had just recently been chosen as his party's choice for the national senate race.

A change of gears that would have been celebrated for a week when Brooke was alive and that had gone largely unnoticed in Sherman's current personal life.

He wasn't sure if Talia had any interest in politics. Let alone any knowledge of the inner workings of the machinery that drove them. He hadn't spoken to her at all since bolting after their kiss Wednesday night. He was purposely giving her breathing room. A chance to figure out if she wanted to explore her interest in him.

And giving himself a chance to cool off, too.

But he'd heard from his son that she'd aced some exam she'd taken. And that Tatum had been with her when she'd picked him up on Friday.

"Jason says that the Lakers have a chance of making it all the way this year," Kent was saying as Sherman led them out of the hotel elevator to the parking garage where they'd left the BMW the night before.

"They have a chance every year," he said, preoccupied with getting them to the mall to buy a new pair of shoes for his son, who'd just announced that he couldn't wear the ones that Sherman had packed because they hurt his toes.

"Yeah, but Jason says that with their three-point percentage they're a real contender this year."

From the time he'd picked Kent up the night before it had been "Jason" this and "Jason" that. As he thought about it, he realized the boy's name had been coming up all week.

"Why don't you ask Jason if he wants to come over sometime," he suggested.

"I don't think he's allowed to leave the Stand right now," Kent said. "He even has school there. His dad's a real jerk and might kidnap him. He put his mom in the hospital."

Sherman wasn't sure if it was the content of the words or the matter-of-fact way his son said them that took him aback.

"Anyway, you never said why I need new shoes," Kent said, climbing into the front passenger seat as Sherman threw their bag onto the backseat. "I can just go barefoot until we get home. And get new shoes online." Kent wasn't a shopper.

"Because we're going to a movie premiere this afternoon and you can't do that barefoot," he said.

"MP," Kent said.

"What?"

"MP on the calendar, that's what you added on Thursday for Saturday afternoon."

He hadn't realized Kent was actually paying attention to the calendar anymore.

"Right."

He crossed his arms. "I guess it's another work thing I'm being dragged to."

"It's a movie premiere, Kent. Most kids would be excited to have the chance to see one."

"I know. Jason says I'm lucky my dad takes me to work instead of hitting me."

Sherman had no idea how to respond to that.

And that was it. No fit. No belligerence. Just a look of bored resignation. Sherman decided he liked this Jason kid.

WORKING THE EVENING as well as the day shift Saturday, Talia took a quick lunch break and ran down to the food court in the mall to grab a salad. The extra shift was going to put her on a tight schedule to get her homework done, but that was the idea. Tight schedules forced her to focus on the life she'd chosen.

Not dwell on one she couldn't have.

Sherman Paulson hadn't loved his wife. He was falling for her. He knew she was attracted to him. He thought she was like the ocean and he wanted to explore her depths forever.

Wow. That had been a good one. A line unlike any she'd ever heard. The first one that had made its way through her protective armor since she was sixteen and believed her high-school teacher when he'd told her that she had the most beautiful eyes he'd ever seen.

Turned out, he'd just had a thing for young girls.

"Ms. Malone!"

There was no way she'd just imagined her son's voice. Then she saw him, his hand holding his father's as he jumped up and down, waving at her, trying to get her attention. "Ms. Malone!"

Talia stared at him. Smiled. And then raised her gaze to his father—whose intent stare melted her bones.

"What are you doing here?" Kent asked as they reached her.

"Are you alone?" Sherman asked at the same time.

"I work here," she said. And then looked at the man who'd been keeping her up at night. "Yes, I'm alone. I'm on lunch break."

"You work here?" He was frowning.

"On weekends." She named the store. "I'm a sales associate." He seemed confused, as though it was disturbing to him that this was a side of her she didn't know about.

Her stomach sank.

What was he going to think when he found out about the job she'd held before this one?

She was going to have to tell him if they continued to see each other. About Vegas at least. That wasn't something she'd be able to keep secret. It wasn't just a onetime event. It had been her life.

"We're going to a movie premiere," Kent said with a groan. "You want to come?"

"I'm working."

Before she even thought about exploring any kind of friendship with Kent's father, she was going to have to tell him what he was getting into. At least as far as her stripper past was concerned.

It was the decent thing to do. And there was no reason not to except to spare herself, and she was done putting herself first.

"How about a late dinner?" Sherman asked, his gaze practically devouring her features.

"I—"

"Yeah!" Kent said. "It's Saturday. I get to stay up late. We could have a fire and show her the colors, couldn't we, Dad?"

"Yes, son, we could." Sherman's gaze never left her face. His smile was warming her skin quite uncomfortably.

For a second—okay, to be honest, for hours on and off since Wednesday night—she toyed with the idea of maintaining a friendship with the Paulson men. Who stood to be hurt except for her? They'd never know she'd given birth to Kent.

And she could have a peripheral role in her son's life. Beyond the few months he'd be at the Lemonade Stand.

The boy was already showing marked improvement in his attitude and Sara had said he was opening up in their group sessions with the other boys. He was competitive when they played games but didn't exhibit signs of aggression when he lost.

"Talia?" Sherman moved them to the wall, away from the crowds of people who were walking around them on both sides.

"I, um…"

"I'll grill steaks," he said. "And maybe you could bring the rest of that bottle of wine?"

She could see Kent's room.

And after the little boy went to bed? What would it hurt to savor, just for a few more minutes, that lovely, sexy, nerve-racking feeling this man miraculously coaxed from her body?

"I'm not off until eight. Which puts me home a little after nine." Tatum would tell her to go. Wouldn't she?

Heck, Baby Tay had had her married to the guy and him finding out she was Kent's mom and forgiving her for everything.

"That works for us. I can have everything ready to go when you get there."

He smiled. So did she. He glanced at her lips. Remembering the touch of his, she glanced away. And saw Kent grinning as he looked from one to the other.

"Okay," she said. It would give her the chance to tell him about Vegas. After Kent went to bed. And see how badly he still wanted to see her after he found out about her pole-dancing skills.

Really, she was worrying about nothing. She'd get to see her son's home so when she was alone she could picture him there. And then her past life was going to take care of the present one all by itself.

THE MOVIE PREMIERE was a marginal success. Kent didn't purposely embarrass him. He fell asleep during the movie, but that was okay. Sherman had a meeting set up Tuesday morning to go over campaign figures with the movie's producer. And they were out of there in time to stop for fresh beef tenderloin filets on the way home.

For most of the drive, while Kent chattered on about the order of household chemicals they should use in the fire to make the most impressive show for Ms. Malone, Sherman was thinking about ground rules.

Kent knew about sex. He didn't need to know whether or not his father was having it.

Not that he was going to that night. But a guy never knew and…

He wasn't going to embarrass Talia by having a ten-year-old boy know that she was having sex with his dad.

Not that she was.

They'd kissed once.

And been halfway to him inside her with that one touch of their mouths.

Just remembering that kiss made him grow. Shifting his thoughts, Sherman came face-to-face with the challenge confronting him.

He was a single father. He couldn't just have sex any time the mood took him.

So be it.

Life was good.

TALIA DIDN'T TALK to Sherman about her past that night. She'd been up before dawn, worked an extra shift and had to be back in LA before the store opened at eleven in the morning. She had home-work to do.

She was too tired to fight the truth tonight. Too tired to stay until Kent went to bed. She didn't want to burst into tears the next time her son tilted his head when he talked in that slightly cocky, mostly innocent way he had. He was so darned cute.

And so was his dad. In an entirely different way.

Bottom line, she was in waaay over her head.

"I'm sorry," she said as Sherman walked her to her car just before 11:00 p.m.

"No reason to be sorry," he said, his usual cheer-ful self. He had both hands in his pants pockets. She was glad.

And a bit let down, too.

Sexual desire was a relatively novel thing for her, and she liked it.

"How about joining us at the beach tomorrow?" His question had her blood rushing like a school-girl's again. He really liked her.

"I have to work." And before he could say more she added, "My schedule this semester is crazy.

I have online classes three mornings a week and classes in LA the other two. My afternoons are spent traveling around to different elementary schools. I'm at the Stand five days a week and now Tuesday and Thursday nights, and I have homework. Weekends I work."

No time for thinking. Or regrets. At least that had been the plan. To give her the best chance of success as she forged her new life.

The whole point in looking up Kent in the first place. So that she could have the closure she needed to put the past fully behind her.

Her schedule was going to solve her problem with the Paulson men for her. No need to talk about her previous career. Or worry about heartbreak.

She didn't have time for Sherman to fall in love with her.

Not that he would have.

"How about dinner at the beach near the Stand Monday?" he proposed. The complete antithesis of her plan.

"You're there, anyway. So am I, picking up Kent. We go to this little Italian place on the beach sometimes. Kent loves their baked spaghetti. And you have to eat…"

He was grinning. Her stomach was melting again. "Don't fight it so hard," Sherman said, his expression serious as he leaned closer to her.

If he only knew…

But he didn't.

He didn't need to know. Because she wasn't going to let anything come of this.

"I, um, okay."

She agreed. And then lifted her chin to the kiss he was about to plant on her lips. She wasn't disappointed. In the kiss.

Yet as she drove home, she was disappointed in herself. Exhausted in every way, she thought about the willpower that had kept her away from drugs and alcohol when the relief would have made life so much easier to bear. Where was that willpower now?

But she knew. This wasn't about willpower. It wasn't even about strength or stubbornness. Or choices. She was fighting a battle she wasn't equipped to fight. She had no arsenal. No experience or knowledge.

The war raged within her. For so long her head had controlled her world. She'd elected it her leader the morning they'd taken her son out of her body and out of the room before she could even see him. It had served her well.

For so long she'd thought her heart was dead. For years it had left her alone.

And now, over the past year, her heart had been staging an uprising. At first, it had been fairly easy to quell. Or at least she'd thought she was still in complete control.

It was quickly becoming obvious she wasn't. Somehow, while she'd been busy moving and taking classes and making amends for deserting Tatum, her heart had been slowly gaining control.

Confusing the hell out of her.

Truth was she had no idea what to do with it now that it was coming back to life.

And wasn't sure she could let it continue.

Sometimes dead was just…better.

For everyone.

CHAPTER NINETEEN

WE AREN'T A FAMILY. We aren't a family. Talia wished she had a sign to wear, a tattoo on her forehead, anything to let the waitresses and other diners all know the truth. It seemed to her that wherever she looked, people were smiling at their cute little family Monday night.

Kent was adorable. His manners were impeccable. His conversation entertaining. And his father could just sit there and do nothing and she was turned on as hell. When he looked into her eyes across the table, she couldn't swallow.

Maybe, given time, her body would get used to the foreign sensation. Maybe not. She'd never know. They weren't a family and couldn't ever be one.

She was going to tell Sherman just as soon as she had some time alone with him. Someday in the near future for sure.

She'd followed them to dinner—which Sherman insisted on paying for—and as soon as they finished, she got in her car and drove home. She had her own classwork to do and tomorrow's collage workshop to prepare for.

She was still considering Mirabelle's offer, too.

And those things had to be her focus. They were her future.

Not the two lonely men that she couldn't get out of her mind.

KENT BURPED AND FARTED, purposely loud, at the table on Wednesday night. If he'd have laughed, Sherman probably would have smiled.

As it was, with Kent ignoring his rude behavior and staring stone-faced at the salt and pepper shakers, his actions were clearly a return to the rebelliousness Sherman had thought they were leaving in the past. Odd, since his son had just come from his session at the Lemonade Stand.

"Can Jason spend the night Friday?" he asked as Sherman was tucking him into bed that night.

"I don't think he can leave the Lemonade Stand," Sherman reminded his son. "I'll tell you what—I'll call Ms. McDaniels in the morning and see if I can get permission to bring him here. No promises, though."

"Okay. Cool."

Yeah. Sherman needed to meet this kid. To see what kind of influence he was having on his son.

"Sleep well," he said, tousling Kent's hair as he stepped away from the bed.

"Dad?"

Turning back, he saw the boy staring at him in

the darkness, Kent's night-light casting a particularly angelic glow on the boy's face.

"Yeah?"

"Sorry about the fart."

He stood still. Processed. This was huge. Choose the right words.

Stifling his first reaction to put Kent on the spot and ask why he had done it, he said instead, "Thanks for the apology. I appreciate it."

Kent's eyes were already closed.

"WHERE'S TATUM?" KENT climbed into Talia's car on Thursday, looking in the backseat.

"A friend asked her to go roller blading down by the beach," Talia told the boy.

"What friend? Not that Jimmy guy."

"Yes, Jimmy." It was Tatum's first date since her time at the Lemonade Stand. Talia was nervous as all get-out for her little sister.

Kent looked out the window. "He's not good enough for her."

"You know him?"

"No."

She was sure that made some kind of kid sense. But it suddenly occurred to Talia that Kent had gotten the wrong idea about Tatum's affection for him.

"You know she's sixteen, right?"

"Yeah."

"And that she's going to be dating. If not Jimmy, then someone else."

"I know."

Was Kent jealous? He was only ten but kids grew up so quickly these days. Tatum was beautiful and Kent didn't know she was his aunt.

"Do you have a girl you like?" she asked him, feeling her way like a soldier in a minefield.

"Nah," he said, his arms folded. His little leather shoes rested on top of his backpack on the floor at his feet.

"You know," Talia said, "even if Tatum goes out with Jimmy, even if she likes him, she's still your friend."

He shrugged. "Yeah."

Oh, boy. What now?

"Did Dad tell you that he's asking if Jason can sleep over tomorrow?"

"No." She hadn't spoken to Sherman since Monday night in the parking lot after dinner. They hadn't bumped into each other.

And he hadn't called.

Which was for the best.

"Well, he is." The boy turned worried gray-blue eyes in her direction and she was a kid again, looking at Tatum and knowing that she'd do anything she could to make her happy. "Do you think you could, you know, help?"

"You want me to talk to Ms. McDaniels for him?"

"Yeah. I really want Jason to come and we've got a good house. You know, you've seen it."

"I'll see what I can do."

"Good, 'cause you like my dad and everything."

She turned into the Stand's back lot. Parked in her usual spot. And wasn't sure what to say. She couldn't give Kent false expectations.

"Your dad and I are friends," she said slowly as they got out and headed across the large expanse of grass side by side. How to handle Sherman's relationship with women in front of his son was strictly Sherman's call.

Until it came to her part in it.

"I know, Dad tells me it's none of my business about who he dates and that he *makes love*," the boy said, breaking into giggles.

"He told you that?"

"Yeah." More giggles. Kent was leaning forward with the weight of his backpack on his shoulders and stumbled but righted himself before she could help.

The man was talking to his son about him having sex? And she was the first woman he'd dated since his wife's passing?

The idea should not excite her. But it did. And that scared the wits out of her.

She was going to have to put an end to all of it. Tatum with Kent. Sherman. Everything.

Kent was going to get hurt.

And she couldn't stand by and let that happen.

WHAT A CRAZY WEEK. Sitting alone on the porch Friday night, waiting for the boys to come out for the fire he'd promised them, Sherman sipped a beer and thought about Talia.

These days she played a part in all of his thoughts. He'd been surprised with an offer that week to head up a state campaign. The offer fell right in line with his career plan.

But he hadn't counted on it until after the next election numbers came in.

And as he'd accepted the position, he'd thought about Talia. About having her on his arm at some of the upscale events he'd be required to attend.

He thought about her all day long, imagining which part of her harried schedule she was keeping up with at whatever moment.

The wood was in place for the fire. The sun had completely set. Chemicals were measured out and ready. The boys should be along any moment. And Sherman thought about another time Talia consumed his attention.

Bedtime.

She was Playboy bunny and sweet innocence rolled into one. He hadn't walked around with hardons like this since he was a teenager.

Life was good and…where were the boys?

Setting his bottle on the little round table Brooke had chosen to go with their outdoor chairs, he went inside. Listening.

He didn't call out as he usually did when looking for his son. Something told him the boys were up to no good and he wanted to catch them in the act. They were in the computer room. He could hear their voices, though they were speaking covertly enough that he couldn't make out the words.

Not really whispering, but close to it.

What was going on?

He'd had reservations about Jason, but the ten-year-old redhead had been respectful and pleasant on the drive home. And at dinner his manners had been better than Kent's. Until Kent burped. And they both laughed. Which resulted in a burping contest.

Heaven help him, he'd joined in.

And been quite proud of himself when he'd won.

As he got closer to the door, he heard Kent say something, a note of excitement in his voice, followed by an equally intense response from Jason.

He wasn't sneaking, wasn't quieting his footsteps on the carpet in the hall. Hadn't even thought to, until he heard Kent's urgent, "Quick, Dad's coming…" just as he rounded the corner.

The computer screen flashed and then both boys were standing there, staring at Kent's home page.

Sherman was 100 percent sure that the boys wouldn't have been speaking intensely about the picture of Sherman and a four-year-old Kent at the ocean that Brooke had had on her screen home page—and Kent had kept there.

He stood before the two of them, took a deep breath and then asked, "What's going on?" His tone was nonthreatening even if the question wasn't.

"Nothing," Kent said as Jason stared at the wall.

"You want to try that again?"

"What?" Kent said, a hint of attitude in his tone.

"That answer. And make it the truth this time."

"Nothing's going on! We were on my computer," Kent said. "Is there a law against that?"

Taken aback, Sherman literally counted to five in his head. "Jason, you want to tell me what you and Kent were doing?"

"No, sir." The boy's voice shook.

Sliding his hands from his hips to his pockets, Sherman surveyed the situation. Or tried to. He was angry. But even more afraid.

"I have a problem in that we can't continue on with our night, can't get out to the fire, or even to bed later, until I know what you boys were doing just before I came in."

"Fine. Here!" Kent said. With jerky movements prompted by obvious anger the boy turned back to his computer, grabbed the mouse and, with a series of clicks, brought up a page of thumbnail photos.

Sherman's heart pounded, and he about lost his dinner. He knew what he was going to see when

Kent clicked open those photos. He just had no idea how he was going to handle the situation.

The boy would be banned from computer use, for sure. That was a given. A promise already made when Kent's computer rules were first established.

The first picture opened full-size, filling the screen.

It was Brooke. All dressed up for election night a little more than two years before—the November before her February death.

Kent clicked again and there was another picture of his mother, smiling for the camera.

He didn't understand.

"This is what you were looking at?"

"Yes!" The word was a hiss.

"So why the subterfuge?"

"I don't even know what that is."

Wow, his son's belligerence was back in spades.

"Why close the screen as soon as I walked in? Why not just tell me you were looking at photos of your mother?"

"We weren't just looking at pictures, Dad." If he didn't know better he'd say there was hate in Kent's voice just then. And he'd never been more confused in his life. What had he done between dinner and their burping contest and now?

"So what were you doing?"

"Talking about how she died, okay!" the boy screamed at him. "Because you sure never do!"

He stood there, trying to make sense of it all.

"You've never even tried to find out who killed her, Dad! He runs off and gets away and no one cares about any of it!" If Kent had been larger his voice would likely have been heard down the block.

Sherman noticed Jason slinking off toward the desk, his shoulders hunched and his head down. "So that's why you're mad at me? Because I'm not trying to find the guy who was driving the other car that night?"

"Yes!"

Jason flinched at the high-pitched screech.

Really? Months of hell for that? He'd told Kent that the police weren't going to stop looking for the person who'd been driving the stolen car. And Dr. Jordon had advised him to leave it at that unless Kent brought it up.

"Did you ever think about talking to me about it?"

"What for?"

"Because you'd have found out that I have been looking, Kent. Every week. For the past two years." He went to his own computer. "See," he said, bringing up different sites he'd bookmarked, and files he'd highlighted.

Kent stepped back, and Sherman saw the boys exchange a surreptitious glance.

"I found a blog," he continued, telling Kent about

the woman in Santa Barbara whose son had left home that same night and never come back.

"I had a call from the police a couple of days ago," he added, feeling that to do so was appropriate given the circumstances. "The boy had packed a bag and stolen his mother's credit card that night, too. She hadn't put that detail in her blog. He used the credit card at a highway diner at the exit just up from where Mom had her accident, an hour before the accident. And he'd definitely been driving a car because the manager remembered him shining his headlights in the front window for a long time."

He'd remembered because he'd noticed the kid lighting up a joint and smoking the whole thing before he'd come into the restaurant. He'd almost asked him to leave without service but it wasn't very busy inside and he didn't want any trouble.

"Was he the one who hit Mom?" Kent's voice was the complete antithesis of seconds before. Subdued. Almost frightened.

"Probably not. The manager didn't see the kind of car it was, but he was headed for LA, the opposite direction. And remember, the person who hit Mom had to have come from the paved turnaround in the median because there weren't any tracks. And she hadn't had time to react…"

They'd discussed this once. With Dr. Jordon present. Because Kent had had questions.

"So you really think it *was* on purpose? That

someone pulled out in front of her to cause the accident?" Jason asked, coming closer to the two of them, looking at Sherman.

Sherman shrugged. "It seems that way," he said honestly. "We just really don't have an explanation."

The boys shared another glance.

"But the police—and I—aren't giving up," he said, looking his son in the eye.

Kent nodded. Jason elbowed him and motioned toward Sherman.

"Sorry, Dad. I didn't mean to yell," he said.

"Thanks for the apology," Sherman said. "Now let's go have that fire."

He gave Jason a good show with lots of pyro. Made ice cream sundaes for the boys. And tucked them both into Kent's double bed.

But he couldn't forget the anger in his son's voice. Or the speed with which it had come on.

He couldn't settle down after the boys were in bed, either. Just kept pacing, hands in the pockets of his jeans, from room to room, indoors and out.

Eventually he dropped down to his chair at the still-burning fire, putting another log into the kiva fireplace.

And the only thing that seemed natural for him to do at the moment was to pick up his phone.

CHAPTER TWENTY

TALIA WAS HOME writing collage reports Friday night. She'd heard from Kent that afternoon that Jason was going to be spending the night.

And had been trying all evening not to picture Sherman there, alone with the two boys. He'd do fine. She had no doubts about that.

They were going to be having another fire. Another pyro demonstration. She wanted to be there.

Giving up on a rather unusual collage a boy had made that consisted entirely of tea cups, Talia dropped her pen and went inside to run a bath. She'd waded in the ocean earlier that evening and wanted to wash the salt off her skin before she climbed between her sheets.

She wanted to soak away the tension in her body, to be alone with her nudity and come to terms with the sexuality that Sherman Paulson brought to life within her.

She couldn't seem to concentrate on much of anything else.

Except for Kent, of course.

But tonight her son was fine. With his father at

home, having a sleepover with his friend. Being a normal, happy, well-adjusted boy.

Tonight, she was the woman who would most likely be spending the rest of her life by herself. Or, at least, the next foreseeable phase of it.

She stripped slowly, almost as though she was treating herself to the show she'd put on for hundreds of men over the years, feeling the slide of the fabric on her skin. Really feeling it. Not just pretending to be aware of the slide of the silky fabric against nerve endings that were long ago deadened to sensation by a shut-off switch in her brain.

She bared her breasts. Rubbed her hands across them as she'd done many times before, pushing them together, up and then hugging them to herself. The latter was something she'd never done onstage. Her breasts were hers. And if it felt good to touch them, that was for her, too.

Stepping into the water, she kept her hands on her breasts, her fingers touching the nipples that had been so sensitive the past few weeks. Rubbing them lightly. Shocked to feel an answering sensation down at her core. Her breasts had always just been a way to get men to part with their money, a toy, a plaything for the opposite sex. She'd had no idea they could give her pleasure, too.

She had seriously thought that the idea of a woman giving herself pleasure was all just a bunch of make-believe created to turn men on. The sex industry was all about playacting.

Curious, she touched her nipples some more. Flicked her thumbs against their tips, her fingers lightly pinching the sides. They were hard and taut and—

Her phone rang.

Jerking in the tub at the interruption, Talia splashed water on the floor as she grabbed a towel, wiped her hands and reached for her phone.

She didn't know anyone who'd be calling just to chat at that hour. Which meant the call was important.

Her heart thudded a hard and heavy beat as she saw the name of her caller. Had something happened to Kent?

"Hello?"

"Talia? It's Sherman. Did I wake you?"

He didn't sound worried. Or upset. "No." He sounded tired. Lonely. "I just finished my collage reports for the night," she told him, feeling incredibly naked in the tub.

"You said you're a night owl so I hope it's okay I called."

It was after ten. "Of course." But why? He hadn't called all week.

She'd waited for the first night or two. Just in case. So she could tell him that they couldn't have dinner together anymore. Because she was just too busy.

And then she'd quit waiting. Knowing that his not calling her was for the best.

"I know this is complicated, but…Kent blew up at me tonight." He told her about an altercation in the computer room, not the details, but that it happened.

"I'm afraid that Kent and I might have done more damage to Jason's already fragile psyche," he said.

Talia felt moisture in her eyes. The man was so kind. So good. So perfect, if only she'd met him eleven years ago.

But then that would put her at sixteen and him at Rex's age and that wouldn't have worked, either.

Odd how Kent was adopted by a man the same age as his biological father, who'd gone to jail for fathering him.

Another one of life's little cruel ironies.

"To the contrary," she said softly after hearing the whole story. "I'd say you two probably just sped up his healing process by months. Anger isn't a bad thing," she said, parroting what she'd learned during more than a year of volunteering at the Stand. "It's a normal human emotion. It's how it's sometimes handled that makes it evil."

"You…talk like you know. More than just from your work."

She couldn't go there. Not tonight. Not while she was naked in her tub, still buzzing with sex…

With her free hand, she reached up and teased her nipple. Then the other. And smiled as the sensation shot downward again.

So life had some little pleasures in store for her. It was…nice.

"I need to see you, Talia. Alone. Just me and you. As two adults."

Oh, God, she needed that, too. With her fingers still at work on her breasts, she slid deeper in the water, letting her legs fall open against the sides of the tub.

"I know this is difficult, with you being so busy and my being a single dad, but you're very quickly becoming a big part of my life."

Her thumb pressed into her nipple. Her other hand held the phone. She was wet and hot all over. "I'm hardly in your life at all," she said, wishing the words weren't true and, at the same time, glad that they were.

She was making the right choice, not seeing Sherman Paulson.

"Are you kidding me?" His incredulousness made her smile. "I seem to be taking you with me everywhere I go."

Which brought up some exciting possibilities. Her overstimulated breasts wanted to be squeezed harder. She spread her legs wider. Did he take her into the shower with him in the morning? Into bed at night?

As she had him?

"It's just sex." The words were strangled. And desperate.

"Maybe. It's been a while, for sure. But I don't think so. It's not like you're the only woman I've been around in a year. But you're the only one who, in my mind, follows me into the office where I'm being offered a promotion just to smile and congratulate me."

"I did that?"

"I'm afraid so."

And then his words hit her sex-fuddled brain. "You got a promotion?"

He told her about it. She congratulated him. He thanked her.

She wanted to give him pleasure like he'd never known before.

But more, she wanted him to give her the same kind of pleasure.

She couldn't.

"Let me come over tomorrow night," he said. "I don't care how late. I haven't had a sitter all week. Sandy has to work, but I know Ben will stay as late as I need him."

One night. Tatum had told her to take one night of happiness for herself.

She'd been talking about a simple date. Not sex.

But Tatum hadn't lived in Talia's world, where sex, or the build-up to it, were pretty much all that existed.

She sat up.

"Are you down at the ocean?" His tone had dropped to a sexy growl. And she almost said yes. Just because it would be safer. Kinder.

"No."

"I heard water."

"Yes."

"You're in the bathtub?"

"Yes."

"You've been lying there naked this whole time?"

"Yeah."

"While I've been sitting outside at a Boy Scout fire, wasting the moment?" His groan made her chuckle.

"If I show up at your door tomorrow night are you going to let me in?"

"Probably."

"Would I be pushing my luck to hope you'll have a bottle of chilled wine waiting?"

He'd mentioned Tanner's wine a couple of times since the night he'd tried it. Had even told the waitress at the Italian restaurant on the beach about it.

"I still have a bottle in the refrigerator so I'm guessing not."

Her free hand moved down her body to come to

rest between her legs. She closed them against it. Pushed her fingers against the throbbing that was growing more intense.

"It's a date, then."

Talia's head was slightly dizzy. Her body thrummed. And her heart…

"There are things about me you don't know."

"I'm not asking you to marry me, Talia. Just to—"

"Sleep with you?"

"Maybe. If that's where our night leads us. But only if that's where it leads both of us."

Trouble was she didn't have much doubt that it would.

"You said it might just be sex between us," he reminded her.

She was clean. Sexually. Most of Talia's years pleasing men hadn't included sexual intercourse. And when it had been introduced, so had condoms. She'd used them every time. She'd also been tested. Regularly. More so over the past year, just out of her own paranoia to feel clean. Unscathed by the years she'd spent in hell.

"I think we should talk first." She had to set her ground rules while she could still think. If, after he found out she'd once been a stripper, he still wanted to take her to bed, she'd go.

"Let me in the door when I knock and we'll see how it goes."

She didn't have the will to argue with him any further. Like he said, it wasn't as though they were getting married.

And lots of nice guys slept with hookers. Not that she'd really been a prostitute. Not a streetwalker, at least.

No. She wasn't going to think about her past tonight. What was done was done. And tonight, Talia was getting out of the tub before she found out whether or not she could actually experience an orgasm.

She wasn't waiting for Sherman.

But just in case…

CHAPTER TWENTY-ONE

DRESSED IN JEANS, a tank top, blouse, sweater and tennis shoes, Talia was waiting when Sherman pulled into the driveway Saturday evening. She'd buried her womanly parts as many layers deep as she could. She wasn't going to have sex with him.

But man, he looked good. In jeans that hugged his thighs and perfectly showcased his delectable backside, a button-down white shirt with the cuffs rolled up and sandals, he was health and virility personified.

She was not going to have sex with him.

"Hello," he greeted, taking her arms to pull her forward—not until their bodies touched. But until their lips did.

Then their bodies touched. Met. Stuck. And they pretty much had sex. While Talia stood there fully dressed.

SLOW DOWN. THE words came from the back of beyond to speak to Sherman. Words. They were just words. Ones he'd vowed, on his way over to Talia's, that he'd listen to. They could have sex. And he was completely convinced it was going to be pretty damned miraculous when it happened.

But he didn't just want a sexual partner.

"How about that wine?" He pulled away from her, dropped his arms to his sides and took a deep breath.

"Sure." Talia's tone gave no indication to what she was thinking as she went into the kitchen, poured the wine and handed him a glass.

"How about a walk on the beach?" she asked. He had the strange feeling that she'd already had the suggestion planned.

And was curious as to the rest of what she might have up her sleeve for their evening. Curious and willing to be patient while the hours unfolded.

He took her hand as they set off. Holding his wine with the other hand. She told him about the private stretch of beach, the other homes, all a bit larger than hers, that shared the beach. Talked about a little boy who used to torment her sister-in-law's little dog. Pointed out his house.

They sipped wine and breathed in the salty air.

"How long have she and your brother been married?" he asked. He wanted to meet them. And the rest of her family. To know everything about her.

He wanted to lie with her in the sand and be consumed by the hunger between them. To listen to the soft swell of the waves against the shore until dawn.

"A year."

"What are the chances of Kent and me meeting them?" he asked lightly. "And I'd like to meet Tatum, too. Kent talks about her almost as much as he does Jason."

She stumbled. "Um, Tanner…and Sedona…asked me to invite the two of you to dinner tomorrow night."

Sunday dinner. A family thing. "What time?"

"I don't know. I didn't ask."

He walked slowly beside her in the dark, sand filling his sandals. Processing. Choosing his words. "You weren't going to ask," he finally came out with.

"No."

"Why not?"

She stopped. Let go of his hand, turned to the ocean and then sat. She pulled sand into a pile between her feet with her free hand and took a sip of wine. Seemed to be content to sit there alone for the rest of her life.

Sherman joined her, lying on his side, propped on an elbow, his glass resting in the sand between his hands. She reminded him of a documentary he'd seen years before about the training of a wild horse. If you pushed too hard, it would turn on you.

Trust took time.

"Last night, in the office when Kent lost it on me…" He looked out to the ocean, relaxing. "He'd been showing Jason pictures of Brooke."

Her pile of sand lay unattended.

"He accused me of doing nothing to find the person who killed his mother. The depth of his anger was…tough to take."

"What can you do? It was a hit-and-run with a stolen car, right?"

"The guy ran, yeah. Just disappeared."

She turned to look at him, her face half-shadowed in the moonlight and still the most beautiful thing he'd ever seen. "You think he was picked up by someone else?"

"It's a theory. But then you'd have to ask yourself why."

"Do you think someone killed her deliberately?"

He shrugged. "I don't know what I think. He had to have come from the paved median turnaround that was almost parallel to the crash site. He'd have to have had enough time to turn so that they were facing each other head-on, but that's it. The coroner said Brooke was definitely awake when she crashed. But she'd had no time to put on the brakes, swerve or react in any way. There were also no tire marks in the grassy median itself, so they know the other driver didn't fall asleep or lose control and cross over from the other side of the freeway."

"You've given it a lot of thought."

"I've been on the internet every week for two years. Trying to find something that makes sense."

"Why?"

That wasn't a question he'd been expecting. Or had asked himself, even.

But he knew the answer. "Guilt," he said. "I'm alive, she isn't. Her life was so short, and that last year or two, they were the last she had, and they weren't… She deserved to be loved better."

"She had a say in your relationship, too, you know."

The last thing he'd expected to do was talk about his wife tonight.

"We'd talked about what we wanted out of life, how we wanted to live it…had an open line of communication, knew the pitfalls. We'd taken a course together before we got married to help us communicate with each other."

Everything had made perfect sense.

"We made a promise to become one with each other, to grow together."

"That's kind of the plan, isn't it? When two people get married?"

He stared at her, knowing, instinctively just knowing, that he could become one with this woman.

"I thought Brooke and I were doing that—losing ourselves to each other, forming something greater than either of us would be alone. Brooke claimed that was what she wanted."

He wanted Talia to know the worst of him. Before he offered the best. Or things got clouded by sex.

"I'd always considered her feelings."

There'd never been great passion between them, but there'd been good sex.

"Maybe she needed more than consideration."

"Or maybe the problem was with the plan in general," he said now, unable to ever see himself planning life with Talia. It would happen as it happened. Be fluid and open to change as challenges presented themselves.

The idea panicked him.

And woke him up, too.

"We were to start a family two years after we married," he said, thankful for the light breeze that wafted over his heated skin. They were hitting record highs for the end of February, but the evenings were cool. "Sex became about that. Everything was timed. For a purpose."

That was Brooke. Everything for a purpose. She'd been a good woman. A good wife. He'd have likely stayed married to her for the rest of their lives.

And never known the passion that was even now wrestling with a mind that told him to take things slowly.

"So you think that this past year, all of Kent's anger is due to him thinking you were just letting his mother's death go unpunished?"

"I'm not sure. Clearly that's part of it. But there's a lot of anger associated with death in general. You know, how could the person leave you? Why did life do this to you? The unfairness of it all. Everyone handles it differently. Dr. Jordon believes that Kent's having a more difficult time than a lot of kids. Probably because he's so cerebral."

"He's been taught to think things through, and this is something that doesn't make sense to him."

This woman's effect on him, the way she'd crashed into his life and made everything different in such a short time, didn't make sense.

"I didn't come here to talk about my son."

"But then, life doesn't go as planned, does it?" She was grinning. It took him a second to realize she was teasing him.

Fire shot through him. Leaning forward, Sherman kissed her. Opening his mouth, he took her lips into his, acting. Reacting. Not thinking at all.

His wine forgotten in the sand, he moved closer, pushing her back in the sand, vaguely aware that her wine had tipped over. He didn't care. Her eyes were wide, glistening in the moonlight and staring at him. Compelling him.

So much was hidden there. Mystery. Sweetness. Longing. And something that made her uniquely woman. Not common woman. Not every woman.

He was mesmerized. On fire. Alive like he'd never been alive in his life.

"I want you," he said. "So bad…" He kissed her again. Over and over. His tongue mated with hers. Shifting until he was lying on top of her, he settled his throbbing groin against her, fitting his penis between her legs and pushing against her, mimicking the act he knew was coming.

Her hips rose to meet his as her tongue played with him. Enticing him. Inviting naughty thoughts and pleasure beyond belief. He wanted her breasts. To touch the soft skin of her stomach.

He wanted her naked…

"No."

Sherman sought her lips again as she broke their kiss.

"Noooo." She kissed him even as she said the word. Through the fog of intense desire, he heard something in her voice. It stopped him.

Talia pushed at him, and he sat up, pulling her with him.

"Did I hurt you?" He didn't think he had, but in all honesty he couldn't be completely sure how much pressure he'd used. How much he'd let his weight sink into her softer, smaller body.

Her eyes were still glistening, but she wasn't crying. Her mouth was straight, her features expressionless as she stared out at the ocean beyond. There were no lights out there. Nothing but darkness on the horizon.

And a chill in the air that made him cold. Even while he still burned.

"I have to talk to you." The words didn't sound ominous as much as pained. And he knew a moment of fear unlike any he'd known before.

Was she dying? Was that the aura of mystery about her? The depth that he couldn't fathom?

He'd hold her until she took her last breath…

"First, I… You… This…" She motioned toward the sand where they'd been lying. "I've…I had no idea it could be… I've never had an orgasm."

Slow down. His earlier words, his admonitions to himself, came back to him. He was overanalyzing. Getting ahead of himself.

"We can take it slowly," he said aloud, needing to reassure her far more than he needed it for himself.

And it hit him.

Whatever she needed was more important than what he needed.

Was this love, then? Was this what love did?

She shook her head. "I'm not…afraid," she said. "Not of having sex." Her laugh was harsher now. As though she didn't like something.

About him? Something he'd said or not said? Something she had to say?

"I just needed you to know that…to thank you, for showing me how wonderful sex can feel."

"But we haven't even…" The shake of her head stopped him.

Really stopped him. No more guessing. He watched her. And waited, confident that he'd handle whatever was bothering her. He'd make it better. Anything she told him was going to bring them that much closer to each other. Give him one more glimpse into her world.

A world he was meant to inhabit. He knew that for certain now. Not because he was turned on as hell by every move she made. But because she'd turned his life—his way of approaching life—completely upside down.

Thirty-eight years of living had brought him to this. He was not a stupid man. He recognized once-in-a-lifetime moments.

The wind blew a few stray tendrils of her hair across her forehead. He brushed them back and her lips found his palm, pressing against it. She turned her head away, and her long, blond hair fell over her shoulders and down across her breast.

"I'm twenty-seven years old and just this past December graduated from college." She was looking at him as though there was some message there.

He didn't get it.

"I graduated from high school when I was eighteen."

Right. So did he.

"I completed my undergraduate work in three years."

Whatever it was he was supposed to be gleaning from this continued to elude him.

"That leaves six years unaccounted for."

He could add and subtract. Just didn't get the significance.

"I…ran away from home, the second time, when I was eighteen," she said. "I'd convinced myself that I was never going to be good enough for my brother, that neither of us was ever going to be happy living in the same state."

He was with her all the way. Eager now for the entry she was giving him. He'd almost forgotten that her story had begun with a "no" to the lovemaking that had been about to occur.

"I was convinced…" She swallowed. "Completely believed…" She swallowed again. Staring out at the horizon, she finished, "That I was my mother's daughter."

Every part of him went on high alert. Not in defense against anything she might tell him, but because she needed something from him, and he had to make absolutely certain he didn't let her down.

"You said she had four children by four separate men and gave up custody of you younger three." He tried to help her, tried to glean where this was leading and make it easier on her in any way he could.

She'd also said her mother was dead.

"Except for Tanner's, our fathers were dealers. At least two were pimps."

This was about drugs, then. She wasn't the first young person to fall into that trap.

"When I was sixteen she took a hundred dollars from her dealer in exchange for allowing him to get in the shower with me."

No. This precious, beautiful, sweet woman had been raped? By a dope dealer? At sixteen?

He'd kill him. He'd find the guy and kill him and...

He had to do something. Wanted to comfort her. But she wasn't crying. She just sat, staring out at the ocean.

What did she see out there? What called to her?

Was there a place for him there? Him and Kent?

She glanced at him then. And seemed surprised to find him still beside her. Wanting her. If she thought a crime against a child was in any way going to change his opinion of her...

"Tanner stopped him," she said. "I was in the shower and didn't even know about it. He beat the guy within an inch of his life and threw him out of our house. Literally."

Thank God. He had to meet this man. Wanted to meet him. To thank him from the bottom of his heart for being a good man. A good brother.

"That day changed us all. Irrevocably and forever," she said, her voice deadpan. "Tanner changed. He grew hard and authoritative. He used the incident against my mother, blackmailed her into giving him custody of us, though none of us knew about any of that until last year."

Sherman thought his life had been rough. He'd felt sorry for himself, having lost a father so young. He'd had no clue.

"He went from being my best friend to being my jailer. He didn't trust me out of his sight. I thought he didn't trust me because I was just like my mother."

He could understand. Both sides. As a young man who'd just come face-to-face with the way other men looked at his little sister, Tanner Malone must have been scared shitless. Sherman would have been. Hell, Malone would only be thirty-four now. Four years younger than he was.

He had questions. Wanted to reassure her. To comment. But waited for her to do things in her own way, at her own pace.

When she was ready, when she invited him, he'd be right there, giving her everything he had.

"By the time I graduated from high school, I knew I was like my mother."

He wasn't sure what that meant.

"I…had an…effect…on men."

Oh, wait. If she thought he only wanted to have sex with her, if he was only attracted to her physically, then he'd set her straight in a hurry.

"I was told once that I *exude*."

She did. Definitely. He'd reacted like a schoolboy around her.

"Didn't matter where I went or what I tried to do, I'd walk into a room and men noticed. And once they noticed, they didn't care about anything else."

That wasn't right. Or fair. He cared about plenty

else. But he'd come on strong. And fast. And felt bad about that.

Because he'd recognized that she was the one. After thirty-eight years of living he'd found what he'd always been waiting for. A partner who interested him, challenged him, on every level.

"I gave up," she said.

And turned to look at him again. His face chilled first. Then his neck. Across his back, down his legs, the frozen sensation passed over him.

She wasn't talking about them. Or him.

"I decided that if I was the type of woman who was meant to entertain men, I'd be the best damn one I could be. I wasn't going to be cheap like my mother. Or give in to drugs and alcohol. I was a businesswoman. With an asset to market. But I wasn't going to sell my soul."

Everything inside of him stopped. Just stopped. His mind was blank.

"I moved to Vegas. Took a week to look around. Visit clubs. Talk to people. I decided where I wanted to work. And I got the job."

"Doing what?"

"I was a stripper, Sherman. For eight years, the last two while attending college classes, I shimmied a pole, completely nude, five nights a week."

Only one thought came to mind.

He wasn't going to have sex that night.

CHAPTER TWENTY-TWO

TALIA DIDN'T CRY that night after Sherman left. She crawled into bed. Closed her eyes. And went to sleep. Sleep meant escape. Had always meant escape. She welcomed it.

She got up when the alarm went off. Got showered, dressed, put on her makeup and jewelry and went to work.

She knew what her life was, what it had to be. She'd known what she couldn't have.

And at least she'd done the right thing. She'd told Sherman the truth rather than stealing one night of happiness for herself. Because she'd have been stealing from him, too.

As much as she'd wanted him, wanted one taste of joy in a lifetime of hard living, she just couldn't take for herself at another's expense.

Not at Sherman's expense.

She cared about him. Like a woman was supposed to care about a man. It was a novel experience for her. One she didn't care to repeat.

The question that remained, that tortured her over the miles of road between Santa Raquel and Beverly

Hills, all during work, and back home again, was Kent. Would Sherman still let her pick her son up and drive him to the Lemonade Stand after school?

She didn't doubt, for one second, that he'd leave Kent in the program now. The Stand had spoken for itself. Talia's integrity or opinion no longer mattered.

Earlier, her reputation had mattered. Back when she'd needed him to listen to her, to trust her, in order to help Kent.

But Kent didn't need her help anymore. And she wasn't his only transportation option.

No, she just needed him. And his father.

And that was *her* problem.

TALIA COULDN'T RISK shortchanging a sixth grader because she wasn't feeling up to par. She wasn't going to take a chance on missing something in a collage reading, so she stuck to her own classwork Sunday night. There was a lot of reading, some of which didn't stick. So she had to read it twice.

She wasn't going outside. Wasn't going anywhere near the beach. Maybe ever again.

Or at least until the sting of her pain had lessened.

Sherman had said he'd be in touch when he'd left the night before. After she'd asked him to leave. He'd been shocked. She'd seen the change in his eyes.

And she hadn't been willing to hang out and talk

things over. Fact was fact and no amount of talking or explaining was going to change it.

She stayed away from her brother's wine. One glass a week was enough for her. As good as it was, she didn't like the effect of alcohol on her brain. The whole "looking like, feeling like, her mother" thing.

Tammy Malone had been drunk as often as she'd been sober. Talia could still hear the slur in her mother's voice as Talia had come home from school. Or gotten up in the morning.

Headlights in her driveway surprised her. Getting up from the table, she crossed to the living-room front window and peeked out.

Tanner had been fine with her canceling on them. He'd understood that she needed time to catch up on her work.

She'd told him, when she'd phoned to say she wouldn't be coming over for Sunday dinner, that her date had gone fine and that she hadn't invited Sherman and Kent to join them that night.

He hadn't asked any questions. But she knew he wanted to meet his nephew. As well as the man who was raising him.

The same man currently walking up the driveway to her back door.

Was he there to relieve her of her driving duties the following afternoon? She'd expected to hear from him about that.

He could have just called.

She didn't wait for him to knock.

The door was standing open when he got to it. She was sitting in front of her laptop and school books at the kitchen table.

"You're studying." He came in. Shut the door behind him, then pulled out a chair and sat down.

His jeans were black. His T-shirt white. Just like him. All black-and-white and neatly planned.

"Just a normal Sunday night," she told him. Nothing had changed. She was on the path of a new life. And she was going to stay the course.

"How was dinner?"

"I didn't go."

He didn't ask why. She didn't offer him anything to drink.

"We need to talk." His look was firm. But personal, too.

She nodded, owing him that.

"I…" Whatever he'd had on the tip of his tongue as he'd walked in her door seemed to have fled. He met her gaze and stopped.

To his credit, his stare didn't travel any farther down, though her unfettered breasts were delineated pretty clearly through the thin T-shirt she wore.

She'd been alone. And she'd wanted to be comfortable.

"It's okay, Sherman," she said. She couldn't do this to him, put him through something that he'd replay in his mind with regret. "I knew when you first asked me out that you were asking the woman you thought I was, not who I really was. The reverse of that is that I didn't let you know, too. Your shock is completely understandable. And expected. And as is the fact that me having been a stripper changes things for you."

It was probably the longest speech she'd made to him. At least it felt that way.

"I have some questions."

She waited.

"You said you were like your mother. But the job you described didn't sound that way."

Still waiting for the question...

"Were you a hooker, too?"

She didn't see why that mattered at this point. Her life was hers. Not connected to his. Unless…he was still going to let her drive her son to the Stand. Give her another few months with him before he disappeared from her life again.

Permanently this time.

"Not by choice."

"What does that mean?"

"I met a guy, an older gentleman who made me laugh. He was a widower and needed a woman to play hostess for him at some very upscale functions. He asked me to marry him. It was a business arrangement. A marriage of convenience."

As seasoned—and life weary—as she'd been, she'd bought his story hook, line and sinker.

And boy, did it sink her.

Sherman's jaw tightened, but as he had the night before, he allowed her to continue in her own time, without interrupting.

She tried not to look at him, not to allow herself to be distracted by what-might-have-beens. Or could-have-beens.

They wouldn't have been. Couldn't have been. Because back when she'd made her mistakes, she'd still been a child. An underage teenager. And the man who'd had sex with her had gone to jail for it.

Of course, if she'd turned toward the college world that Tanner had offered her instead of running away to Vegas, the what-might-have-beens would have stood a chance. In the present.

"When you work in the sex world, there is no desire," she said baldly. "I hadn't been turned on since I was a kid in high school and even then it was more curiosity and a craving for love than it was any physical drive."

It was as close to Rex, Kent's biological father, as she was going to go.

"I was also completely aware that I was not the type of girl a decent man took home to meet Mom. I wasn't ever going to marry for love, raise a family and live happily ever after. I was my mother's daughter."

Talia had accepted her past. It was her present that she struggled with.

"The marriage proposal was a sound business arrangement that would provide security for my future when my body was no longer tempting enough to make money at the pole."

He took a sharp breath. And continued to study her, gaze for gaze, as she spoke, giving away none of what he was thinking.

"We were married in a chapel in Vegas. For the first couple of weeks things were actually nice. He had his room. I had mine. We met for dinner every night. He was intelligent and witty. I enjoyed our conversations."

And then she hadn't enjoyed anything about the man. Looking at Sherman, seeing the decency shining from his eyes, feeling the heart of him, she almost couldn't continue.

"He sold me to his friends," she blurted. "And if I didn't do as he asked, just private lap dances at first, he'd beat me so badly I couldn't work. Who wants to gape at a woman with bruises all over, you know?"

The ugliness brought bile to her throat. And in that moment she realized how far she'd come. When she'd been in that life, things had happened one step at a time, baby steps, so going from one thing to something a little bit worse hadn't been so traumatic. When her husband had sold her out she'd been angry. But not all that shocked.

Tonight, reliving it, she was shocked.

And devastated for that girl she was talking about.

"The one line I drew was that no one was going to have sex with me without protection," she said. "I'd rather be beaten to death than die of a disease some jerk gave to me.

"And I wouldn't kiss. No exchange of bodily fluids. Period."

This distinction, which had, in her mind, been huge, seemed insignificant now.

"I made it about a month before I knew that the life was killing me," she said. "I tried to get away from him, to divorce him, and that's when I found out how powerful he really was. And how deep I was in. If it hadn't been for Tanner…"

Her brother had shown up like the damned knight in shining armor she'd always thought him to be. "He paid to have me for a night and then whisked me into a woman's shelter where I stayed long enough for him to win my freedom. I'm not sure what else was said or done, but the next thing I knew I had a divorce and was free to do whatever I wanted."

"And that's when you came home?"

Of course not. She was her mother's daughter, after all.

"No. It was another couple of years before that," she said. "I enrolled in college, and went back to work at the club—at the pole only—until last year when Tatum disappeared."

That was when she'd come home. When she and Tanner had finally been forced to be honest with each other. When everyone found out the secrets—and burdens—her older brother had been carrying on his own.

And all because their lies and secrets had left Tatum ripe for, and vulnerable to, the manipulation of an abusive rich boy.

Talia had gone into her marriage willingly. Walked on stage willingly.

Tatum had been raped. "You'd needed to make your own way, not be reliant on Tanner."

Sherman's words were not at all what she'd been expecting.

But they were true.

"Because you aren't your mother's daughter."

That was when her tears fell.

CHAPTER TWENTY-THREE

HE'D NEVER MET a woman like her. He'd been to a strip club once. For a bachelor party when he was in college. He and his friends had whooped and hollered and made crude jokes about what they'd like to do to the girls onstage.

The tears welling in Talia's eyes made him feel a little sick at the memory. Strangely her tears didn't fall.

Just as the woman didn't ever seem to fall. She was soft and feminine and hard as a rock at the same time. Sexy, vulnerable and completely capable.

He wanted her so bad he hurt with it. And would feel safer with her in a tough situation than anyone else he could think of.

She was wild and unpredictable and completely reliable.

"You're staring."

He was.

"You confuse the hell out of me."

Her chuckle broke some of the tension in the room. "Join the club."

"Seriously? You seem to have a pretty good handle on things."

"I'm a showgirl, remember?" Her smile was still there, but it was the slight hint of loneliness in her gaze that captured him.

"Dressed like that?" He brought it back to her body. Her looks. Anything deeper was going to sink him. He couldn't care about this woman. Not now. Not anymore.

When she glanced down at her simple but revealing T-shirt, her long, blond hair brushed her breasts and he wished he could brush them with his fingers.

So maybe focusing on her body, her looks, hadn't been such a good idea. Maybe leaving was his only option.

"Why are you here?"

"We have unresolved issues." Clearly, that much was obvious.

"You could have phoned."

He'd called Sandy and Ben over again, leaving Kent with a sitter two nights in a row. A first for him.

"You deserved better than that." She'd been honest with him. She'd tried to tell him from the beginning that he didn't know her. She'd clearly fought with herself about seeing him at all.

And what had she owed him? She'd been there to help his son. Period. And in that capacity she'd pretty much worked a miracle.

Her past was none of his business. Nothing to do with what had originally brought them together.

He'd pushed her into more.

"So what do you want?" she asked, looking him straight in the eye. Talia didn't waste time.

It was another reason he appreciated her so much.

"I want to take you to bed and make love to you until the world goes away."

"No, you don't."

"Why do you say that?"

"Because if you did, you'd be doing it."

Eyes narrowed, he stared at those big blue eyes, at the hardened nipples visible beneath the thin fabric of her shirt. Had she just told him she was willing?

His penis pushed against the fly of his jeans.

The darkness outside was a stark contrast to the bright light shining down on her at the kitchen table.

He should go. He wanted to stay but couldn't do it right. "My job, my career...powerful public figures trust their reputations with me."

He could have been speaking a foreign language for all the reaction she gave him.

"If it ever became known that I was spending my time with an ex-stripper, I could lose everything."

The fact stood between them.

"For every campaign there's another side that's constantly looking for dirt to use to take our votes. Politics should be about the issues, but so often, during a campaign, it's more about perceived reputation. I can see the potential PR nightmare of a headline that reads Campaign Manager in Bed with a Stripper."

The words were cruel, and yet he guessed that they were exactly what Talia Malone would want. The complete truth. "If I do my job right, I'm invisible. When that changes I'm no longer of value."

"What do you want from me?"

He knew. And had a feeling she did, too.

It wasn't right. Wasn't fair. But it was why he was there and they both knew it.

"YOU WANT TO hire me?"

Talia knew better. The question was pure defense. "No."

"You just want the goods for free?" She could tell him to leave. She had absolutely no doubt he'd do so.

"No."

"So what is it?" If they were going to do this... obliterate this...this sex thing...she had to know where she stood.

She needed him to know.

He took her hand, turned it over, ran his thumb along her palm and then raised it to his lips. That soft kiss sent shock waves through her body. Looking at her, with her hand still at his lips, he said, "I want to spend what will probably be the most incredible night of my life making love with a woman who has me enthralled."

Wow. "You're good."

"Stop it, Talia."

What? Stop getting turned on by every breath he took? Stop wishing things could be different?

Stop liking the man so damned much?

"We're calling it like it is, right? What guy hasn't fantasized about bedding that girl up onstage?"

"I'm fantasizing about the woman standing right here, right now. I'm picturing her naked in my arms because from the second I met her I've been unable to get the thought of her out of my mind."

"You have to face facts, Sherman. I deserve that. If you're going to take me to bed, take me knowing what I was."

"I don't see you on a stage. I'm sorry."

"If you could see me there, if this was just a strip club fantasy, would it stop it from happening?" She was scared to death, couldn't he see that? Scared that it wouldn't happen. And that it would. Scared that it would be too good. Scared that she couldn't ever be good enough to make up for her past.

"Probably not."

If she was actually going to embark on a sexual odyssey with this man, she had to be sure that she had no illusions. No hope that some miracle could happen and they could all live happily ever after. Her. Sherman. And their son.

He sat there with his elbow on the arm of the wooden kitchen chair, propping his chin on his hand, his pants tight enough that she could see how badly he wanted her. "If we're going to call this like it is, then it's a matter of me being mesmerized by the most fascinating woman I've ever met and need desperately to know in every possible way there is to know a woman."

A pithy response didn't spring immediately to mind. She was too busy trying not to be mesmerized right back.

She was going to have sex with him. Going to have that one night of joy. And find out if she could actually have an orgasm. There was nothing holding her back now. She had nothing to lose.

Except maybe her heart.

"If you don't mind, I need to adjust a bit here," Sherman said, watching her face while he unbuttoned his waistband. Her gaze flew to his hands.

Very deliberately he unzipped his fly, and pulled back the corners of his jeans to expose the head of his penis protruding from the top of a pair of black briefs.

And then he stopped.

Sitting there exposed to her gaze. She looked up at him and read the message there loud and clear.

The next move was up to her.

TALIA LIFTED HER T-shirt. She didn't pull it off. Just lifted it up past her breasts and let him see them.

Sherman almost came right then and there. She

was every man's fantasy. Or maybe just his, but God, she was hot. Her breasts were full and tight, the nipples large enough to satisfy a man's sucking urges, and as hard as his penis.

She was art, sitting there. Beautiful. Every man's dream. Art.

He pulled off his shirt. And waited.

Staring at him, she untied the pajama bottoms she was wearing. He couldn't tell if she was wearing panties or not. And wanted to know. Bad.

Neither of them spoke any words. They weren't needed. They were perfection, sitting at that kitchen table together. Just him and her and an attraction that was bigger than either of them.

Or a world that was going to have them spend their lives apart.

He'd kill for her.

Not to have her but to protect her.

Kicking off one sandal, he dared her to take her turn.

She took an arm out of the sleeve of her gray T-shirt.

He lost his other sandal.

She wore her shirt around her neck.

And he was no closer to knowing whether there were panties under her thin cotton black-and-gray-striped pants.

So he showed her his. Still sitting, he pulled his pants down to his knees, exposing the black cotton briefs in their entirety, caressing her breasts with his gaze. First one, then the other, paying particular attention to those nipples. Needing to know how sensitive they'd be to his touch.

Talia pulled her T-shirt over her head, letting it trail down her long hair as she parted her hair in the back and pulled it forward to cover her breasts.

He pulled his feet out of his jeans and spread his legs.

And waited. She was going to have to show him now.

Soon he would see her feminine beauty in its entirety. He'd be able to worship her there, to show her how a man touched a woman when he cared about her.

He'd show that gorgeous body reverence. Coax more pleasure from her than she'd ever known before.

And then he'd claim her as his own.

Just as soon as she showed him whether or not she was wearing any panties.

TALIA KNEW HOW to tease. But she had no idea how to make love. Her few experiences with actual intercourse had been strictly mechanical. And quick. A man using her for his own pleasure. No communication between them.

Without words, Sherman was saying so much she

could hardly take it all in. He was stripping for her and allowing her to give him whatever she chose.

He was everything she'd once longed for. A real man.

One who was willing to be a partner to her, not a boss.

One who would give, not take.

But tonight she didn't dare allow herself to long for anything. Neither could she extricate herself from the most exquisite experience of her life.

Standing, she held the tops of her pajama pants in place and, looking back over her naked shoulder at him, walked slowly toward her bedroom. As soon as she knew he was following her, she let the pants drop.

The thong she was wearing was a turn-on in itself as she felt the thin piece of fabric move against parts of her that were so sensitive she didn't even recognize them as her own.

He kept a good two feet behind her. Still watching over her shoulder, she purposely enticed him as he matched her, slow step for slow step, following her into the moonlit darkness of the master bedroom, his gaze glued on the tight backside she was rather proud of.

When they were both in the room, leaving everything but the anticipation of what they were about to do outside, she turned around to face him.

He gaped hungrily at the V of fabric covering her.

"You first," she said, hoping she sounded sexy.

Naked females were a dime a dozen in her life. Naked men were not. Men who wanted to be naked, yeah. Men who actually got the chance…never with her permission.

With one thumb, he hooked the waistband of his briefs, lifted them out and away from his protrusion, shoved them down and stepped out of them.

Overcome by an incredible urge to spread her legs, Talia stood still, more alive than she could ever remember feeling, and laughed out loud.

Before she realized that he'd think she was laughing at him in all his naked glory.

Backtracking as quickly as her befuddled brain could, she opened her mouth to make matters worse when he approached, jutting his hips forward with exaggerated pride, a huge grin on his face.

"Let me help you with those," he said, prodding the waistband of her panties with the tip of his penis.

He wasn't going to let her strip. Or make her strip. And that's when Talia knew she was going to care for this man for the rest of her life.

Sherman played with her for hours. Touching every part of her. Lying back while she explored every part of him. She teased him. And he found her sexy as hell. He worshipped her, and she looked at him with confusion. He brought her to orgasm, holding his fingers inside her the first time as she pulsed around him, and her surprise brought a surge of protection from deep within him. He would take care of her. She would never want for anything again.

When he finally positioned himself above her, touching the head of his condom-covered penis gently to her opening before very slowly driving himself completely inside her, he knew that a lifetime of this wasn't going to be enough.

One way or another he had to make love with this woman for the rest of his days.

CHAPTER TWENTY-FOUR

TALIA KNEW BY the way he was dressing with his back to her that nothing had changed as far as Sherman and their future was concerned. She'd known going in that it would be that way. She'd been under no false pretenses.

So why in the hell did she have to choke back tears?

And then anger?

"Was it worth your money?" she asked to his back in a hardened voice she hadn't heard coming from her in over a year.

He spun around, zipping his fly. His chest, still bare and covered with dark hair, taunted her. It had been hers to touch, but only for a short time.

"I didn't spend any money." His tone was upbeat as always, though the narrowing of his eyes hinted at a different story.

"Not literally, no," she said. And then before she could stop herself, the years of disappointment, of trying so hard to be decent, deserving of respect and failing time and again, spilled out of her. "But you might as well have, right? How was it, having sex with a woman who's not respectable enough to be your date? Was it as exciting as you thought it would be?"

"More." His stare was hard. And pinned her to her spot. "Far more. And I've been thinking about it, exactly the same, from the second we met. Not since I found out what you did for a living." Still shirtless and barefoot, he stepped closer to her on the plush carpet of the bedroom. "And that's really what we're talking about here, isn't it?"

Was it? She hoped her nonchalant stare spoke the question.

"Why don't you just ask, Talia?"

"I don't know what you're talking about."

But she did. And couldn't bear to voice the question.

"You want to know if, in my mind, while I was making love to you, I was fantasizing about bedding a stripper. You want to know if it was Talia the collage reader I was sleeping with or Talia the Las Vegas pole dancer."

She didn't slap him. Or cry.

"And the answer to your question is…" He took her bare shoulders in his hands, caressing them so gently her whole body tingled. "Both. I was making love to you, Talia. All of you. Think about what just happened here. Think about how my body touched your body and then look me in the eye and tell me you think I was with a stripper."

She couldn't.

And he knew it.

But it didn't change things. Not really. He still couldn't have her in his life. Not in any real sense.

And that wasn't anything new. Not from that night or the night before. Not from the beginning.

Because she'd known all along there was no chance for a life with him.

Because of Kent.

Because of who she was.

And whose son he was.

"Where does that leave us?"

"I don't know. I'm not going to be able to stay away from here."

He would if she told him to.

She nodded. Pulled on a robe as he finished dressing and followed him out to the back door.

"May I still pick up Kent tomorrow?"

His surprise was clearly genuine as he said, "Of course."

He bent and kissed her. She kissed him back.

"Your past... I wish it was different, more for your sake than for mine," he said softly. "But it doesn't change how I feel for you privately," he told her.

She nodded again. She understood.

And as he walked out she understood something else.

After years of refusing to take male clients, of

refusing to have sex without commitment, she'd just succumbed.

Standing there alone, her body still wet from his touch, she felt like Sherman Paulson's much appreciated whore.

She watched his back, watched him approach his BMW, wanting to call out to him. To tell him not to return. That he wasn't welcome in her home.

But she didn't. She couldn't.

Because regardless of the fact that he was never going to marry her, there was never going to be another man in her life.

She was in love with this one.

SHERMAN WAS IN his car, on the way to a breakfast meeting Friday morning, when his phone rang. Pushing the hands-free talk button, and with his mind filled, as always, with thoughts of Talia, he took the call. He hadn't spoken with her since leaving her place Sunday night, but he'd heard about her every day from his son. And taken her to bed with him every night.

"Mr. Paulson?"

"Yes?" He hadn't known the number and didn't recognize the voice. The area code was local.

"This is Detective Lacey with the Santa Raquel Police."

Kent!

"We've found Eddie Billingsley," the detective

continued, naming the young man who'd left home the night of Brooke's death. "His mother identified the duffel bag we found on him."

Identified? "Is he dead?"

"Yes, sir. And we have reason to believe that he was the driver of the car that killed your wife."

Sherman pulled over to the side of the three-lane road, hardly aware as horns honked and vehicles sped past him.

"What reason?"

"He had the keys to the stolen car on him," the detective said. Sherman understood that it was the guy's job to deliver sensitive information. But he sounded so...

"Where was he?" Sherman couldn't rally his thoughts. Couldn't really put it all together. Or know how to respond. For two years he'd been waiting. Looking. When had he begun to believe that he'd never really know what happened?

And been relieved by that fact?

"Not far from the site of the accident," the detective relayed in the same prosaic tone. "We're waiting for forensics and the coroner to confirm, but it's highly probable that while he sustained injuries in the accident, they might not have been life-threatening. He likely had his bag over his shoulder and left the scene, crossing over the median a short distance down the highway, ducked into some trees and unfortunately went over a cliff that overlooked the ocean. He probably heard the water, was heading for it, but didn't see the drop-off. Once we had reason to suspect that he was our driver, and couldn't find any sign of him after that night, we put searchers out. A team in a boat scouring the shoreline spotted what they thought might be a duffel bag and we put someone down on a line."

"His body's been lying there all this time?"

"What's left of it. Yes, sir."

Sherman didn't want to imagine the decomposition. Or the pain Tricia Billingsley must be suffering.

And then something else struck him.

"But we know that he was at the diner at the exit up ahead of where the accident took place," he said, confused. "Which means he wouldn't have come from the median turnaround like everyone thought."

"Yes, sir, it does. Unfortunately, it now appears that Eddie, who was under the influence, entered the highway going the wrong way, and that your wife drove straight into him."

"She wasn't asleep at the time of the accident," he said slowly, his peripheral vision red-tinged. "The coroner said that she was awake, fully reactive at time of impact."

"Yes, sir. It is my duty to inform you that the accident is now being ruled a suicide. I'm sorry. If you collected on any life insurance, you'll want to contact your agent."

Life insurance? The man had just told him his wife likely killed herself, that the accident could have been avoided but for her conscious choice to let it happen, and he thought Sherman would care about life insurance?

"I didn't," he said, because something was expected of him. He was pretty sure he thanked the man. And then he sat there, his car running, and tried to figure out what it all meant.

TALIA HAD DINNER with her family on Friday. She'd taken Tatum with her to pick up Kent from school and then drove her home afterward. Staying for dinner had kind of been expected.

"I got a call from Osborne," she announced, naming an elementary school on the outskirts of town as she helped set the table. Tanner was getting drinks. Tatum was helping Sedona in the attached kitchen. "Some stuff I wrote in my report triggered a meeting with a girl's mother and the school counselor. Turns out the girl was being sexually harassed by her stepfather. The mother filed for divorce and thankfully things were caught before he actually touched her. I guess they'd been having problems, but the mother hadn't known just how much of a creep the guy was."

"Wow!" Tatum brought a basket of hot rolls to the table. "That's one lucky girl."

Talia agreed.

"Thanks to you," Tatum added. And Talia wanted to believe her.

It wasn't until they'd finished eating that she told them that she'd told Sherman about her former career. And that she didn't think she'd be seeing either of the Paulson boys again after Kent completed his program at the Stand. Maybe even before then.

"But you're going to continue seeing both of them in the meantime?" Tanner asked.

She couldn't lie to him. But she couldn't look at him when she told him she was.

"I'm worried about you." They were still at the dinner table. They'd baked chicken enchiladas, Sedona's mother's recipe, and the only thing left were some chips and salsa in the middle of the table.

"I can't not see my son every chance I get while I've got the chance."

"The more you see him, the harder it's going to be to say goodbye." Sedona's warm gaze showed concern.

"It's going to hurt like hell no matter when it happens." The truth was right there in front of them. Had been all along. "I don't regret the choice to help him," she added, maybe a tad defensively.

They could judge her if they wanted to, but she knew she'd done the right thing for Kent. In the end, that was all that mattered.

"Have you thought about the fact that he might have a hard time letting *you* go?"

"I'm just another adult in his life," she said. "I've been very careful to be supportive without getting too close. He's far more interested in his new friend Jason than he is in me."

Which was as it should be. A memory came to her as she thought about those words. A movie that she and Tanner and Thomas had watched together once.

"Do you remember *Mary Poppins*?" she asked her brother.

His grin told her he did. "You tried for weeks after that to get liftoff with an umbrella."

She remembered that. "She loved those children, and they loved her, too, but when it was time for her to go, the kids turned to their parents."

Mary Poppins had said that was how it should be.

And little Talia had wondered about that for a very long time.

Kent was fond of her. Like he'd be fond of a teacher. And when their time together was done, he'd move on. Hopefully remembering her now and then with a smile.

Tatum offered to spend the night with her. It wasn't a school night, she reminded Talia. The teenager was supposed to be going to the movies with Jimmy and another couple that evening. While Talia would have loved her sister's company, she didn't want to be an excuse for Tatum to give in to her fear of leaving the safety of her family and having a social life. Assuring Tatum that she really wanted to be alone, that she needed to do homework, Talia helped her little sister pick out an outfit for her date and then left for home.

Where she sat at her table, as she had each night for a week, and wondered if she'd have a visitor.

She was alone. Lonely as anything. But she still had her family. She'd helped her son. And another little girl.

Her life was on course.

SHERMAN WAITED UNTIL Kent was in bed Friday night before calling Ben over. Sandy was working and the older man was just as happy to fall asleep in front of the television at Sherman's house as he was at his own.

Changing from his work clothes into jeans and a black, long-sleeved pullover, he slipped on his sandals and left in a hurry.

He hadn't planned on going. Knew he shouldn't go. But once his mind was made up, he couldn't get to the ocean fast enough.

Her light was on. He'd known she'd be home. Talia Malone was always home. Unless she was working or in class. He'd never met a more responsible woman.

Or a more beautiful one.

Just as she had the previous week, she had the door open for him by the time he got out of his car.

And, as before, she wasn't standing there to greet him. Books, papers and her laptop were spread out on her worktable. From the almost-full glass of iced tea on the table he figured she'd been there working, but as he closed the door behind him, he still couldn't see any sign of her.

No sign of life in the darkened living room, either. Or in the dimly lit attached kitchen. No Talia in there getting him a glass of wine.

Not that he'd expected her to be.

Knowing he should leave, Sherman moved quietly through the house, leaving the master bedroom for last. He told himself that he had to make sure she was safe. Out there alone, with no close neighbors and her back door unlocked, she could have come to harm. And might need his help.

More likely, he was the threat.

When he reached the bedroom and saw her there, on her bed, in a scrap of black silk and lace, he went hard instantly. He had his shirt off before he was all the way through the door and his pants weren't far behind.

Her opened arms welcomed him. Her lips as hungry as his as they satisfied a thirst that had been building all week.

Or maybe a lifetime. He just didn't know anymore.

All he knew was that this woman owned him.

He was her slave. She called to him even when he stayed completely away.

Leaving her lace lingerie on, he accessed her breasts. Her nipples. Not as gently as he had the previous week. Egged on by her urgency, he spent the next hour doing things to her body that he'd never have imagined he'd be doing. She cried out in pleasure more times than he could count. And she brought sounds he didn't recognize to his lips. And then swallowed them up. Once wasn't enough. He made love to her a second time. And then a third. And when it was over, he lay there, staring at her ceiling, wondering what in the hell he'd done.

CHAPTER TWENTY-FIVE

TALIA COULDN'T LIE with him. Having never spent the night in a man's arms, she knew that she couldn't afford to allow herself the luxury with Sherman. She was already in way too deep.

If she spent the night with him, letting him go might just break her.

Sliding off the far side of the bed, she adjusted her lingerie—an expensive piece purchased for her by a girlfriend in Vegas—and headed for the bathroom.

When she came out, Sherman was dressed, leaning a shoulder against the wall as he peered out the window into the darkness that hid the beach and ocean beyond.

He turned. "I'm s—"

"No," Talia interrupted. "Do not apologize to me." Why the idea that he would made her so angry, she didn't know, but it did. Anger was better than hurt. Easier. She clung to it.

"Brooke committed suicide."

Whatever she'd been expecting, that was not it. Meeting his gaze, she saw the shadows in the depths of his eyes.

"How do you know?"

He told her about the phone call from the detective. Followed by a second conversation with the detective who'd been on Brooke's case from the beginning. It would be a while before all of the tests came back, but the results were pretty clear even without the science necessary to confirm them.

"Why?"

Feeling cold in her negligee, Talia wrapped her arms around herself. Sherman grabbed the robe she'd left lying on the chair by the window and brought it to her, but didn't help her into it.

"I don't know," he said, stepping away from her. "Truthfully, I have no idea. Things weren't great between us. We weren't gloriously happy. But we weren't miserable, either." He threw out a hand and let it drop again. "We had good careers that we both enjoyed. And the rest of our lives revolved around Kent, whom we both adored. And Brooke and I... if nothing else, we remained good friends."

"Had she been seeing a therapist or anything?"

"No. She'd never had problems with depression or chemical dependence. She wasn't on any medications..."

He sounded as though he'd already been asked those questions. And probably had been. For the police report.

She'd promised herself to keep her time with

Sherman what it was—a sexual release for both of them.

After the last time he'd been there, when she'd had the idea that she loved him, she'd promised herself that her heart would not be left open to him again.

If he visited, they'd have sex, and then part ways with kindness. Period.

For a critical second she forgot that. And found herself in the kitchen, pouring him a glass of wine. And one for her, too.

Taking his hand, she led him into the living room, sitting with him on the couch. "Have you talked to anyone?" she asked.

She was no psychologist. Her classes weren't doctorate level. But she knew enough to know that the unanswered questions created by suicide were hell on those left behind.

"No," he said. "You're the first person I've told. I have no idea what to say to Kent, but I'm fairly certain that telling him his mother chose to die isn't a good idea right now."

"Talk to Sara, she'll be able to help you. And Dr. Jordon, too, because he knows Kent's history."

He nodded. And in that moment it wasn't Kent she was worried about.

"You blame yourself?"

Staring out into the living room, Sherman sipped his wine.

"I think suicide is a personal choice," he said finally. "No one can make you do it. It's your reaction to dealing with life's challenges."

A generic response if she ever heard one.

"They say people commit suicide when life's pain is greater than their ability to cope with it."

"I was reading this afternoon..." He paused again. Took another sip of wine. "I should have been working. We're having a seafood fund-raiser tomorrow afternoon down at the pier, but...it said that suicide is the direct result of an overwhelming sense of hopelessness."

She couldn't imagine the horribleness he had to be going through. And couldn't help her heart from hurting for him, either.

"I have no idea why she'd have felt so hopeless," he added.

"Obviously she didn't want you to know. She did a great job of hiding whatever was going on with her."

She wasn't a therapist. Had no business passing judgment or theory on this matter. No, she was just a woman whose heart was driving her to help this man feel better.

"I feel responsible..." He broke off. Shook his head. And stood.

Talia followed him out to the kitchen where he set his half-empty wineglass on the counter.

His gaze met hers. Held it. For too long. Talia

needed to fold him into her arms, lay his head on her breast and let him stay there until morning. She needed to chase his demons away.

"Thank you." He touched her face with his thumb.

And was gone.

TALIA CALLED HIM the next day while he was at the fund-raiser on the pier. Sherman had just left Kent at a table with Cole Vanderpohl and the teenage daughter of Sadie Bishop, their country auditor. He was on his way to give last-minute speech suggestions to his brand-new senate candidate when his belt started to vibrate, signaling an incoming call.

He recognized her number immediately and, keeping Kent in sight, stepped far enough away from the private party to snag some privacy.

"I've been thinking about you."

His dick rose up to say hello.

About to tell her that now wasn't a good time, but struggling to find the words, he forced his mind to think thoughts that left his body unengaged.

"I'm on lunch break and just wanted to make sure you're okay."

She was still the only who knew about Brooke.

And Sherman was ashamed for his immediate assumption that her call had been of a sexual nature.

The assumption had come from his constant hunger for her.

"I'm fine," he told her when what he'd wanted

was to use the sounding board she offered. He'd
been up most of the night reliving more than a decade of memories of his life with Brooke and needed
a female perspective.

From a female he trusted.

From Talia.

"If you need to talk…"

It was as though she was reading his mind. And
that didn't surprise him.

"Can I call you later?"

"Yes. I'm off at six."

The long night he'd just spent faded a bit farther
into the distance.

A COUPLE OF single women Talia worked with,
Kelsey Banes and Wendy Marshall, asked her to
go out for dinner and to a club with them Saturday
after work.

She'd had lunch with them a time or two. Found
things in common with both of them. Missing the
camaraderie of feminine companionship—one thing
she'd had a lot of backstage in Vegas—she hesitated
before declining the invitation. She could always
have written her collage reports later.

Studied in the middle of the night.

But her pretty, peaceful cottage on the beach
called to her. It was all she'd ever wanted—a safe
place that felt like home. Still, their invitation gave
her another idea. She told them she couldn't do

dinner, but invited them to come out to the ocean the following Saturday. They could ride home with her, spend the night and they could all return to Beverly Hills together in time for work on Sunday. They could have a little fire on the beach. Make salad. And enjoy a bottle of her brother's wine.

They accepted, and she was glad. She was building a life, one step at a time.

And now she had one night filled so she wouldn't be available to Sherman. Should he happen to stop by. Maybe, as time passed, she'd find more and more ways to fill her nights.

She was out on the beach when he called. He'd waited until Kent was in bed, which didn't surprise her. The fact that he'd stayed home didn't, either. He'd called a sitter the night before.

She'd built herself a fire that night—not far from her back deck. Sitting out there in cotton pants and a hoodie, she was content.

He told her he was in his room, sitting up in bed in the dark. Exhaustion from a lack of sleep the night before had led him there. And then he couldn't sleep.

"What did you and Kent have for dinner?" she asked, even now interested in every single thing her son did. Every breath he took.

Interested in keeping his father on the line, as well.

She was storing memories of the Paulson duo

for the years when she would no longer be privy to them.

"Hot dogs with chili."

"At home or out?"

"On the way home." He told her about the afternoon function—the seafood samplers they'd munched on, the game of beach volleyball Kent had played with some other kids. "He was the smallest guy out there, but he made a couple of good plays," he said.

She wasn't surprised. Sports were huge in the Paulson household. Before she'd met Kent and Sherman, Talia hadn't even known if the Lakers were basketball or football. And to her, every golf club looked exactly alike. She'd never been fishing. Or picked up a tennis racket. And didn't feel particularly deprived.

But for Kent, she'd spent some time educating herself.

Sherman talked about the people who'd attended, the pledges they'd received. He talked about speeches and dignitaries and probable vote counts. He talked about a couple of the wives who were assets to their husbands' political aspirations. And about the kids Kent had hung out with.

"So it was a family affair," she summed up, trying to picture the afternoon from a ten-year-old's perspective.

Sherman's response was too long coming. "Yeah."

In other words, it was the type of gathering she would not be welcome to attend with him. Her past was not impeccable enough.

And she'd bet that most of the others weren't saints, either. It was just a matter of whose sins came to light.

Even if Sherman had been willing to take a chance with her, even if she'd been crazy enough to agree to a relationship with him with the secret of his son's birth forever hidden between them, she wouldn't be willing to risk his career should her past somehow become disclosed.

"It's going to come out," he said softly.

"Not if we quit seeing each other." So they'd had sex a couple of times. In today's world that wasn't such a big deal. Even in some of the more conservative societies.

His pause was overly long again.

"I was talking about Brooke's suicide. She was fairly well-known, or at least associated with some well-known names locally. I don't think I'm going to be able to keep this out of the paper."

"How long before the ruling is official?"

"I don't know. Could be months."

"The accident was two years ago—you really think it will still be news?"

"Maybe, maybe not. My mind just keeps jumping to different aspects of this thing, you know?"

"You'll need to let Kent know before anything comes out."

"I've got an appointment with Dr. Jordon on Monday. And plan to talk to Sara Monday night."

Of course he did. Because he really was a great dad.

"I just feel so responsible," he said. "Not like I'm to blame, but like I should have known she was that unhappy. She was my wife and I had no idea…"

"It's possible that the fact that you didn't know was deliberate on her part."

"That doesn't sound like her. Brooke didn't like to hide things, or allow them to remain hidden. Because secrets prevented resolution."

"Maybe she was sick, you know, terminally. Maybe she was trying to spare you and Kent the pain of watching her die slowly."

Flames jumped into the night, and Talia watched them, wondering what it would be like to be inside the fire for once. It felt as if her whole life had been lived on the outside looking in.

"Maybe. But the coroner's report should have shown that."

"Unless he was just determining cause of death and collecting evidence for the accident report."

"So what you're saying is we may never know these answers."

Was she? She'd just been talking. Because he'd needed someone to talk to.

Sherman said he wondered if Brooke had grown tired of being a mother. If she'd felt so trapped by their marriage that she'd no longer wanted to live. And suggested the possibility that the accident had been premeditated by his wife. That she'd made up her mind and had just been waiting for an opportunity to present itself.

He was all over the board. Spewing thoughts so fast she figured he couldn't possibly be using his usual filters. He contradicted himself. He said things that didn't make sense.

Her flames died down. She stirred them. And if she hadn't already been in love with Sherman Paulson, she'd have fallen in love with him as she sat there accepting the gift of friendship he was offering her. The gift of trust he'd bestowed upon her that night.

CHAPTER TWENTY-SIX

BOTH SARA AND Dr. Jordon suggested to Sherman that he wait until there was an official ruling before telling Kent about the possibility that his mother had committed suicide. The boy was showing progress, but wasn't far enough out of the woods that anyone wanted to impede his progress if it wasn't necessary.

Sherman was relieved.

And on Monday night he went home and had a brief conversation with his neighbor. Two minutes later he was whistling as he came back into the house to supervise as his son fixed dinner. Ben was more than happy to watch Kent again the coming weekend—though it would have to be Saturday, not Friday, as he and Sandy had a dinner engagement with one of Ben's clients. His neighbors made it clear to him that they thought it was about time Sherman started dating.

No matter how many times he explained that he wasn't seeing someone, that he didn't have a girlfriend, they just smiled and looked at each other.

A little on edge about that, he decided he'd worried enough for a few days, decided not to borrow trouble and whistled all the way through sorting laundry while Kent grilled some cheese sandwiches.

As soon as Kent was out for the night he climbed into bed and called Talia. He told her about the advice he'd received from Dr. Jordon and Sara first.

"What if it does hit the news as soon as a ruling is made?" she asked. She'd told him she was sitting at the kitchen table, doing an online assignment for an effective-thinking psychology class, and he pictured her there, braless, in her sleep pants and gray cotton T-shirt.

"I'll get at least a few hours' notice," he told her, after explaining that he'd already called the detectives to ask. He answered the rest of her questions, and realized just how much he'd missed having someone to share the burden of decision making for the precocious ten-year-old he loved more than life.

When he knew that he'd kept her from her work long enough, knew she had a full week ahead with very little time to make up slack, he mentioned the weekend ahead. He wanted their time together locked in. Solid. For her as much as for himself.

"I'm sorry, Sherman, I can't," she said, shocking the hell out of him. What did she mean she couldn't? She worked and she came home. That was her weekend.

As he sat there, considering his response, he realized something else. He wasn't just shocked. He was panicked.

She was calling it quits on him. His response wasn't negotiable.

"If you've had enough, you need only to say so." It wasn't as if there was any permanence to their relationship. Implied or otherwise. He'd still hear about her through Kent.

Until the summer. Or Kent no longer needed to go. Or she no longer had time to take him.

"I know that."

Of course she did. The woman had him going all directions of crazy. Not anything he'd have believed possible for a thirty-eight-year-old guy with his head firmly on. A guy whose life was dedicated to thinking before he acted.

"I can't do Friday," he told her, so she'd understand the dire straits they were up against. "Ben and Sandy have a business engagement."

"I understand."

No, she didn't. Because if she did, right now she'd be telling him that she could get out of whatever she had planned for the next weekend. Unless…

He relaxed against the pillow. "So, next Saturday, you've got something with your family…"

That family of hers seemed to be the only thing besides work and study that mattered to her. And he'd lost his right to meet them when he'd had sex with her without any intention of dating her.

"No. I'm…entertaining."

If she'd meant to send him skyrocketing without

a ship, she'd succeeded. And he had a pretty good idea that was exactly what she'd meant to do. Even if she was having Tatum spend the night, she'd presented it in a way that put him in his place. Because he deserved it.

And why shouldn't she entertain? She was staying out there in that seductive little cottage all alone. She'd accepted him and his son into her life while he was refusing to acknowledge her in his own. She'd never be the woman on his arm at a political function.

Which meant to him that there'd never be a woman there again.

Who? The question pounded against his brain. Who was she entertaining?

He had no right to ask.

Sherman forced himself not to think about the next weekend. He asked about her collage workshops. And heard that she'd helped save a girl from possible future sexual abuse by her stepfather.

Something he should have already known—if they were as close as he felt they were. He should have been on her speed dial for that one.

With an aching head, a tired body and an exhausted heart, he knew he was going to have to tell her goodbye. She had homework. He needed to get some rest. He had a busy day ahead and a son to keep ahead of.

He couldn't do it. Couldn't just let the next weekend drop.

"We need to talk about something," he said, and then wished he could rephrase his statement. The old "we have to talk" line usually meant "I want to break up."

But they weren't even a couple.

Talia's silence wasn't as demeaning as it might have been considering her usual reticence.

"I need something." That was better. He thought.

"What?"

"Monogamy."

"What are you saying? That our…interlude…is over? You've found someone you can both date and have sex with?"

He cringed. Rubbed his hand over his eyes. He'd deserved that.

"No," he told her softly, closer to breaking than he could ever remember being. "I need to know that you aren't sleeping with anyone else."

"Is that what you think of me? That I'd be with you like…well, you know…and then take someone else into my bed?"

"No." He'd known this was not the right way to go about this. "I'm scared to death that I'm going to lose you." The embarrassing childish words poured out of him. "Because I can't give you as much of me as you deserve to have in your man."

Her pause was painful at best.

"So you're telling me you want us to be mutually monogamous," she said. The soft husky note in her voice raised a completely different but equally powerful emotion in him.

"Kind of like we're a couple without the dating," she added.

It sounded horrible. And glorious.

"Yes."

"Good. Because if I ever find out you so much as kissed another woman you aren't getting near me again. Ever."

That was his Talia. Up-front and out with it when it really mattered.

It was on the tip of his tongue to tell her he loved her.

He said good-night instead.

TALIA DIDN'T WANT to take the sales promotion. She hadn't told anyone about it. The question was, why? Because she really didn't want to travel? Or because she was afraid she wouldn't be good enough at it?

One thing she'd never lacked before was confidence. She'd always known she could be successful in the sex industry. Even just the edges of it that she'd inhabited.

She'd had offers of more. Plenty of them. They were quite lucrative and a lot of her friends made a good living that way.

Talia had chosen to go to school instead.

And she'd never posed for a camera. There were just some things that were wrong for her.

So why the hesitation now that she had a dream offer on her plate? In her chosen field of study?

She could visit all of the best and most famous fashion design houses on someone else's dime and gain entrance into the most elite circles. Which would put her one step closer to her original dream of being a designer. She'd wanted to create and sell her own designs. Beautiful, tasteful clothes that would accentuate a woman's beauty without laying it bare. And then she'd started working with the women at the Lemonade Stand—hoping to help them find their inner beauty through art. To encourage them to make choices based on what they wanted, not what anyone else told them they should do.

It was Sara who had convinced her to take her program to the school board. It was still hard for her to believe the success she'd had with it. It didn't pay. Might not pay for some time to come. But if she accepted the promotion Mirabelle was offering she'd have to give up on the collage program altogether.

The dilemma of what to do with her future plagued her as she waited for Kent after school on Thursday. It had been a few days since she'd seen or spoken with his father. But seeing her little boy kept the smile on her face.

Except that on Thursday, as he came out of school, he wasn't smiling.

"What's wrong?"

He settled his little preppy self with a sigh, fastened his seat belt and crossed his arms over his chest.

"What happened?" she asked, her stomach in knots.

"Nothing."

She was a driver. Not a mother. She didn't start the car.

"You've never lied to me before."

Those gray-blue eyes, so like Tatum's, looked her way. "I got in a fight," he said.

She'd watched him walk toward the car. And did a once-over now. He didn't have so much as a smudge on his knee.

"With who?"

"A girl."

This was bad. Visions of big teary eyes and bruises struck fear in her heart.

"Tell me what happened."

"She said that boys don't have best friends like girls do. Because boys do sports and fight."

She wasn't going to touch a gender stereotype. Not at the moment, anyway. Not without Sherman's input.

"Why did she say that?"

"Because the teacher asked why I didn't have my

math done and I told her because I'd just found out last night that my best friend was going away and I wouldn't be seeing him anymore and didn't feel like doing homework."

Oh, no. "Jason's leaving?" she guessed. It was a given, at some point. On average, residents only stayed at the Stand for three months.

"Yes." The word was a short hiss.

"Just because he won't be at the Stand doesn't mean he's moving away. Maybe he'll be even closer. And if not, you can still spend the night at each other's houses. It would be pretty cool to see Jason at his house, wouldn't it? And play with his things?"

His big eyes had tears in them now.

"He has to go to San Francisco to live with his grandparents because his dad won't let his mom have their house and it's going to be a long time for the divorce to get done so he can come home."

"So he's just going away temporarily." She drew out the only positive she could find.

"Till the end of the school year, which is just about forever."

She could remember when three months had seemed like forever.

"Maybe you and your father can go see him. Or maybe he can come stay with you during spring break or something." As soon as the words were out of her mouth, she regretted them. She had no business putting false hopes in a little boy's head. No business at all.

And she most certainly couldn't offer to drive or facilitate the meeting, though she'd have lots of free time over spring break since she'd have no sixth-grade art classes to work with.

"Yeah," Kent said, sitting up straighter. "Maybe. I'll ask Dad."

They still had an issue at hand. The fight with a girl. It obviously couldn't have been as bad as she'd envisioned, considering the fact that he hadn't been expelled.

"So what about this fight? What did you say to the girl?"

"I told her to go to hell."

Okay. Not good. Must be when the fight started.

"Then what happened?"

"I walked away."

"That was it?" That was the fight?

"No, she told on me and I'm in trouble for saying 'hell.'"

Talia knew the situation was serious. That Kent would need to be disciplined. But she held back a smile, too.

All in all, he was a good boy.

CHAPTER TWENTY-SEVEN

SHERMAN WAS ASLEEP when his phone rang. Flying upright, he had his phone to his ear and was saying hello before he was fully awake.

Before he'd realized where he was and that Kent was in bed asleep. Safe and sound.

"Did I wake you?" The voice brought him to a consciousness that was buffered by the residual of dreams.

"Yeah."

"I'm sorry, I—"

"I'm not," he interrupted. "Talking to the real thing is much better than dreaming about her and waking up alone."

"Oh."

"What's up?"

"I guess I didn't realize it was so late. I'm used to…"

Late hours. Because she'd worked a night job. Once again he was face-to-face with their differences. They were elemental. And huge. He'd been to a strip club once. She'd practically lived in one.

He was eleven years her senior and felt like a boy to her woman.

"I debated with myself all night about calling."

"Don't do that."

"Do what?"

"Debate with yourself. If you need or want to talk, just call. I'll answer."

Silence met his statement. At the moment he didn't care. He was lying in the dark, his head on his pillow, talking to the only woman he ever wanted to have head-on-pillow conversations with.

"I said something to Kent today and I had no right, and I want to apologize."

"I can't imagine what it might have been. He was in a great mood when I picked him up from the Stand. Didn't even seem to care that he was losing his internet and TV privileges for the night because of his language in school. He told me he told you about the incident in school. He has to learn to differentiate between what he hears and what is appropriate for him to repeat."

"It's a tough world in which to be raising a kid."

"Yeah." He supposed. He couldn't imagine a world without Kent. Not anymore. His son gave life meaning.

"So what caused the great mood?"

"I'm not sure. He said he had this idea that maybe he and Jason could get together over spring break."

"Oh. What did you tell him?"

"That I'd talk to Jason's mom. I'll have to take some vacation days, though, and unfortunately, with the new campaign, time off is going to be hard to get. If Jason's mom will let him come here, I'll work something out." There was a pause.

"I'm going to be off that week—no school, you know. I could watch the boys for you."

"That would be great." He didn't even hesitate. "If you wouldn't mind…"

Because the idea of Talia in his home with his son seemed right. And then he woke up.

"But…that's not really fair to you," he said. "I'll let you watch my kid, but I won't take you to dinner." Not anymore. Not since he knew that her past posed a potential risk to his future.

"I know the score, Sherm." *Sherm.* Only one other person in his life had ever called him that. Brooke.

"You're not angry?"

"What would be the point? I made my choices. I'll pay for them. I'm okay with that."

She shouldn't have to be okay. Shouldn't have to pay. Her choices had been born from a life that no little girl should have had to live. Her impressions about who she was had been formed by that life. Still, he should let her go. There were men, good men, who could love her, whose careers wouldn't be affected by the fact that she'd been a stripper for eight years.

"Are you at the table?"

"No. I'm outside. On the deck."

"Are there boats on the ocean?"

"I see a bobbing light."

"Tell me about your first time."

"My first time what?"

"Having sex." She'd had such an unhealthy up-bringing. And then…Vegas. He knew about her husband. Knew she hadn't whored herself out, but…

"Why?"

"Because I want to know you that well."

"When was your first time?"

"I was seventeen. A junior in high school. It was after the prom. I came as soon as I was inside. And we broke up the next week."

"She didn't love you or she would have understood."

"We were kids. And I wanted to break up as badly as she did."

He pictured her on the deck, sitting in her chair with her feet up on the seat, staring out at the darkness. And wished she was inside with the doors locked.

"I was sixteen," she said when he'd convinced himself not to ask a second time. "I thought he was in love with me. I thought we were going to get married as soon as I turned seventeen and could legally marry without parental consent. I thought I was finally going to have a real home…"

There was no call for sympathy in the telling—

just a relaying of a memory. One that obviously went bad.

She'd been a kid, like him. In high school. Experimenting...

"Was he in your class?"

Her chuckle was tinged with an uncharacteristic bitterness. "You could say that."

Sherman sat up. "Was he or wasn't he?"

"Depends on what you mean by *class*. If you're talking graduating class, then no. In my classroom, yes."

"He was a year or two ahead of you?" Couldn't be more than that. She'd been sixteen. So at least a sophomore.

"He was the teacher."

He almost lost his dinner. And was so angry he'd have hit the man if he were in the same room with him. Bashed his head against a wall until it was pulp.

"Your teacher took your virginity?" He had to be sure he was getting this right.

Because it was very, very wrong.

"Yeah."

"How old was he?"

"Twenty-seven."

Eleven years older than her, then. The same age she was now. Which would make the guy his age.

Shit.

He'd been married to Brooke eleven years ago.

About ready to give up on artificial insemination and accept that they'd never have a baby.

"What happened?" He had to know. And wished she was in bed with him so he could hold her. Just hold her.

"Tanner found out. Turned him in. He went to prison."

Something else she'd told him clicked. "And you ran away."

"The first time I ran away to be with him. The second time I left was the night of my high-school graduation."

"Was this guy in love with you?" He couldn't have been. He'd have waited to have sex with her if he'd been in love with her. Because she'd deserved that from him.

"I thought so. For years. Later I found out what Tanner knew."

"You weren't the only student he'd…" *Screwed* was the word on the tip of his tongue.

He couldn't use it with her.

"Nope. I wasn't. I wasn't even the youngest."

"Is he still in prison?"

"I don't know. But if he's out, he's registered as a sex offender. It was part of his sentence. He can't ever work around kids again."

He supposed, as long as the guy left her alone, it didn't matter. But he had another question.

"So when was your second time?"

"When was yours?"

"Brooke."

"Mine was the jerk I married."

The older guy who'd offered a business proposition with separate bedrooms. And then forced her to entertain his friends. Red-hot rage burst inside him. It burned. And left him hurting and helpless to do a damned thing. For her. For any of them.

She was one of the most decent women he'd ever known.

"I...I'll be home Sunday night."

His reaction was instantaneous. And physical. The switch in gears so swift he had no hope of containing it.

"I'll talk to Ben." He couldn't leave until after Kent went to bed. Sunday nights were family time.

He'd have liked to invite her for dinner. But as things were now, he couldn't afford to give his son any false hopes. As far as Kent knew, Sherman and Talia hadn't seen each other in weeks. She was an art teacher. Period.

As far as Kent knew...

"You're friends with my dad, aren't you?" Kent's question on the way to the Lemonade Stand on Friday afternoon was far more difficult than handling the fight discussion the day before.

What had happened to those ten-minute rambles about who farted in the lunch room?

"I know your dad—you know that," she said. Were she and Sherman friends? Lovers, for now, but she could hardly tell his son that.

"But you're not, like, seeing each other."

For better or worse. "No."

He looked at her, his expression so serious. "Can I tell you something?"

"Of course." She slowed her driving.

"I found something on the external hard drive my mom used."

Oh, boy. Foot to the gas, Talia sped up again. This was Sara territory. But Kent was only going to talk to who he chose to talk to. That had been the problem from the beginning—the boy not opening up.

He'd chosen her.

"When was this?" she asked when he didn't offer up more.

"I don't know. A long time ago. Last summer maybe."

Before all the trouble had started at school.

She had to push. In case this was the only shot they had. "What did you find?"

"Stuff. Like emails and things. She…" The fear in his eyes when he looked at her struck her cold.

"She what?"

"She… I think she had a boyfriend."

Talia's nerves went into a tailspin. She wasn't trained for this. "What makes you think that?"

"I read them."

"The emails?"

"Mmm-hmm." His precious face was so twisted with concern she wanted to hug him.

"And you think you're going to be in trouble for that." She made a stab in the dark.

"Yeah."

"I can't say for sure, but I don't think you will be."

He nodded. "I don't want my dad to know," he said, settling back into his seat. "It might, you know, hurt his feelings. But I think he might have had something to do with why she got killed."

"Your dad?"

"No." The disgust her question elicited was clearly obvious. *"Him."*

She turned into the Lemonade Stand. Parked. And sat for a second. "The boyfriend."

"Yeah." He was staring at her as if she was going to know what to do with this information.

"Did you tell Sara about this?"

"No."

Because Sara wasn't friends with his dad? He wanted Talia to do something about the situation without hurting his father?

"Do you know his name?"

"Alan Klasky."

"Isn't that the man your mom had a meeting with that night?"

"I don't know. She was working is all Dad said."

Was it possible Brooke had been having an affair with the shady reporter? It didn't fit anything Sherman had ever told her about the woman.

But what if he'd been blackmailing her?

Would she have taken her life to protect her integrity? Or her family?

Kent might be right. There might be some connection.

"Anyway, Dad came in on Jason and me on the computer when I was showing him the emails and I passed it off as just showing Jason pictures of Mom and all, and told him we were talking about her, so it wasn't really a lie, but now Jason's leaving and I don't know who else to tell about it…"

"Your dad has to know about this, Kent." It was the only way.

"Can you tell him?"

"Of course."

He opened his door. She got out, too. They walked, just as they always did, side by side across the complex. She'd deliver him to his room. And go on to hers. She had three fourteen- to sixteen-year-old girls waiting to find beauty in their worlds.

Opening the door to the main building, she stood back, waiting for Kent to enter before her. He did. But instead of continuing down the hall to see Jason, he stopped.

Without warning his little arms were stretched

around her middle, squeezing tight. "Thanks," he mumbled into her stomach.

And just as quickly he was gone.

CHAPTER TWENTY-EIGHT

SHERMAN GOT TALIA'S voice mail Friday evening on his way to pick up Kent from his session at the Stand. Jason and his mother and little sister were going to be leaving for San Francisco in the morning, and as much as Sherman needed to hear what Talia had to tell him—her voice had sounded pretty urgent, while assuring him that it wasn't an emergency—he wanted to be there to meet with Jason's mother, Belinda, after the session and firm up some arrangements for the boys to see each other over spring break.

He'd made a promise to Kent.

As it turned out, Jason's mother had arranged to have Kent spend the night with them there at the Stand, assuming Sherman gave his permission. They were having a movie night in the main building, and there was an extra twin bed in the little bungalow Jason and his mother and sister had called home for the past few months. And Kent had clearance to stay at the secure shelter.

Belinda's parents had purchased a used car for her, which she would be using to drive her small family to San Francisco. She offered to bring Kent home the following morning before they left. She wanted to see where her son would be staying for the week of spring break.

"Can I, Dad? Please?" Kent begged as they all stood in the hallway outside the room where Kent had his sessions. Sara was there, too, but remained silent in the background.

"Yeah, Mr. Malone, please?" Jason asked without a hint of the timidity the boy had shown around Sherman the entire time he'd spent the night at their house.

Seeing Sara nod in the background, Sherman agreed. On one condition. "You need to be home by nine in the morning," he said. "We're playing golf."

"Come on, let's go!" Kent said to Jason, and then turned back. "Thanks, Dad."

Sherman gave Belinda directions to his house, agreed to see her at eight o'clock the following day and thanked Sara, as he did every single night when he collected his son from the Stand.

He walked out, infused with his son's enthusiasm. At least he told himself it was Kent's excitement he was feeling as he turned the BMW in the direction of the beach...

SHE'D TAKEN A long walk on the beach before settling in for the night. Sherman would call after Kent was in bed, and she'd needed to clear her mind.

She couldn't keep doing this—living on the fringes of a life she couldn't have. The point was to build a new life. To leave her past behind, not live a slave to it.

And that was what she was becoming with Sherman—and Kent, too.

She'd never turn her back on her son. As long as she could find a way to be at least a little part of his life, she would be.

But she could no longer be…whatever she was… with his father. It was time to be completely honest with herself. She was in love with the man. Being his clandestine sex partner wasn't enough. It was like saying to herself that she wasn't good enough to have it all.

So, it didn't work with Sherman. There'd be another man out there for her. One who could handle her past.

Because it wasn't just Sherman's career keeping them apart. He might believe it was. He might just want her to believe it. But the truth was, if he loved her, really loved her, he'd find a way to make things work for them.

She had no idea what that way would be. But she knew, as her hair blew around her face in the early-evening breeze, as she listened to a little boy calling out to his father on the beach, that the way would exist for her.

Someday. With someone.

She'd left the past behind. She'd come home. And found herself again.

In one small hug from her ten-year-old biological son.

SHE SAW HIS car in her driveway before she noticed him, standing on the beach up by her deck, watching her. With her sandals in her hand and her white eyelet ankle-length skirt billowing in the breeze, Talia felt…healthy…as she walked toward the man who'd given her back her sexuality. She would always be thankful to him for that.

He was walking out to meet her before she realized that he shouldn't be there. Not yet. His step was easy. Not filled with alarm.

"Where's Kent?" she asked as soon as he was within hearing distance.

"Spending Jason's last night at the Stand with him. They're having movie night."

His smile was filled with promise. Sexy promise. The second his responsibilities were met, he came running to her.

Would always come running to her.

Because she meant something to him. A lot. Just not enough.

She wanted more than moments. She wanted a lifetime.

"Your phone call sounded serious." He'd reached her. He slipped an arm around her waist, and Talia leaned into him. Memorizing the feel of his warmth supporting her.

"Kent told me something today," she said, focusing on the moment instead of the lifetime. Because she'd promised Kent she'd talk to his dad before she'd promised herself that she wouldn't settle for less.

"He asked me to talk to you about it."

"Okay." His leather loafers remained steady on the sand.

"He…found some emails. On an external hard drive. He's afraid he's going to be in trouble for reading them."

"He might be. What emails?"

"They were his mother's. Between her and Alan Klasky. He thinks, from reading them, that Alan was her boyfriend."

Talia watched him while she spoke, memorizing everything. The hair that was long enough to fall naturally across his forehead. The strength in his jaw. Lips that were masculine and generous, too.

"Alan was the man she was meeting that last night, wasn't he? That reporter who goes for sensationalism rather than truth."

"Yeah." His frown didn't detract from his good looks at all. It added to them. Hinted at the well of emotion buried inside him. "I can't imagine why Brooke would have been emailing with him. As far as I knew, that night was the first time she'd actually met with him. Believe me, Alan Klasky was a guy we made a point to steer clear of."

"I wondered if maybe he was blackmailing her. Kent seemed to think this guy had something to do with her accident."

Because Kent hadn't been told they'd found the driver. He didn't know his mother had committed suicide. Not until an official ruling had been made.

"I need to see those emails."

Wrapping her hands around her arms, she said, "He said they're on his mom's external hard drive."

"I had no idea he knew how to access that."

"He said he found it last summer. Did you have someone staying with him at the house while you were at work?"

He nodded, his look intense. "The daughter of a guy I work with," he said. "She was home from college."

"And didn't you say his problems really escalated at the beginning of this school year?"

He nodded. Watching her. She could almost see the facts adding up in his mind.

"Come with me."

"What?"

"He's gone for the night. Come with me to my house. Help me find the emails." He held out his hand.

The emails and whatever was in them. She loved him. She couldn't send him off to face that alone.

After running inside to grab her purse and lock up, Talia placed her hand in his and allowed him to lead her away.

THE FIRST EMAIL WAS dated almost a year before Brooke's death.

Brooke, so unexpected, meeting you. Thank you.

More followed. Just one-liners of two people keeping in touch. No hint of something more.

Sitting at his desk with his wife's external hard drive plugged into his computer, Sherman read the emails as though reading a newspaper. They were interesting. Things he should know.

But they didn't contain anything personal.

Until he came to the one dated six months before his wife's death. Talia, who'd pulled up Brooke's chair, was reading right beside him.

I'm going to be at the governor's fund-raiser this weekend. Sherman will be home with Kent.

And the reply.

I have a room. Can you stay all night?

He felt her hand on his arm. Talia's hand. A gentle touch. Keeping him in the chair. Reading.

More of the same followed. Clandestine meetings.

A sentence or two along the way expressing their surprise, their disbelief, in the connection they'd found together.

He and Brooke hadn't been meant to be married. After meeting Talia he'd understood that. Apparently Brooke had figured it out much sooner than he had. They'd thought being so alike would keep them together. Instead, they'd each been attracted to someone more their opposite…

So what had kept her there? Kent?

There were more emails. He had to get through them. Had to know everything Kent knew. To know what his son had read. He had to know what had happened the night that his wife had apparently chosen to die. His hand fell off the mouse he'd been using to scroll.

"I thought…that whole last year…we didn't have sex. At all. I thought it was me."

Talia didn't say anything. She didn't need to. Just having her there helped.

He scrolled. Opened another email. And then another.

While nothing was overt, Brooke had clearly been having sex with Alan. In her own office. While Sherman had been right down the hall in his.

I'm sorry for pushing you out so quickly this morning. You know I have my lunch meeting with Sherman every day.

How could she have done this? What if Klasky had been seen coming from her office?

Maybe he had. Growing warm, then cold, Sherman considered the possibility that the entire firm had known about the affair.

But no, they wouldn't have stood for it. Personal integrity was the number one job qualification in that firm. Their goal was to get voters to trust them. To trust their choices and to believe what they had to say. To rely on them to steer them through all the political backstabbing to arrive at the truth...

Roland thinks I'm courting you to tell our side of the story from now on. That was a close one. Don't come to my office again.

All he had to do was keep reading. The answers were all there.

Talia glanced at him as he paused. Did he look as foolish, as pathetic, as he felt?

I need to end things.

The email was from Brooke to Klasky.

What? Fingers moving more quickly, Sherman read on.

I made a mistake. A big one. I love my family. My son. I almost screwed it all up. I want out.

Klasky's reply read, Meet me tonight. We'll talk. You're just getting cold feet. You're my sexy kitten. You don't think I can just sit back and know that you're going to be purring in his bed again, do you?

The threat was there. Veiled, but there.
Still it didn't make sense.
Until he read the next email.

I love you, Alan. You know that. But I made promises. I married a man. I have a life with him. Debts and savings and a home we own together. We adopted a child together. Our futures are planned. I won't be able to live with myself if I just walk away from those obligations. I also can't not see you one more time. I love you so much...

The email was sent fifteen minutes before Brooke had left their house for the last time.

"She went to meet him that night to break up with him." Sherman had offered to make dinner for Talia. He was scrambling eggs. She was making toast—finding her way around his kitchen and promising herself she'd forget the experience of being at home with him just as soon as it was over.

"And was so devastated that on the way home,

when she saw that car coming at her, she just let it…"

He was standing at the stove, but no longer stirring the eggs. They were starting to congeal in the pan.

Taking hold of his hand, she helped him stir. And then moved away to butter the toast. He got out plates. Silverware. She found jelly in the refrigerator. Together they moved to the table.

And she didn't know where to sit. Didn't know which chair was Kent's. Sherman's. Or Brooke's.

This wasn't her home. She would never be his wife.

Talia needed to be a wife.

And a mother.

CHAPTER TWENTY-NINE

"Brooke was exactly opposite of the way we lived."

They'd finished their light dinner. Sherman knew he had to get up, maybe do the dishes and then take Talia home. He couldn't hold her hostage there in his home.

But he didn't want her to leave.

He wanted to take her to his bed. To make wild and crazy love with her until he forgot any ugliness existed. And then to sleep beside her until morning.

Just one night. That was all he asked for.

"In what way?" she asked, seemingly in no hurry to go. He knew she had homework to do. Friday nights were reserved for homework.

"We chose to live deliberately." He tried to explain a way of life that had seemed like the surest bet to happiness. "We didn't let ourselves be swayed by the moment. We considered every response, no matter how big or small, weighing them against the big-picture goals that we'd laid out together."

He didn't get it.

"It sounds like you were trying to make yourselves live solely according to your heads." Talia's soft words fell like boulders. "Brooke found out that she couldn't shut out her heart, no matter how hard she tried."

And she had tried. The emails had made that clear.

"And she couldn't control it, either."

Right. But the human experience granted one the right to control his or her life. He'd made the choice to exercise that right. Every moment of every day.

Back in college, Brooke had made the same choice.

Thoughts pushed at the back of Sherman's mind. He shook his head. He had to stay the course. It was what he'd always done.

It was easy to slow down and consider one's choices when the choices were easy. The critical moments, the hard times, were when he most needed to think. Not just react. Years of practicing self-control held him in good stead.

Sherman cleared the table. Did the dishes. Talia helped. Then she picked up her purse, and he kissed her. Just leaned over in the middle of his kitchen with his hands still wet from the sink and kissed her. Long. Adding more pressure as he went along.

He needed her. In his bed. With shaking, damp hands he lifted the white shirt that had been teasing him all night, and kept lifting until it was over her head and gone from his sight. Her bra was next. He took it off quickly. Before he could think. Before she could.

"Are you going to stop me?" He needed to know.

"No."

"You need this, too?"

Her gaze wasn't clear. Or open. "Yeah." He took her at her word and left the rest.

TALIA WOKE AT three in the morning, naked, in Sherman Paulson's bed. In his arms. If her son had been down the hall, she might have thought she'd died and gone to heaven.

But if Kent were down the hall, she wouldn't be there.

She was Sherman's Alan Klasky. The person he had sex with in secret. Never to be acknowledged or legitimized.

Because he'd made promises. Adopted a child. Had obligations.

He'd said it himself. He and Brooke walked the same path. Except that Sherman had never even told her that Kent was adopted like Brooke had told Klasky. Proving…what?

But at least that answered one of her questions. Kent obviously knew.

So did her son ever wonder about her? Was he at all curious about the woman who'd given birth to him?

Sherman moved next to her.

"You awake?" she asked.

"Yes."

She wanted to make love with him one more time. For the last time. "Can you take me home, please?"

"Of course."

Without another word, he dressed, grabbed his keys and turned the BMW back toward the ocean.

When they arrived he walked her to her door, waited for her to be safely inside and then, hands in his pockets, he stared at her. She stared back. She loved him. But she couldn't be who he needed.

Seeming to get that, he nodded, turned and left.

Talia was pretty sure they'd just said goodbye forever.

SHERMAN DIDN'T GO back to bed. He walked over to the calendar on his refrigerator, saw the list of chores for Saturday and set to work.

Everything was going to be fine. Things always looked darkest before the dawn and all that.

He'd already known he'd lost Brooke. Even before the accident. Now he knew why.

The sun would shine Saturday. He and Kent would go golfing. He'd do some business. And after they left the course, he'd take his boy out to eat wherever he wanted to go. Maybe they'd head to the batting cages after that. Kent would be sad, knowing that Jason had left. Maybe they'd stop by the animal rescue and adopt a dog.

At some point he and Kent were going to have to talk about his mother. About what he knew.

And then it hit him. What Kent knew. Not just about the affair his mother had been having, which was what he'd mentioned to Talia. Brooke had written to Alan that they'd adopted a son. He couldn't believe he'd missed it. He'd been so busy dealing with the fact that his wife had been unfaithful to him. That she'd fallen in love with a man known for having questionable integrity. Hearing her mention Kent's adoption hadn't been unusual for him. They talked about it between the two of them. Hearing her mention it to her lover had hurt him—because it was more sign of her unfaithfulness to him, her sharing their secret.

But Kent had read those letters...

Sherman had been so poleaxed, and so tuned in to the woman at his side—who didn't know that Kent was adopted, and so didn't know that Kent didn't know he was adopted...

He'd known his son was as safe as he was probably ever going to be again, spending the night on the secure grounds of the Lemonade Stand. Truth was, he hadn't been thinking about Kent at all.

While looking for something to explain why Brooke would kill herself, he'd stumbled on the real explanation for Kent's sudden change in behavior the year before.

Oh, my God.

Kent knew he was adopted.

HE HAD TO get to Kent. Had to explain. To make sure that his son knew how very much he loved him. How much of a miracle he was to him. Then. Now. Always.

Grabbing his keys for the second time in the dark early-morning hours of that night, he made a rush for the door.

And stopped himself.

The more of a big deal he made of the circumstances behind's Kent birth, the bigger they'd be to him.

Now more than ever he had to stop. To think. The next few hours or days could affect the rest of his son's life, depending on how he handled them. He had the chance to make all the difference. To do this completely right.

Sherman dropped to the living-room couch, playing different scenarios in his mind. Rejecting one, then trying out another. Exhausting himself, but refusing to give up. He did this until he finally fell asleep.

And never knew that eight o'clock came and went.

TALIA WAS AT work on Saturday, in the middle of her largest sale of the month—a bridal trousseau—

when her phone buzzed with a call. As soon as the bride-to-be was back in the changing room, trying on yet another option for the suit she'd wear to walk from the hotel room to the limo on her way to the church the day of the wedding, she glanced at her missed call.

Tatum.

Motioning to Wendy, who'd just finished with a customer, she slipped outside to return her little sister's call. Tatum knew she was at work that morning. She wouldn't call unless it was important.

"Tal? Oh, my God. Did you get my message?"

"No," she said, her heart hammering. "I didn't waste time with voice mail. Tell me what's going on. Is it Tanner?" Their big brother nearly ran himself ragged tending to the vineyard that had been providing for their family for almost ten years.

"No! Listen, Tal, I wouldn't do this like this over the phone and all, but you're there and—"

"What's going on?" She tempered her response. Tatum had a tendency to be dramatic. Please, God, let that be all this was. A boyfriend crisis or some such thing...

"It's Kent, Talia! I wouldn't even have known, but I was at the center this morning talking to Sara because of my date last night and...oh, it doesn't matter. Kent and Jason ran away."

"What?" A couple walking into the mall stared at her. She turned her back to them and faced the brick wall that made up the exterior of the mall.

"On the way to Sherman's this morning. They told his mom that Jason felt like he was going to throw up and made her stop at a gas station. Then they went to the men's room. It had an outside entrance, and she waited outside with his little sister."

"Slow down," Talia said, already heading into the store for her purse. She'd lose a sale, maybe even her job. She didn't care. "How do they know they ran away and weren't taken?"

"That's the crazy part," Tatum said. "They were lurking around the back of the gas station, sneaking away, and some girl saw them. She asked them if everything was okay and they told her their mother was out front with a car problem and they were going to get help from someone they knew down the street. She thought it was kind of odd so she went out front and found Jason's mom, waiting for them. But by the time they went back to where the boys had been, they were nowhere to be found."

"But they've located them by now?" She had her purse and was heading out. If she saw someone on the way she'd tell them she was leaving. If not, they'd figure it out.

"No. They just vanished into thin air. Then a little bit later Jason texted his mom. He told her not to worry and they'd be back. They just had one thing to fix."

"One thing to fix? What does that mean?" She was in the employee section of the parking garage.

"I'm pretty sure it has something to do with Jason's dad. So that Jason doesn't have to move to San Francisco. But...anyway, Belinda, Jason's mom, came back here and they called Sherman and when the boys didn't show up there, he came here, too. The police have someone watching his house. But they can't do an Amber Alert because the boys ran away—they weren't snatched."

Two ten-year-olds on their own could be snatched...

But it wasn't likely. Not in Santa Raquel. Kids still played outside in their neighborhoods in the small coastal town. They played on the beach.

She was in her car, starting it.

"Did they check the beach?" she asked. "Kent loves the beach. You know how much he talks about it."

"I know. And they aren't there. I think I know what's going on, Talia."

"Then tell the police! Now!"

"No, I mean I think I know what they're doing." The girl was frantic. Talia could hear it in her voice.

"Tatum, if you know something you have to tell them!" They'd all paid enough for their family's penchant for keeping secrets.

"Listen to me!" Tatum snapped at her, getting her attention. "I'm trying to tell you something and I don't want anyone to hear me. I'm in the bathroom."

"I'm listening."

"Something is going on with the police is what I'm trying to tell you. Sherman wanted to go look for Kent and they wouldn't let him. But listen, I was talking to Jason, and he was telling me about his dad. You know, those of us who've lived there, we talk sometimes and try to help one another out, and…oh, that doesn't matter. Anyway, he was telling me how his dad used to hold them hostage." She'd yet to take a breath. "He told his mom that his dad would kill them before he'd let anyone take them away from him."

Talia was heading for the freeway and hitting every damned stoplight on streets packed with Saturday tourists who didn't know where they were going.

"Jason said there was this cellar beneath the shed, in case of a nuclear bomb or something. He said his dad had all kinds of stuff down there. Like a gun and everything. Now here's what I know. Everyone was frantically sending out search parties for them, afraid that they were going to do something crazy. They found out they took a bus to Jason's old neighborhood. Which is between here and LA." Tatum named the town.

Talia was trembling and sick and entering the freeway.

"I think they went to do something to Jason's dad, Talia! That class they're in, it's all about not having to feel out of control. About choosing how to handle things that make you mad and—"

"You think Jason's dad has them in that cellar?"

"Yes, I do," Tatum said. "Shoot. Someone's coming down the hall. I know the police are all there, and no one else is supposed to be in the area. But he's your son, Tal, and I knew you'd want to know... to do something if you could."

Her little sister gave her the address and though Tatum was filling her with teenage drama, Talia took the next exit off the freeway. She had no idea what she was going to do. Certainly nothing that would impede the work of the professionals.

But her son was in danger. She couldn't not be close to him.

She couldn't walk away.

Not this time.

SHERMAN HAD SEEN the teenager on the periphery of the room where people had gathered to wait for news about Jason. It was very clear that these people considered themselves his family. Certainly they were Jason's friends.

And now some of them were Kent's, too. He'd charmed the few people he'd met during the time he'd been attending his sessions there and claimed more admirers the night before at the movies and the ice cream social afterward.

Then there was that girl—she'd left and was back

again. He felt as though he'd met her before, but knew that he hadn't.

But what did he know, really? His son had been halfway to LA that morning while he'd been asleep, had been in the home of a man who'd sworn to kill before giving up his family, a man who'd followed threats with his fist—many times.

"I'm so sorry." Belinda came up beside him. She was dry-eyed at the moment. He admired her ability to carry on.

"It's not your fault." But he was blaming her. Because he wasn't himself. Because he was scared to death and couldn't get control of his world.

Not any part of it.

He needed Talia. But he wasn't calling her. There was nothing she could do. And…she'd said goodbye to him the night before. They both knew that. The fair and decent thing to do was let her go.

Kent was going to be fine. The police had assured him on that score. Jason's father had already sent Kent out and the boy would be on his way back to Santa Raquel just as soon as they'd gotten what information they could out of him regarding the situation in the house. Jason was still in there, being held hostage by his father.

No one knew yet just what the boys had hoped to accomplish by pulling this stunt, but Sherman knew one thing.

His boy was going to think long and hard before

trying anything like it again. Kent would be lucky if he wasn't cuffed to his father's wrist for the rest of his life.

Belinda was still standing there, and Sherman realized that she needed him. And that he was being a selfish prick.

"Kent's a smart boy," he told the woman. "He'll be able to tell the police whatever they need to know to get Jason out safely."

She nodded.

"And Jason knows better how to handle himself since his sessions here." He'd seen a change in the boy just in the couple of times he'd been around him.

"He thought his father was going to be gone," she said, her face pained as she spoke softly enough that only he could hear. "He used to work Saturday mornings. It was our safe time."

A family routine. He got that.

"He said in his text that he just wanted his mitt and his signed Johnny Bench card. And the tablet my mother gave him for Christmas. It's a cheap one, but he kept saying then he could email Kent without having to wait for his turn at the computer—my folks only have one."

He listened. He ground his teeth. He swayed back and forth in the sandals he'd put on with his jeans to take Talia home in the middle of the night.

And he watched the young blonde woman across the room, looking worried, talking to no one. Watching him.

CHAPTER THIRTY

SHE FOUND THE street easily enough. Getting down it was another story. She could see the police cars forming a roadblock from a quarter of a mile away. And knew she had to get down there. One way or another, she had to be close to her son. To let him know that he wasn't alone. To make everything okay.

How she'd do that didn't cross her mind at the moment.

Getting to him was all she could think about.

With her heart in her throat, she pulled behind a car parked in front of a nondescript white house. Forty or so people were milling around, craning their heads to see what was going on. A couple of uniformed officers held them back.

She had to get by them. So tried just boldly walking through. She'd always heard that if you approached with confidence, as if you knew what was going on, people would leave you alone.

"Miss? I'm sorry, miss, but you can't go through here. You'll have to wait back there like everyone else."

A camera went off. And another. A woman was talking on her phone. And she realized that some of the people in the crowd were reporters.

"I... My mother," she said. "She's in that house over there." She swung her arm haphazardly, holding back none of her worry and fear. "She's in a wheelchair and needs her medicine. I have to be able to get to her. I promise, I'll just go up and cut through to the backyard," she improvised without missing a beat. Tammy's daughter and all. "Please, sir. She just called and said she's having an episode. I have to get her nitroglycerin for her."

She had no idea where she'd come up with that.

Even more shocking was that it worked. The man let her pass. And several cameras went off, catching her as she acted on her lie. Was she breaking the law? She didn't know. And didn't care, either.

Hurrying up the yard two houses down, she prayed there was no fence in the backyard that would prevent her from moving farther down the street. There was a fence. She climbed it in her dress pants and heels. Ran through the yard and scaled the fence on the other side, as well.

Pole dancing might look like easy work, but it took a lot of training and a hell of a lot of physical strength. For once in her life she was glad for the experience.

Once she'd made it past the watchful eye of the officers holding the small crowd at bay, Talia moved more easily, skirting a couple more fences, until she was only a door or two down from where the recovery team was gathered.

SWAT team? Bomb squad? She couldn't be sure. She just knew their uniforms were different.

And that was where she stopped—two doors down. Watching the team that was surrounding the house where her son and his friend were obviously being held. Just like Tatum had feared.

If there was anything she could do, if Kent managed to escape or someone brought him out, she'd be there. She just had to be able to see him. To know that he was okay.

Her little sister had steered her right.

Again.

Lila McDaniels called out to Belinda, taking the woman over to speak quietly with an officer on the telephone. Sherman watched. And knew that he couldn't lay any blame at the battered woman's door. She'd trusted their boys when they'd told her Jason was sick. He'd have done the same.

She was paying a price far worse than any he'd ever paid. Had been doing so for years, by the sound of things.

A couple of women smiled at him. Employees, he could tell by their shirts, but beyond that he didn't know who they were.

There was still no word that Kent was on his way

to the Lemonade Stand. He had no idea when he could take his son home.

The blonde teenager had taken a seat on a couch by the door. As though she needed to be ready to bolt. She'd looked at her cell phone no less than ten times while he'd been talking to Belinda.

Sherman moved closer to her. He suspected who she might be. Talia's little sister, Tatum, had sessions at the Stand. She'd befriended his son. The blonde was about Tatum's age. And was clearly agitated.

Just as he drew near enough to speak to her Belinda was back. "There's been some kind of explosion," she said softly. "From inside the house. Someone tried to breach it from the back and—"

It was all she got out before the teenager jumped up, crying, "No! No! Oh, my God, no!"

Lila and Sara were there immediately, flanking her on either side.

"Tatum? What is it, sweetie? What's wrong?" Sara asked. Lila guided her back to the couch.

She *was* Talia's sister!

Sherman moved closer.

"Oh, my God." The girl's wail chilled him and he stood there, completely helpless but feeling as though he should be taking action. "Call Tanner." Tatum was crying now. "Please, someone call Tanner."

Sara nodded at Lila, who slipped away, pulling her cell phone out of her pocket.

"Tatum." Sara's voice was more firm than he'd ever heard it before. "Tell me what's going on."

"It's Talia!" she said, sobbing as she looked at Sara. "She's probably the one who breached the back of the house."

The therapist looked as confused as Sherman felt.

"Talia?" Sara asked, while Sherman, unable to stay away, sat down next to the girl. Tatum glanced his way, but other than that didn't acknowledge that she was aware anyone else was sitting there.

"Yes," Tatum said. "I called her. From the bathroom."

"She's at work in LA today," Sherman said without thinking.

The girl looked at him. "I know. But I knew she'd want to know about Kent. She left work and was going to the house."

"How'd she know where to go?" Sara asked with a glance at Sherman over the girl's head.

"I gave her the address," she said. "I heard Belinda tell the police."

"You're telling me that Talia was going to the house to break into the middle of hostage negotiations?" Sherman wasn't a player here.

But he couldn't just sit there and calmly take any more. Not only did nothing make sense, it was now bordering on ludicrous.

"No…she said she was going to stay back. She'd never get in the way of official police business. But if she saw something…if Kent was in danger…she'd have stopped at nothing."

Sherman's blood froze in his veins. She'd risk her life for his son because she loved them. Just as he loved her. Something was finally making sense and he didn't want it to.

Not if it meant Talia was in danger.

"Why would Talia even go there?" Sara's frown was deepening. "I don't understand. Why wouldn't she just come here and wait with the rest of us?"

"Because he's her son!" Tatum's words split through the room. Conversations stopped. People looked over at the three of them sitting on the couch. And Tatum started to babble. "He's my nephew! I love him. No one was telling me anything, but I figured out what was going on and called Talia. I knew, no matter what, she'd want to be there and…"

The girl kept talking, but Sherman didn't hear anything she said. He sat there, but couldn't feel the couch beneath him.

Talia Malone was Kent's mother?

Could it be true?

Was it even possible?

She'd had sex at sixteen. With a teacher who'd gone to prison. About eleven years before. Kent had been conceived close to eleven years before.

The math worked.

Nothing else did.

WHEN THE EXPLOSION SOUNDED, Talia felt it clear to her bones. Emotionally. She wasn't physically hurt, but she was in pain. More afraid than she'd ever been. And couldn't continue to hide in the bushes like an onlooker to her life.

She ran for the street first, and then moved up it toward the house that still looked intact. Nothing was burning. She saw no smoke.

A band of police officers saw her.

"Please," she said, crying now. "Kent Paulson—he's in there. Do you know if he's okay?"

They'd been standing there in a group, talking. As if they were waiting. Just like her.

"I'm sorry, ma'am, you'll have to step back…" A woman broke away from the other officers and took Talia by the arm, leading her across the street, away from the house. "I didn't catch your name," the woman said, clearly trying to calm the situation.

Talia looked over her shoulder, not letting the house out of her sight.

"Ms. Malone?" She heard his voice. And thought she was imagining it.

"You know this woman?" The police officer spoke, and Talia knew it was real. Glancing over, she saw Kent with police officers on both sides of him, getting out of a car.

"I'm in trouble, huh?" the boy said, looking up at her with tears starting to fill his eyes.

He was fine. It was all she could comprehend at the moment. Kent was fine.

Forgetting everything that stood in the way, she ran to him, grabbed him up into her arms and hugged him as if she'd never let him go.

SHERMAN HEARD ABOUT the small homemade device that Jason's father had set off as a warning to police.

Other than to know that Jason was still alive, and as fine as he could be still in his father's custody, he was hardly aware.

"You're Talia's sister," he said, finally sitting alone with the blonde teenager.

She nodded. "And you're Sherman. I know. I've seen you pick up Kent."

Nothing in life had prepared him for this moment.

"Talia's going to kill me," the girl said, having calmed down once she heard that Kent was out of danger. If anyone had realized the stake she had in the situation they'd have told her much sooner.

She'd been among them all morning, but suffering on her own.

She reminded him of her sister.

Kent's mother.

He shook his head. Angry. Hurt. And unable to leave the emotional teenager until her brother arrived to care for her.

Lila had told them Tanner was on his way.

"She's probably going to leave again and never come back," Tatum said.

"Why would she do that?"

"Because I told you her secret. She didn't want anyone to know. Ever. Kent most of all. She thinks that knowing she's his mother will somehow ruin him. I think he's lucky. No one will ever love him more than she does…"

The girl broke off and looked up at Sherman, her eyes widening. Eyes that reminded him of someone else.

Someone close to him. A little boy who'd looked at him just like that on many occasions. Pretty much every time he was in trouble.

He saw the truth there.

And he wasn't ready to deal with it.

"I'm sorry," she said now, still staring at him. "Other than you, of course. You love him more than anyone."

As backtracking went, the attempt failed. Sherman wanted to throw something. To scream at a world that was careering so far out of control in spite of his playing by the rules every single second of every day.

But he couldn't blame this young woman. Her heart was in her eyes.

"She's his mother," he said, half to himself. Still not able to accept what was staring right at him. The way she'd taken to Kent from the first. Had been able to read him like a book when no one else could.

Her eagerness to drive a virtual stranger to counseling every afternoon. Sherman had thought it was because of the compelling attraction between the two of them.

The attraction between them, the sex…had that all been an act just to get closer to her son?

"She was at Kent's school, helping him, because she was his mother?"

"No!" Talia said. "Well, only in part."

He heard how Talia had started helping the women at the Lemonade Stand. How she'd developed a program for high-school girls, only the school board had voted for a trial program with sixth graders first. How Talia had just needed to know that her son was okay so she could leave the past behind and move on with her new life. And how she'd witnessed him going off on a teacher the day he'd been expelled.

It all made sense. Sickening sense.

All but the part where she'd seemed to love him. He'd thought she was "the one."

The rest he could understand. Maybe even someday forgive.

But having sex with him? Pretending to return his feelings?

That he couldn't accept.

CHAPTER THIRTY-ONE

KENT WANTED TO ride back to the Lemonade Stand with Talia. He'd started to cry, to cling to her, when the officer tried to lead him back to the car that was to take him to his father.

The officer made a phone call. Presumably to Sherman. So Talia wasn't all that surprised when she was given temporary custody of the little boy. She'd been driving Kent for weeks. Of course his father would trust her with him.

He talked to his son for a moment, and then asked to speak with her.

At which point she panicked. How was she going to explain being there? At a crime scene she should know nothing about?

She wasn't going to involve Tatum, she knew that much. But wasn't enough Tammy's daughter to come up with an alternative feasible explanation. "Is Kent right there?" was the first thing he said when the officer handed her the phone. Thinking that he wanted to tell her something about Jason, something he didn't want his son to know, she stepped away, watching to make certain that the officer had Kent firmly within her sight.

"No."

"I know that he's your biological son." The voice on the other end was not the man she knew. Not one she'd ever met before. "That doesn't concern me at the moment. What concerns me is that he's been through a traumatic experience and right now his emotional health is the only concern."

He *knew*? But how? And…oh, no. Please, no. Just no.

"To that end, I am allowing him to ride with you because he thinks he knows you. He's comfortable with you. And because the officer suggested, based on Kent's agitation, that riding with you is what's best for him."

Wow. "Okay."

She deserved his anger. His mistrust. She just…

"Further, I need your word that you will not, in any way, speak to him about his adoption or about your part in it."

And she understood. She was going to be out of their lives. Permanently. As soon as she delivered Kent to his father. One more time.

"Per our agreement, I am legally bound to leave any telling to you." Where she found the voice, or the courage to say the words, she didn't know.

His silence, in light of how much he'd had to say seconds before, confused her.

"It's really true, isn't it?"

Had her mention of the agreement confirmed it? Had he only been guessing before? But how could he have made such a leap on his own?

At the moment, it didn't matter. Their son did. And getting him home.

"Yes," she said. "But don't worry, Sherman, I have no intention of telling him. Ever."

"Just get him home to me safely."

"I will."

"Thank you."

He hung up before she could reply.

Not that she had any response to give him.

OTHER THAN WHEN he was on the phone with Talia, he sat with Tatum until her brother arrived. He wasn't obligated to speak to her at all.

And yet, he felt as though his place was there.

Not because she was family. In any way. He couldn't consider the ramifications of the announcement she'd made. Wasn't sure anyone could, based on the way the few who heard the news were looking over at them.

Sara, who'd been watching them, left Belinda to come over.

"You two okay?"

"Fine," Sherman assured her.

"I screwed up, didn't I?" Tatum asked her.

"If you did, it wasn't on purpose," the other woman assured her. She was looking at him.

When he didn't respond, she said, "Talia was in a no-win situation."

Maybe.

"She had no intention of getting involved with Kent or even meeting you. She just needed to know that he was okay."

He nodded.

"She doesn't believe she's worthy of him…" Tatum started in.

"Tatum," Sara interrupted. "Whatever else remains to be said has to be between your sister and Sherman."

Tatum, looking like Kent in trouble, nodded.

Right about then, a tall, dark-haired man entered, perusing the room in one glance with a clear objective in mind. Sherman noticed him first.

"I'm guessing that's Tanner?" he asked as he stood.

"Tanner!" Jumping up, Tatum ran to him, throwing her arms around her brother and burying her face in his shoulder. "I told him, Tanner. I'm so sorry. I…just… I thought she'd been hurt, and all because I'd told her where he was and…I've made a mess of everything."

The man held his little sister as though he'd never let her go. He whispered something Sherman couldn't hear, all the while studying Sherman.

"I'm Tanner Malone," he said, holding out a hand to him, while he still held his sister against him with the other. A woman appeared beside him then. Someone else new to the room.

"Tatum, sweetie? Let's go get some cold water for your face." Letting go of her brother, Tatum allowed herself to be led away.

"My wife, Sedona," Tanner said, watching the two of them leave the room. "She's a lawyer."

Was the man giving him a warning? Asserting his power?

"She volunteers here," Sherman said, letting him know that Talia had told him all about them.

"Talia…she's had a hard time."

"So I've heard."

"I hope you'll go easy on her."

He couldn't make any promises. But he had to know something. "Have you seen him, too?"

Did this biological family of Kent's have designs on him?

"No."

He processed that for a moment.

"You aren't curious about him? He is, after all, your nephew." Why he'd said that he had no idea.

"Of course I'm curious. More than curious. I also know what's right. He's your son. You gave him a home, love, a life. If I meet him, it will be when you bring him and introduce him."

Sherman didn't know what to make of that. Of any of them.

"My sister did what she thought best," Tanner said.

"I'm sure she did."

"For the boy," Tanner clarified, his eyes narrowed. "Not for herself."

She'd been sixteen. Betrayed by a man who was supposed to protect her. Teach her.

"She was petrified of bringing a child into the world we'd grown up in." The words didn't come easily from the other man. Sherman saw the struggle on his face. Heard it in his voice.

"She was afraid she was like our mother. She chose to break her own heart to give her son a chance at a better life."

He had one. The words sprang to Sherman's tongue. He didn't give them release. Because he wasn't sure they were true.

At the moment he wasn't sure of anything. Except that he needed to see his son. To hold him like Tanner had just held Tatum. And take him home.

To their home. Where it would be just the two of them living happily ever after.

THE SECOND HARDEST thing Talia had ever done was walk her son into the Lemonade Stand that afternoon. She knew she was seeing him for the last time.

The hardest had been to give birth at sixteen and

let them take the baby from her body and out of the room in the same breath.

But she'd done it for him then and would do it again. For the same reason.

Sherman Paulson was a great father. The best. He was everything she'd hoped for her son. And more.

Getting this over and done with was for the best, too.

"Let's go," she said, walking him down the hall to the room she'd been told to take him to.

The second she walked in she saw Sherman. Standing and talking to another man. A familiar man.

The other man turned.

Tanner.

Everything happened at once after that. Kent ran to his father, crying as Sherman picked him up, and Kent threw his arms around his father's neck, holding on for dear life.

Tatum came out of nowhere, running over to Talia. "I'm so sorry," she cried. "I'm so sorry."

And she knew how Sherman knew that she was Kent's mother.

"Shh." She comforted her sister automatically, pulling her close. "It's okay, Baby Tay. It's okay."

She said the words. But she believed them, too.

She'd lost the man she loved. The boy who would always be a part of her.

But she was glad that her secret was out.

Sherman was talking to Lila and then left through another door without a backward glance.

She watched them go. Waiting for either of them to look back at her. To wave goodbye perhaps.

"Let's go home." Tanner had his arm around her waist. Sedona came up on her other side.

"What about Jason?" Talia was fine. But the day wasn't over yet. A little boy...

Tanner said something about a negotiator going in unarmed after the explosion. They couldn't take a chance on another, more deadly blast.

"His father surrendered to the police shortly after you left. Jason's unharmed."

So it was over.

So much was over.

Maybe everything.

She'd done what she had to do.

CHAPTER THIRTY-TWO

"WE DIDN'T SAY goodbye to Ms. Malone." Kent put his club in his bag, slung the junior-size gear over his shoulder and walked beside Sherman.

They'd missed their foursome the day before, heading straight to Dr. Jordon's office from the Lemonade Stand.

"I'm sure she understood." Estimating the distance between his ball and the green, Sherman chose a five iron. It was just the two of them today. He liked playing golf alone with his son.

"Why do you think she was there? I mean, how did she know where I'd be?"

He wasn't ready for the questions. They'd talked about Kent's adoption in Dr. Jordon's office the day before. He'd told his son the story of his birth, and his and Brooke's reasoning behind the choice to celebrate the adoption as part of his tenth birthday.

Kent had cried a little bit, telling his dad how alone and lied to he'd felt when he'd first found out. But mostly, they were discussing old news. Kent, through all of his counseling, but mostly through his friendship with Jason, had figured out how very much his father loved him.

His son had largely dealt with the news without him. So much for his and Brooke's careful plan.

They'd also talked about Brooke's affair. Kent had felt that double whammy—the fact that his mother had lied to his father, that even his adoptive family hadn't been what it had seemed—more deeply than Sherman had realized. He was certain now that they'd solved the acting-out problem, although he still hadn't told Kent that Brooke's accident was most likely being ruled a suicide. There'd be time for that in the future. If the ruling became official. And only then. The rest was speculation that a ten-year-old boy didn't need to be concerned about. If he figured it out for himself in the future, Sherman would trust that it happened because he was ready.

"Tatum called her. She was on her way home from work so she stopped to see if she could help." He'd told Dr. Jordon, in private, that Talia was Kent's birth mother. He'd wanted—no, needed—validation that his choice to keep the information from his son was the correct one.

The therapist had been frustratingly noncommittal on the subject.

There are no easy answers.

"We really should have told her goodbye."

Sherman swung, and hit the ball flat-on.

"Wow, Dad, you really overshot that one."

Yeah, he seemed to be doing a lot of that lately.

TALIA MADE UP her mind that she should take the promotion. She'd be in training for the first couple of months and could finish her course work. The following semester would have to either be completed online, or...she'd have to defer her graduation. Maybe she'd eventually get her degree. Maybe not.

She'd approached Mirabelle with a plan that would allow her to travel no more than fourteen days a month. The woman had surprised her with more freedom than that. Her schedule was up to her. She could come and go as she pleased as long as she brought in money commensurate with the company's expectations.

"You have a rare talent to know what looks good on women," her boss had told her. "I've been watching you," the woman continued. "You dress a woman and she immediately feels different. More beautiful. Confident."

Talia couldn't explain what she did, but she understood what Mirabelle was saying. "A woman is not just the sum of her body parts," she said softly. "She is a combination of many complicated and sometimes warring factions. I just try to bring those factions together."

And in the process, she was bringing herself together.

"You fill our store with your vision, and I have faith that our associates will be able to sell whatever you bring them."

"I'd like to try."

Because she was doing something she was good at. And traveling so much wouldn't be a problem for a woman who lived alone.

Talia also concluded her trial period with her sixth-grade art classes. One young man was getting help for his fixation with fire, thanks to the report she'd written. A few other kids had exhibited self-esteem issues in their collage work that might have been contributing to bad grades.

And hundreds of children now had a piece of pretty artwork to hang on their parents' refrigerators for a time. Until it was taken down either to be tucked away for safekeeping, or thrown out in the trash.

At the end of April she met with the school board to discuss the trial program and to explore the possibility of taking her program to high schools to work exclusively with young women as she'd originally intended. They offered her a part-time paid position to continue her work in the sixth grade and add the fifth grade the following year.

At first, her heart leaped at the opportunity. She'd loved her time in the schools. And while she'd veered far off her intended career course, she knew she'd found value in being able to give something back to others. Something more than just helping them look good.

Sitting in the private board meeting at the conference table that night, in a conservative blue suit with a cream-colored silk blouse buttoned up to her neck, she faced the elected parents and community business members who made up the board, words of grateful acceptance on her lips.

They didn't spill forth. As she considered her response and processed the ramifications of accepting their offer, she realized she had to be completely honest with her new employers.

"I'm sorry," she said. "As much as I want this, and believe that collaging is a formidable tool in exposing the hidden demons that lurk within all of us, I'm afraid that I'm not the best candidate to work with your children."

Nine shocked faces stared back at her. Talia focused on the woman directly across the table. Her kindly expression seemed to encourage Talia to continue talking.

"I worked for a time in Las Vegas," she said, the words coming calmly, clearly. "I was a dancer. A stripper."

The entire room seemed to shift uncomfortably. She could feel male eyes on her, undressing her. Whether they were or not.

Conversations broke out, quiet ones, members leaning over to whisper to their neighbors, until someone realized she was still sitting there, watching it all.

"Can you excuse us a minute, please?" The board's president, a kindly looking older gentleman in an impeccable suit and tie, stood as he made the request, looking Talia in the eye.

"Of course." She'd been prepared for this. Had told Tatum and Tanner and Sedona that she didn't expect to get the job.

"Wait." Another member of the board, a mother of seven children, five of whom had graduated from the Santa Raquel school district, stood. "I don't see why this should change anything," she said. "I'm as surprised as the rest of you—I've never actually met a…an exotic dancer before. But I don't see how this affects our business here tonight."

"Well," another woman spoke up. "I think we need to be free to have a candid discussion here. This woman will be working with our *boys*. Can you imagine? What if a photo of her…you know… turns up? I mean, we all know what strippers are about. Their sole purpose is to get men going…"

Talia turned to leave.

"I disagree," a third woman said.

And a man Talia didn't know added, "So do I." She turned to see him stand.

"Really, Reverend?" the woman who was so concerned about her "boys" said.

"Ms. Malone has a gift that can help our children

where other traditional means have failed. In just a few short months she's made a difference. Her past was another time in another place. Furthermore, she's never alone with the children. Their teacher is always present when she's working with them—not that I'd have any problem with her being alone with them, mind you. She also doesn't spend more than a couple of weeks in any one class, and isn't in any one school for a long period of time, either.

"Who among us doesn't have a past? The key issue here is that she made the choice to change her life. She went to school, got a degree and moved home. She comes from a good family. Many of you are aware of her brother Tanner, who turned the old Beachum farm into a successful winery, and from what I hear is growing some pretty valuable grapes. Another brother, Thomas, graduated from our district with a full scholarship to Harvard. And her little sister, Tatum, just received some of the highest SAT scores we've seen in our district."

Talia swallowed. And tears welled in her eyes. If only her brothers and sister were present to hear this. They deserved this gift, not her.

The *Malones* a good family? Tanner, Thomas, Tatum—they'd done what they'd all grown up believing was impossible. They'd become respectable citizens in a community of people who'd once refused to let their children play with them.

Maybe she was the only one who'd thought the

transition was impossible. Maybe the rest had made something of themselves because they'd believed they could.

"And what do we do when one of our sons turns up a picture on the internet?"

"In the first place," the school board president, standing at the head of the table, interrupted. "Any boy of ours who would be on a site where photos of that nature would show up is breaking the law himself."

"Excuse me." Talia stepped back to the table. If she was going to be there for the crucifixion, she was going to at least stand in the light—not the shadows. She'd purposely and consciously left those behind. "Just to make this a little easier…there are no photos. It was part of my contract that photos of me were not taken. And just to clarify, in case it ever were to come up, I was a dancer. Period. I didn't do private parties. Or take personal clients." She was speaking for her family now, not a job. She couldn't change having been a stripper. But her family had worked hard to clean up their reputation, and if by her very existence she was hurting that, she was at least going to do as little damage as possible.

"I don't know any of the Malones," another man said from his seat at the table. "But I don't see why this should be an issue. She's not dancing now. She dresses appropriately. Acts appropriately. And most importantly to me, she has ethics. Which is more than can be said for some others in our district."

He didn't name names, but the board seemed to know who he was referring to. One by one, they sat back down. Talia took her seat, as well.

"Ms. Malone didn't have to tell us about her past," the man continued. "We'd probably never have known. She did so because it was the right thing to do. It couldn't have been easy." He gave a brief glance in her direction. "But she did it, anyway. This is the type of behavior, the type of example, I want for my children."

The room was silent.

"Would you like me to leave so you can reconsider your vote?" Talia asked.

The board president looked around the table.

Then all heads turned as the door to the room opened. "I'm sorry for the interruption."

Talia's heart pounded, her skin getting instantly hot. And then cold. The reaction had nothing whatsoever to do with the job at stake.

And everything to do with the man whose voice she heard in her sleep. And in her mind when she lay awake in the middle of the night.

Whispering delicious compliments in her ear while he took her to heaven.

The man who'd taken his son from her, left the Lemonade Stand and never contacted her again. Except to leave a message on her cell phone the following day to let her know that he'd made other plans for his son's travel arrangements.

Sherman Paulson, wearing a full suit and tie, looked as though he was dressed for a funeral.

Hers.

"I WAS TOLD to wait outside and that I would be called if I was needed," he said, addressing the board's president. "I couldn't help but overhear— I'm not sure if you know, but the room's speaker is on."

The boardroom wasn't large enough to accommodate members of the public, but the meetings were open to the public. Benches in the outer vestibule allowed members of the public to sit in on board meetings.

This meeting, however, as Sherman had been told, was *not* open to the public.

"Oh, my gosh." One of the female board members jumped up and tended to a control on the wall. "I'll just go out and apologize and... Oh, my, I am so sorry."

"There's no one else out there," Sherman said, approaching the table. "The meeting was designated private." And if there had been anyone else present, he'd have interrupted far sooner and asked to have the intercom switched off.

"I came specifically because I'd asked about Ms.

Malone's status with the district and had been told that the topic was the agenda for tonight's meeting."

He didn't look at Talia. He couldn't. He'd get hard, or go soft, and he couldn't afford to do either. His presence had one purpose and one purpose only.

Addressing the president, Walter Pendergrass, a man whose campaign he'd run, he said, "I am aware of Ms. Malone's past. Because, like with you all, she told me about it. She worked with my son. As some of you know, Kent's been struggling a bit this year. He's been through several therapists, is still in therapy, has worked with school counselors, his teachers and Mrs. Barbour, his school principal. But even with all the extra attention and help, no one had been able to get through to him. Not even me. He was sitting by himself in the office after being expelled from school when Ms. Malone noticed him. She offered to do a collage with him, on her own time, and the end result has been miraculous. Through her work, her insights, we were able to get Kent the help he needed. She gave my son back to me.

"Mr. President and members of the board, as a long-standing member of this community, I recommend that if you are considering rescinding your job offer because of a job she held in the past, you talk to some of the parents of children she's had contact with first. I think you'll find the support you need to hire her full-time, which was my original reason

for being here tonight, to request that the position
be full-time. Thank you."

Turning, he left the room, then left the building.
And went home to his son.

CHAPTER THIRTY-THREE

ONCE AGAIN, TALIA had to rethink her life. Thanks to Sherman Paulson, the first week in May she received an offer for a full-time position with the Santa Raquel school system. The position was only for one year starting out, and fluid. She'd be working with grades four through twelve, conducting traveling art classes with the elementary-school grades and working one-on-one with older students as an alternative or complement to other options of assisting those who were struggling—either emotionally or academically.

She talked to her family before accepting the position. And afterward, sent a note to Sherman, thanking him for his support. She didn't hear back from him.

Mirabelle was gracious, though not pleased, when she told her she wouldn't be taking the buyer position, after all, but she agreed to let Talia keep her sales position through the summer, and for as long after that as she chose.

She'd be taking classes all summer, as well, and

hoped to complete her psychology course work by December.

All in all, she was pleased with herself. And starting to feel like a real Malone. Worthy of being a Malone.

So much so that she'd talked to Sedona about letting her buy the beach house, on a land contract. They'd signed the deal the day after she signed her contract with the school board. And Talia was spending her free time—now that she was done with collage reading for a few months—looking for new furniture for her place and adding other little changes to make the place her own.

One of the first things she'd done was take down a couple of decorative mirrors and change out the mirrored closet doors. She still wasn't at the point where she felt good looking at her own nudity.

Her first major undertaking was to paint the kitchen a pale yellow to mimic the sunrise over the ocean.

Her social life had also picked up a bit. She'd been invited to the theater—by the brother of a woman she'd been dressing for more than a year. She'd already had dinner with him. Found him charming. Funny. Entertaining. And…lacking in spark. She wasn't going to waste his time. Or her own.

On this third Friday in May, she'd pulled back her hair and, dressed in cutoff jogging shorts and an old T-shirt, was taping the windowsills in the kitchen to prepare them for painting. The tiles she'd purchased for a backsplash border around all of the countertops lay in neat stacks along the wall behind the table. As did the thin set and grout. Tanner was on call if she needed help.

With her iPod blaring her female empowerment playlist, she didn't know a car was in her driveway until she heard the door shut. A single door.

She glanced out the front window and saw the tail end of a silver BMW.

Sherman.

She had no time to think. He was probably counting on that. Damn him if he thought he was just going to walk in her unlocked back door, unannounced, and take her to bed.

The old Talia might have thought she deserved no better, but the new Talia, the healthier Talia, knew better.

She'd lock her door. And keep it locked until he called her and asked her for a proper meeting. Even then, it was debatable whether or not she'd let him in.

Decision made, she grabbed her keys and went over to the only unlocked door. The one he'd always used. She'd just locked the keyed dead bolt when she heard steps on her back deck.

Heard them because while she'd been locking the door, she'd somehow managed to position herself on the outside of it.

So she'd talk to him. It had to happen at some point. They lived in a small town. And neither of them appeared to be going anywhere anytime soon.

If he wanted assurances that she would stay away from Kent while she was in his school, she'd give that to him. She loved her son. She wasn't going to confuse his life.

"Hi."

The voice was male. Definitely Paulson. But it wasn't Sherman.

"Hi."

She stood there, barefoot, in her ugly painting clothes, and tried not to cry.

Her son looked so…grown-up. Easily an inch taller. His hair was still as short. His clothes as preppy. Today he was wearing light-colored khakis, a white short-sleeved shirt and a blue, sleeveless sweater vest.

The boy needed some serious help loosening up.

And he was absolutely perfect to her.

God, she'd missed him.

"Where's your dad?" Kent might look all grown-up, but he was still ten. For another two months, three days, six hours and seventeen minutes, give or take a second or two.

"In the car." He shrugged. Trying to look so manly. His right thumb and forefinger were working each other to the bone at his side. "He offered to come with me but I said no."

She nodded. She was just so glad to see him she didn't want to ask any more questions.

"I came to give you this." He pulled an envelope out of his back pocket and held it out to her.

An invitation? To his birthday party? A formal thank-you from his father for agreeing to leave him alone?

That didn't make sense. Not when the boy was delivering the missive himself.

With shaking hands, she opened the envelope. Pulled out the worn piece of folded paper. Lifted the top from the middle and recognized it immediately. She didn't need to open it any further to read a word, to know what she held.

A generic copy of the letter, minus names, they'd all later signed, giving each other permission to access the other's information. It was a copy of the generic letter she'd chosen to use for their contract. Before their contract had been drawn up, Sherman and Brooke had been sent a copy, given the opportunity to approve the generic letter. Then Talia had signed and they'd signed, separately and separate copies of the same letter. Neither had seen the other's names.

Now every part of her was shaking.

"I know it's not signed and that it's not official, but Dad says there's a signed one at the adoption agency. But since we knew where to find you, we didn't need to wait to call them. 'Cause it says there that anytime I want to find you I have your permission."

Sherman didn't know she'd revoked that permission.

Tears streamed down her face. She couldn't move. Couldn't wipe them away.

"So...here I am."

"I think this is where you take your son into your arms." The voice came from just beyond the deck steps.

"Maybe we got it wrong, Dad..."

The vulnerability in that voice, that hint of not being sure you were wanted, catapulted her. "No, no, no," she said, touching his hair, running her fingers through the short strands, staring down at him. "You didn't get it wrong. I just... Can I hug you?"

Another shrug. "I guess it would be okay. If you wanna." Talia pulled him up against her, held him close. Felt his small arms wrap around her middle. And hold on. Tight.

She laid her head on top of his.

"I love you, baby." She'd been told not to name him those nine months she'd carried him.

"I'm not a baby." His words were muffled against her. Until he pulled back. "But...can I call you Mom?"

SHERMAN STOOD OFF to the side for as long as he could.

"Can I come up now?"

"I haven't said the other stuff yet."

"What stuff?" Talia's voice floated down to him.

"About how Dad thought the most important thing was standing for what looks good, but you taught us that what's most important is standing for what feels good."

"He didn't get that quite right," Sherman said, climbing up to the top of the deck to face the woman he loved with all of his heart, but didn't deserve. "But close enough. It went more like, what looks good on the surface isn't what's worth standing for. It's what's underneath that matters."

She glanced over at him. And he saw all of the pain she'd kept hidden inside her. Not because she looked any different, but because he was looking at her differently.

"You didn't answer my question." Kent shook his hand, which was attached to hers, but didn't let go. He was getting her attention in a way that was all too familiar to Sherman.

But brand-new to his mother.

"What question?" she asked.

"Can I call you Mom?"

"Did you ask your father?"

"No, I'm asking you. It's your name."

"Then, yes. Please, yes!" She hugged him.

He pulled back again. "Why did you give me away?"

All of Sherman's coaching had been for naught.

The questions would come, had been coming ever since Kent had insisted on knowing about his birth parents. With Dr. Jordon's coaching he'd told him the who, but said the why was up to Talia to explain to him. He'd also suggested—okay, ordered him—to give her some time before bombarding her with questions. He'd tried to explain how painful they might be for her.

It was clearly a concept Kent didn't yet grasp.

And how could he blame him? He was thirty-eight years old and he was just starting to get it himself.

While Sherman stood there, his hands in his pants pockets, Talia took Kent down on the beach. He could hear her voice, even hear her words, but he knew that this moment was not for him.

It was between a mother and her son.

SHE TOLD KENT that she'd wanted him desperately. That his father had been taken away from her. And that she'd given him up because she wasn't going to be married or have a job and wanted him to have a safe, happy place to live with people who wanted him and loved him as much as she did.

He asked who'd taken his father away.

She asked him if he'd mind waiting a few years for that part of the story. She asked him to trust her that it would be better. He scrunched up his sweet face. Had asked if his father—Sherman—

knew about his biological dad. She told him yes. He wanted to know if the other man was around now. And when she said no, he agreed to wait to hear about him. And then asked if he could build a sand castle.

They all three built one.

"ASK HER, DAD." They were sitting on the beach, watching Kent dig a moat around the castle they'd built.

Sherman loved his son. But there came a time when a man needed some time to himself. Or with another grown-up.

"Do you mind if I take your mom for a walk?" The words flowed naturally off his tongue. Until he saw Talia's look of shock. And the tears that sprang to her eyes.

"Don't ask me, ask her," Kent said, still digging. The boy wanted to know that he was going to have a family again. A real family.

And was scared to death that his dad had blown their chance.

"Will you walk with me?"

She stood, brushing off her ridiculous shorts, looking more beautiful than he'd ever seen her.

Sexier, too.

Sherman didn't touch her. He wouldn't. Not until she gave him that right. *If* she gave him that right.

"I screwed up, Talia." He started in as soon as they were far enough away not to be overheard.

"No…"

"Please, let me get this out. I was so busy trying to control my life, I missed out on living it. Brooke figured it out, but didn't know how to tell me. Frankly, I'm not sure I'd have heard her if she tried. Hell, maybe she did try."

Digging her toes in the sand, Talia quit walking, and looked up at him. "Just tell me where we go from here," she said. "You told him I'm his mother…" Her voice broke, and the trembling in her chin choked him up, too. "Thank you," she said in between holding her breath.

Tears blurring his eyes, he nodded. She was so gorgeous. And he'd done her so wrong.

"From what I can see you've spent your whole life trying to spare the people you love from having to be around you."

Her head pulled back. She frowned.

"It's like you thought you were diseased and would make them sick if they got too close."

"I don't—"

"I'm not saying I'm right," he interrupted. "I'm just telling you what I see. You asked where we go from here, and I know where I want to go, but it's going to be up to you."

"That question Kent wanted you to ask."

She wasn't smiling.

Because she didn't get it? Or didn't want it?

It was time for him to follow her example. To be as brave, as selfless, as she'd been. "Will you marry me, Talia?"

Her mouth fell open. "I... My past... Your career..."

"If it becomes an issue, we'll face it. You took down the school board, Talia."

"With your help."

"You had them without me. I just might have helped you get the full-time position a little sooner. And that was completely selfish on my part, you know."

"How so?"

"I wanted to make sure you'd be sticking around. And as much as you love your collage work, as good as you are at it, as much as you love kids, I figured..." He broke off with a shrug. "If your past becomes a problem, we'll deal with it together," he said, completely serious. "We might have a problem when the news of Brooke's suicide hits the press. If it hits. There are going to be bumps ahead. We can count on them. One thing I've learned is that no matter how carefully you prepare, life is messy. Another is that a career is worth nothing when compared to standing up for the woman you love."

"You love me?" Her blue eyes were huge, searching. The vulnerability he read in them would be with him until the day he died.

"I do. Very much. More than I believed it was possible to love another human being."

"I love you, too. Like that."

He started to pull her into his arms. She held him off with one hand to his chest. "What about Kent?" She nodded toward the little boy who was watching them from a distance. "What happens when he hears about the career his mother had in between having him and finding him?"

Sherman braced himself, knowing this was going to hurt her. "I've talked to Dr. Jordon about that. He suggests that we tell Kent, together, as soon as possible. Before he has a chance to hear it somewhere else. We'll need to give him tools to use, words to have to respond in the eventuality some jerk kid tries to make a big deal of it."

When she bowed her head, he lifted it up again with a finger under her chin.

"He's a smart boy, Talia. He lives by his heart, not his head. Like his mother."

"I don't get that."

"You… All your life you've been trying to make up for the woman your mother was—to the point of when you thought you were like her, taking yourself away to a world where you wouldn't be able to hurt anyone."

"I—"

"You're all heart, my dear, sweet Talia. Thank

goodness for you. Those of us who know you and love you get that you don't see that yet."

"Tanner said something to me several months ago…"

"Whatever it was, I'd believe him." Sherman was grinning.

"Why are you so happy? I haven't said yes yet."

"Because I'm a positive thinker. You know that. And right now I'm feeling pretty positive that we're going to have a pretty spectacular family."

He turned toward the ocean and raised his voice, calling, "Santa Raquel, world, watch out!"

"Did you say 'have' a pretty spectacular family?" Talia asked, smiling as he turned back to her. "As in, maybe another baby someday, too? Assuming we can conceive?"

About to tell her he was up to begin trying as soon as possible, to tell her that according to all of the tests that had been done, there'd been no apparent reason he and Brooke had been unable to conceive, he was interrupted as Kent came running up behind him.

"Did she say yes?"

Hooking an arm around his son's shoulders he pulled him forward, a vital piece of their circle. "Not yet…"

"Yes! I say yes!" Talia's laugh was a new sound to him. Full bodied. Full of delight.

And something else.

Something he didn't think either of them had ever fully known before.

Happiness.

* * * * *

LARGER-PRINT
BOOKS!

◈ HARLEQUIN *Presents*

PASSION GUARANTEED SEDUCTION

GET 2 FREE LARGER-PRINT
NOVELS PLUS 2 FREE GIFTS!

LARGER-PRINT BOOKS!
GET 2 FREE LARGER-PRINT NOVELS PLUS
2 FREE GIFTS!

(H) HARLEQUIN®

Romance

From the Heart, For the Heart

YES! Please send me 2 FREE LARGER-PRINT Harlequin® Romance novels and my 2 FREE gifts (gifts are worth about $10). After receiving them, if I don't wish to receive any more books, I can return the shipping statement marked "cancel." If I don't cancel, I will receive 4 brand-new novels every month and be billed just $4.84 per book in the U.S. or $5.24 per book in Canada. That's a savings of at least 19% off the cover price! It's quite a bargain! Shipping and handling is just 50¢ per book in the U.S. and 75¢ per book in Canada.* I understand that accepting the 2 free books and gifts places me under no obligation to buy anything. I can always return a shipment and cancel at any time. Even if I never buy another book, the two free books and gifts are mine to keep forever.

119/319 HDN F43Y

Name _____ (PLEASE PRINT)

Address _____ Apt. #

City _____ State/Prov. _____ Zip/Postal Code

Signature (if under 18, a parent or guardian must sign)

Mail to the Harlequin® Reader Service:
IN U.S.A.: P.O. Box 1867, Buffalo, NY 14240-1867
IN CANADA: P.O. Box 609, Fort Erie, Ontario L2A 5X3
Want to try two free books from another line?
Call 1-800-873-8635 or visit www.ReaderService.com.

* Terms and prices subject to change without notice. Prices do not include applicable taxes. Sales tax applicable in N.Y. Canadian residents will be charged applicable taxes. Offer not valid in Quebec. This offer is limited to one order per household. Not valid for current subscribers to Harlequin Romance Larger-Print books. All orders subject to credit approval. Credit or debit balances in a customer's account(s) may be offset by any other outstanding balance owed by or to the customer. Please allow 4 to 6 weeks for delivery. Offer available while quantities last.

Your Privacy—The Harlequin® Reader Service is committed to protecting your privacy. Our Privacy Policy is available online at www.ReaderService.com or upon request from the Harlequin Reader Service.

We make a portion of our mailing list available to reputable third parties that offer products we believe may interest you. If you prefer that we not exchange your name with third parties, or if you wish to clarify or modify your communication preferences, please visit us at www.ReaderService.com/consumerschoice or write to us at Harlequin Reader Service Preference Service, P.O. Box 9062, Buffalo, NY 14269. Include your complete name and address.

HRLP13R

Reader Service.com

Manage your account online!

- Review your order history
- Manage your payments
- Update your address

> *We've designed
> the Harlequin® Reader Service
> website just for you.*

Enjoy all the features!

- Reader excerpts from any series
- Respond to mailings and special monthly offers
- Discover new series available to you
- Browse the Bonus Bucks catalog
- Share your feedback

Visit us at:
ReaderService.com